TUMBLED

Margaret Johnson-Hodge

PUB DAY PRESS

THE NOVELS OF
MARGARET JOHNSON-HODGE

Tumbled

Promised (chapbook)

In Search of Tennessee Sunshine

Red Light Green Light

This Time

A Journey to Here

True Lies

Some Sunday

Butterscotch Blues

Warm Hands

A New Day

The Real Deal

ANTHOLOGIES
Proverbs for the People

Black Silk

Long Journey Home

Visit Margaret's website at *www.mjhodge.net*

PRAISE FOR THE NOVELS OF
MARGARET JOHNSON-HODGE

"Johnson-Hodge's popularity continues to grow. Audiences tired of buppie antics will respond favorably to the earthy dramas she describes." –*Publishers Weekly*

"Johnson-Hodge offers a poignant and lyrical tale of dreams lost, dreams deferred and dreams reborn."
–*Booklist*

"A book so memorable it will become a classic in years to come." –*Midwest Book Review*

"Attention grabbing from the start."
–*Black Issues Book Review*

"A wonderful job." –*Quarterly Black Review*

"Bestselling writer Margaret Johnson-Hodge delivers a powerful story about love, relationships and the choices people make…" –*Ebony Magazine*

"Fresh writing and an honest recognizable heroine."
–*Publishers Weekly*

"A captivating sequel that loyal readers and new fans will devour." –*Publishers Weekly*

"…a sassy and endearing story." –*Publishers Weekly*

"An engaging novel…a moving tale." –*Ebony Magazine*

"Audiences will respond favorably to the earthy dramas she [Johnson-Hodge] describes." –*Publishers Weekly*

Copyrighted 2012 by Margaret Johnson-Hodge
Press Pub

Margaret Johnson-Hodge
2774 N. Cobb Parkway, Suite 109, PMB 180
Kennesaw, Georgia 30152

Printed in the United States of America
First Printed 2013

ISBN: 978-09754026-7-2

This book is dedicated to a phenomenal woman of whom I was blessed to have in my life—Writer, Teacher Extraordinaire, and Poet Laureate

Brenda Connor-Bey Miller
(July 8th 1944 – August 18th 2012)

She was my friend, my mentor, my rabbi, my priestess, my *Obi Won Kinobi* and my *Glinda the Good Witch.* I am grateful to God for her. She believed in my works before I could find the courage to believe in them for myself.

So when you pick up a MJH book, remember that Brenda Connor Bey Miller is truly the 'wind' beneath every single word I write…

Brenda, I love you. Thank you for being my angel on earth…
Love,
'Maya Joy'

and to

Valerie Jean Jefferson Barnes Escoffery
(VaJeJeBa)
~ one of my longest, dearest, sweetest friends
who was
the first to believe in me
as a writer….
I love you and appreciate you,
'Mai-yin'

Love is as ordinary as an opened window on a balmy afternoon. It's a steady hand. That devoted smile. These are the tiny bricks that create forever: the mortar that holds; the emotional glue that binds. Durable or weak, it leaves some feeling blessed, others, simply unlucky. But luck has nothing to do with it. It's about those things that bind or destroy; what keeps us together or apart. But always, always, it's about the choices we make, for better or for worse; the choices we make in the good times or bad...

CHAPTER ONE

After the love is gone is a riff from a song that no one wants to sing. Dajah Moore was no different. But that song could have surely been playing inside the one-bedroom apartment on Merrick Boulevard in Jamaica, Queens, New York as she stood surrounded by boxes.

It wasn't supposed to be her background music, especially after being so sure that the love she'd sought was finally hers. Especially after the imperfect Jeff had changed his flaws into near perfection, with monogamy and ring talk and I'm-ready-to-walk-down-the-isle talk and Dajah had taken his words and meld them into her heart with a good enough fit to say: Okay, we can do this. We can get married, have babies and live that happily *ever- after.*

Love wasn't supposed to leave after that. Love was supposed to stay and grow and swell like a seed planted in springtime soil with heavy rains and plenty of sunshine. Love was supposed to be like a summer melon ripening, ready to burst under the slightest touch.

Someone's touch did burst Dajah's and Jeff's 'love,' exploding sanguine chunks all over her emotions, the walls of her soul; leaving her drippy and messy and messed up.

No woman wanted to be. No woman wanted to be so victimized by a crime of the heart that in the aftermath, who they were, how they thought, walked, talked, behaved, analyzed, was changed.

But Dajah was changed, her life, her thoughts, her heart, all different.

Now, her *after* were the cardboard boxes from U-haul marked 'bathroom', 'kitchen' and 'shoes'. Her *after* were the sad eyes of Jeff's Irish setter Kelly, who sat silent and guiltily, as if the dog had been a part of the undoing.

"I think that's everything," Jeff decided, looking around.

"Yeah," Dajah said absently.

With wedding plans and honeymoon dreams, she'd moved in with Jeff because his bedroom and closets were roomier than hers. Living together suited them. They'd taken drives out to Glen Cove to look at three million dollar homes on the waters edge, hosted dinners with her friends and his; their guests *oohing* and *ahhing* over lobster macaroni and cheese and Thai-styled grilled tilapia.

They'd come up with names for their children. Planned to honeymoon in Cozumel. Placed the promise of that first grandchild in their parents hearts. But all there was to show was her departure.

"Gonna take these down," Jeff's able hands holding the biggest box. It was those hands that had brought forth the damage; hands controlled by a mind that convinced him that one last fling before the ring would be okay because Dajah would never know and trusted him completely.

He was supposed to be beyond his philandering ways, beyond wanting to stick his jank into Syreeta and Joy and Lisa and Jill and who ever else welcomed the fine, smart, handsome, wise Jeff between their thighs.

But what had been loosed from him reappeared; the proof was Jill coming to the apartment, armed with text messages and a cell phone picture of Jeff naked and sleep in a bed that wasn't his.

Jill had been one of the many women Jeff had been seeing when he'd first met Dajah. At Dajah's insistence, Jeff had let Jill and the

rest go. But Jill had made a come-back, showing up at Jeff's front door, proof of their affair on her Nokia cell.

Dajah didn't remember lunging, only that Jill's phone ended up in her hand. She'd been on the verge of throwing it when Jill grabbed her wrist. It could have gotten nasty but Dajah realized that that was exactly what Jill wanted—she wanted a Jerry Springer moment full of hair pulling and name calling.

Only her thoughts—*I'm so much better than this*—stopped her. She took a breath, handed Jill back the phone. Thanked her for telling and opened the door to let Jill out, finding Jeff, key in hand, on the other side.

The look on his face brought it home. The sheer shock and guilt made it real. Jill and Jeff's voices collided around her as she stepped out the apartment and headed for the stairs. She took them quickly, bursting out into the warm early spring air, breathing hard and long and forever.

Dajah was still standing on the sidewalk when Jill brushed by her. Still there when, a few seconds later, she felt Jeff's touch. She didn't resist his pulling her close. Didn't resist the arms that held her or the tears she shed. Didn't resist his request to come back up stairs.

Sat stoic and numb on the couch as he tried to explain the why.

She had no strength to tell him to keep it. There wasn't enough 'whys' on all of God's green earth to make her stay. She was gone from him by the time her head hit the pillow that night, the king size bed empty of Jeff, swallowing her whole.

That had been two days ago. Now with her things packed, she was exiting his apartment and his life, forever.

"These are light." Dajah blinked, surprised to find Jeff back gathering up more of her boxes. "I can probably handle two." His tone — conversational. Did he really expect her to say one word more than what was necessary to leave his life? Did he really? "If you put that one on top," he was asking.

"What? So I can be gone faster?" Her nasty tone betrayed her. Dajah wanted to snatch the words back and shove them into her mouth. She wasn't going to be bitter or mean or cruel or unkind. She was better than that.

"No Day, that's not what—,"

She stopped his talk with her hand. Refused to add 'keep it.'

She was moving in with Frieda because her old apartment had been rented and she hadn't found a new place yet. Dajah was going to live with her best friend because her best *man* had done her dirty.

Not a failure, she reminded herself as she piled one box on top of another. *Not*, she reminded herself as Jeff left the apartment and Kelly got up and nuzzled her hand.

Not, she whispered as Kelly whimpered and sat at her feet; large brown eyes, beacons of pain that hurt her in the worse way.

Soon there were no more boxes. Soon all that she owned was packed into Jeff's SUV. Soon he would follow her down Merrick Boulevard, making a left on Baisley and a right on 129th Avenue. But it didn't feel soon enough, as she started her car and put on her signal. Not soon enough as she moved into the flow of traffic, the midnight blue GMC right behind her.

She had been sure, so damn sure. Sure that Jeff could be the man that Rick hadn't, that she didn't think David was, Michael before and Christian before that.

There had been a long line of men who couldn't, wouldn't, shouldn't. Too long of a line. She wasn't a spring chicken. Wanted babies and a real life as a real wife. *Want doesn't have a thing to do with need.* She chuckled to herself, the sound, disturbing.

I'm not going to trip over this. I'm not. I never have tripped over a man. Not about to start now. But she had. Dajah had tripped and fallen over Jeff. Despite her best intentions to protect herself, she'd crashed. And the landing hurt. It was throbbing by the time she pulled up to Frieda's, with no relief in sight.

*

"He forgot." Her voice was soft, distant and hushed in the dark night.

"Forgot what?" Frieda asked in between a yawn. It was late. She was sharing her bed and just wanted Dajah to stop talking so she could get to sleep. But best-friend duty was upon her, so Frieda yawned again, waiting for an answer.

"Who I was."

"Yeah." Frieda didn't know what Dajah was talking about, but she didn't have to. It wasn't about Frieda understanding. It was about Dajah talking.

"He did," Dajah said with a little more fire.

"I agree."

"Do you understand what I'm saying?"

Frieda paused. Enough truths had done her friend in. She didn't dare add more to the pile. She reached over and turned on the side lamp. Adjusted her head scarf as she sat up. Looked at her friend with sad eyes. "No, I really don't. But it doesn't matter Day. I don't have to as long as you do."

Dajah nodded, some great truth unburdened from her. Turning her back to her friend, Dajah moved her head around the pillow that smelled of a softener she didn't use and was too soft to support her neck.

"He still loves you Day. He really does."

Dajah knew that, so hearing it from Frieda didn't help. "Please make that the last time you tell me that."

"Okay." Frieda turned off the light. Tried to get comfortable in her own bed. Didn't, not once.

*

Desperation, like dried river beds, carved Jeff's face. His eyes were somber, saddened. Gloomed. "Another?"

It was already late and Martin had a wife at home waiting. Martin shook his head no. "Nah man, I'm good." He swallowed the last of his Heineken. "What about you? You feeling better?"

Jeff sat back, smiled. Lost it as his eyes drifted over the neon Bud sign on the back wall of the bar. "No, I'm not." He blinked back tears. Felt the need to hit something. A wall. His own stupid head.

He had called Martin because Martin was the oldest and wisest of all of his friends. He'd called Martin who had been successfully married for a few years, in need of guidance. But so far Jeff hadn't gotten anything he could use.

"You messed up, big time. No getting 'round that." Jeff nodded. "And Dajah ain't the type of woman who's going to forgive you."

"I know that."

Martin leaned forward. "So what you going to do? Sit in this sad ass bar every night and drink Heinies? Cause as much as you're my boy, I can't sit here with you."

"I know you can't."

Martin patted Jeff on the back. "Well, good. Least you know." Leaned back. "Now, you told me why you stepped out on Dajah with Jill, but you need to figure out the real reason."

Jeff looked at his friend, trying to latch onto an answer too fleeting to grasp. "I don't know."

"You gotta know. You may not like what the real answer is, but you got to figure out what the real answer is. If you don't, twenty years from now, you're going to be making the same damn mistake, 'cause that's what it was—a mistake. Cost you much, but I'm going to give you the benefit of the doubt."

"I. Don't. Know."

"Yeah? Well I see a couple choices here. You can go on with that line of 'I don't know' and end up like our boy Casey, clueless and lonely as shit, or you can get to the root cause and, with every cell of your being, make sure you don't do it again. Dajah ain't regular. You messed up on a damn good thing."

Jeff raised his hand again. "Enough, okay?"

Martin stood, tossed some bills on the bar. "I'm out." He extended his palm. Jeff slapped it, both of them snapping their fingers in the aftermath. "I'm here for you, but at some point, you have to be here for yourself."

Jeff watched Martin leave. Looked at the clock over the bar. It wasn't quite eleven yet. He pulled out his cell phone and dialed Casey. "Yo, Case. What up?"

Fifteen minutes later Casey was coming through the door. Jeff didn't need judgment, just a drinking buddy. As long as Jeff was buying, Casey was down for his cause.

*

The next morning found Dajah aching. She had pain in her shoulder, the dip in the back of her neck. It hurt to roll over, her reward for sleeping in Frieda's bed. "Uhh." Dajah didn't mean to utter that. Had no intentions of announcing to Frieda or anyone else how this first night without Jeff and the comfort of his Sleep Number bed had done her.

But the bed was empty. Dajah listened for sounds of life in the apartment. There was none.

She was alone.

CHAPTER TWO

*D*ajah entered the lobby of her office, a full work day ahead of her. She looked towards the elevator bank. Saw Mr. Elias, the elderly black gent who worked building maintenance. Waved.

"How are you today Miss Moore?" he asked.

"I'm fine Mr. Elias." which was a lie. "And you?"

"It's a good day."

Dajah nodded, forcing herself into an agreement. "Yes, it is." She and Mr. Elias had exchanged morning greetings nearly every day since she'd starting working at General Management out in Seaford, Long Island many years ago. It seemed every day was a 'good day' for Mr. Elias. Dajah couldn't say the same.

In the elevator, she pushed the three, eyes toward the shiny aluminum panel, seeing nothing. Her mind wasn't on what she did for a living—corporation accountant, or what the end of April meant – coming off an extremely heavy tax quarter.

Still she was glad for both as she got to work, losing herself in the world of numbers.

Numbers were faithful. They never changed. Always stayed true. But lunch time forced her back into her real world. Back to what had become a priority—finding a place to stay.

She ordered a sandwich and an Arizona ice tea from the concession stand downstairs. Scanned the internet for apartment listings as she munched on roast beef with Monterey jack. But even as she licked mayo from her fingers, scrolled through dozens of listings, there was only one place her soul desired—to go back home.

Not the home of her parents, but the placed she lived before there was a Jeff in her life. Dajah wanted the one-bedroom, one bath with the living room that gave her northern exposure and the bedroom that gave her soul strength.

She wanted to slip her key into the lock, open the door and hear the apartment whisper *welcome home*. But it had been rented a week after she'd moved in with Jeff. 'Home' now belonged to someone else.

Her office phone rang. "Dajah Moore speaking."

"Just wanted to see how you're doing."

"How I'm doing?" Dajah laughed, the sound unkind. "I'm doing. Okay?" She was about to hang up, but his voice stopped her.

"Can we meet? After work maybe? Manhattan Proper or somewhere close?"

Dajah wanted to say no. Wanted to say it with all the vengeance she was feeling. Couldn't. Though she had rallied and fumed and cursed and cried and howled and nearly beat Jeff with her fist, there were still things inside of her that needed to be released upon his lying, deceiving, cheating head. There was still fury in her and she needed it gone.

She told him yes.

*

Just April and the winds from the south were stirring up waves that pounded the Atlantic Ocean. Sand the color of ground oats took the beating, sparkling like diamonds in each aftermath. That's where Dajah fixed her eyes as she sat on the bench on the boardwalk of Jones Beach. That's where she stared as Jeff settled down besides her, his silence adding to the burning that filled her bones the moment they'd gotten out of their cars.

He had only said "Hello," and "Let's go to the boardwalk." Not another word did he utter as they headed towards the beach. Since he was the one that wanted to talk, she was decidedly mute.

His expression was masked. Nothing to read about how he felt. But that was Jeff, wasn't it? Master of disguises. Hadn't he banged Jill for two weeks and came home to her every night? But here she was back to the very place they had met over a year ago. The only thing missing was Kelly, running up to her, bent on a formal introduction.

Dajah smiled at the memory and Jeff misread the expression. "What's funny?"

Everything she wanted to say. She shook her head. There were too many words in her brain to release in any semblance of order.

"I'm sorry." *Yes you are*, she thought, hot eyes lashing his face. *You are so fucking sorry, aren't you?* "I don't know—,"

Her hand rose to shut him up. Inches from his eye, Jeff blinked, feeling the heat that rolled off her skin. "Don't you dare say that. Don't you dare."

Her eyes went back to the ocean. Back to the waves beating a shoreline that still sparkled in the aftermath. That's who Dajah had been once. She'd taken a licking and kept on ticking, shining bigger and brighter with each pounding. But this time her shine was lost. Gone. She needed to re-group, find herself. Being there with him wasn't helping.

She stood up. "There's nothing you can say to make it better. I don't even know why I came."

"Because you still love me."

Dajah wanted to laugh out loud, snicker at his assumptions. But truth was truth and it made her heart beat hard enough to sting her chest. Her head may have been ready to flee, but her heart was stuck in cement.

"And I love you too, Dajah. I know I messed up, big time....I was scared."

She could feel his gaze. Could sense the pain in his eyes. There was no need to check, but that part of her that loved him made her. A tear glimmered on his cheek. She'd never seen him cry.

"I was scared," he said again, "and I messed up. And I'm hoping you can forgive me."

Yes, he messed up. And yeah, he was probably scared. But his fear sent him into the arms of someone else. Do it once, he'd do it again.

"In all my life," Jeff continued, "there were only two women I wanted to marry. One of them is you." She remembered the story about how he was supposed to get married but the chick cheated on him right before the wedding.

Things came together. The fire in her bones returned. "So you pulled this little stunt because somebody did it to you, is that it? How fucking twisted is that?"

She didn't wait for an answer, just started walking fast; the sound of her high heeled boots, palms against a hollowed drum. Jeff would pursue. Would pursue her and catch her and then what? For as much as the victory was now hers, some closed window in her heart had been cracked open.

Her feet picked up speed. *Run Dajah. Just run.* She wanted too. She wanted to take off like she was doing a hundred--mile dash. She needed to get away from him before he caught her. Before he touched her. Before the love between them ruined what was 'best for her.'

But it became too late as his hand latched around her arm. Too late as her feet gave up the ghost; as he turned her around, uttering "I do love you, Dajah."

She nodded, "I love you too," lost. There was no way she could not say it. Truth was truth, and the power of her confession took her under. Made her forget how this even came to be. But when he tried to kiss her, reality stepped in and she pushed back. "It's over Jeff. You did this. Not me. And I'm done."

For the second time in as many minutes, her feet began moving, far and fast away from him. This time, there was no pursuit. This time, her word became deed.

*

The past could not be conjured through longing, wishful thinking or sitting in a car staring up at an apartment window. Rick Trimmons knew this, but he had been doing it anyway. Maybe it was because Brea had broken up with him two months before. Or maybe it was because despite it not working out, what he'd had with Dajah felt like the best time of his life.

Maybe Rick was just a glutton for punishment. Whatever the reason, he'd begin parking across the street, a few doors down from Dajah's place, hoping...*for?*

Rick blinked. Looked away.

There was nothing good here, just old ghosts from a past that had no intentions of being his future. But he couldn't get himself to turn the key in the ignition, pull away from the curb. Rick couldn't get himself to leave the street that once, long ago, knew and welcomed him.

The last time you saw her, she was with some other man and you were with Brea and that was over a year ago.

Go home Rick. He wanted to, but there was nobody there waiting. Not his daughter Kanisha and certainly not Brea.

He liked Brea, appreciated Brea, but in the end, did not love her. When it became evident that he couldn't, she didn't hang around. It wasn't a part of her philosophy to be with someone who couldn't give her what she needed. Rick respected that.

He missed her afterwards. Tried calling her, asked her out. But Brea kindly refused him. It wasn't the first time a woman had turned him down and even though there was no love for her, he did miss her. The missing turned into other things and the other things turned into him window-watching Dajah's place.

And if you saw her, what could you possibly say that she'd want to hear? I still love you, he decided, as he saw her car drive by, her face sad, her eyes wearied.

He watched as she slowed near her house then kept on going.

Instinct made him reach for the key, turn on the engine. He glanced quickly in his side view mirror and pull out of the parking space. But by the time he did, Dajah's car was gone from sight.

*

If she had really thought about it, Dajah would have understood that she was in the midst of trying to return to who she had been before Jeff. But Dajah wasn't really thinking as she left behind the place that used to be hers, a Chevy claiming her parking space. She hadn't been thinking when she slowed in front of the two-family home, hurt coming as she saw that they had taken down the blinds and replaced them with curtains.

Dajah wasn't thinking as she tried to imagine who stepped into her tub every morning and if they kept the stove as clean as she had. Just that maybe she'd ring her landlord's doorbell to say hello. See if the apartment would be available soon. Hole up somewhere until it was empty again.

But at the end of her trip down 'maybe' lane, reality set in. No doubt the tenants had signed a two-year lease. There was still a year to go. Did she really think she could 'hole up' somewhere for a whole year?

Let it go.

But she didn't want to. She was tired of always having to give something up in the name of love, and the thought of spending another night with Frieda made her head hurt. If there was ever a time she needed to be alone, it was now.

She needed her own space to go over all that had happened not forty minutes ago on the boardwalk with Jeff. Dajah needed music, soft and sad around her as she thought, felt, hurt and cried. She needed to expel the latest chapter of her life with Jeff and there was no place to do that at Frieda's.

So she'd hold it in. Wouldn't tell any of it. Lie to her friend if asked about her day. Lie and let the truth between them take a hit.

*

Frieda wasn't there when Dajah let herself in, just a post-note stuck to the back of the front door that said "Going to Barry's for the night." Barry was Frieda's boyfriend and that simple decision gave Dajah the solitude she'd wanted.

But by seven thirty when night had stained the world, being alone didn't feel so comforting. Her music CD's were in storage and Frieda's taste didn't quite match her own.

The bluish-grey walls and brown accents of the living room seemed to mock her, letting her know with every look that she wasn't a part of the space. Even the fit of the couch against her spine made her feel like a stranger.

Overwhelmed, Dajah let loose the tears. Mouth opened, she let the hurt that clawed the inside of her chest free. When the last tear had fallen and she'd gone through her twelfth tissue, Dajah left the living room and got on Frieda's computer. She'd find a place to call home. Had to. There would be no type of peace inside of her until she did.

*

Saturday morning, Dajah and Frieda were out early checking out new places. The apartments Dajah liked were in the wrong neighborhoods. The neighborhoods she liked didn't have any apartments that suited her. After checking on six different places, Frieda suggested a rental agent. "It can save you a whole lot of time and energy."

Frugal Dajah didn't want to use one because there was always a fee but her back was against the wall, so she agreed. She dropped Frieda back home and headed to a real estate office on Linden Boulevard. She filled out an application, talked with a real estate agent named Ms. Baldwin, and made look-see appointments for Sunday afternoon.

The first place she was shown was too tiny. The second place had a nice size bedroom, but the bathroom was small and outdated. Dajah couldn't believe where the third place was. Pulling in behind the realtor's, she didn't want to get out of the car.

Rick's house was two blocks away and on the very same street.

She gripped the steering wheel, heart beating fast. This must have been some kind of a joke.

"Miss Moore?" she heard Ms. Baldwin say through the rolled up windows. "Are you coming?"

Dajah looked at the row of fairly new homes, at the realtor, then back at the houses. The neighborhood was fairly decent. She already knew the layout because Rick had the same exact floor plan.

The living room, dining room and first bedroom was on the left. The kitchen, bathroom and second bedroom were on the right side. There would be central air conditioning and an updated kitchen and bath. The floors would not squeak and new insulation meant it would be cozy in the winter.

The rent was a great price. There would be that extra bedroom and tons of windows. Had it been in a different part of town, she might have smiled.

The sun was setting behind the house, which meant the day light exposure was east, perfect for morning coffee and reading her New York Newsday. It was empty, available, and move-in ready. She'd be able to start a new life, one baby step at a time. But it was just two streets down from Rick.

When she'd met Rick, he was still living with his baby's momma. When he left his baby's momma, he invited his baby's momma to live on the second floor apartment of his house so he could be 'close to my daughter,' his words.

Though Dajah tried to work within those crazy dynamics, including the crazy baby momma Gina being crazy with her, in the end, it didn't work out. In the end, Rick still had feelings for his crazy baby momma, feelings that Dajah could not accept.

So she'd left him and even after he tried to make a come back in her life, she shut that and him down, meeting Jeff soon after. Jeff had had his issues but he addressed them and life got good for her. No, not good—great.

Three quick raps hit her passenger window. "Miss Moore?"

Dajah looked up at the creamed colored siding with the dark beige trim. Looked at Ms. Baldwin, who was waiting a little impatiently on the street. Got out the car.

*

She didn't want to love it. Didn't want to like it even a little bit, but from meeting the landlords, an older black couple name the Dents, to stepping into the bedrooms where the sun made golden rays of melody on the walls, her soul was hijacked.

Natural light dusted everything in a soft glow. The walls were clean and spotless. The air smelled of nothing but freshness and the kitchen sparkled. The closet space was more than adequate and the sounds of the busy avenue three blocks away didn't penetrate the walls.

"What do you think?" Ms. Baldwin asked.

She was *home.* Dajah nodded emphatically.

*

"Are you serious?" Frieda's first words upon hearing the news.

"I am Frieda. And I know it's crazy, with Rick being up the street, but you know how many places I looked at and this place…" she couldn't finish.

"You've only been looking for two days. Are you sure you want to settle for that one."

"I'm not settling Frieda. It's where I'm supposed to be. Two bedrooms for what I used to pay for just one? Everything new and *sparklely?*"

"And when you run into Rick?"

"Who says I have to?"

Frieda didn't answer. Frieda knew, but kept it to herself. Some things just had to play themselves out.

*

Dajah had no plans of ever seeing Jeff again, but necessity dictated that she see him, his friend Martin and his other buddy Casey. It was moving day and Dajah needed strong backs to take her couch, bed, tables and chairs out of the storage unit and haul them up the flight of stairs. She needed willing souls who would move furniture around until it was to her liking.

It had cost her a pretty penny just to get the apartment and she always tried to be penny-wise. Jeff jumped at the chance and enlisted his friend's aid without even asking them. He also rented the U-haul.

The weather was in agreement, with sunny skies and moderate temps. Windows were cracked and soft spring air filtered around as boxes were put down, furniture assembled and the place began to take on the look of a home.

Eight hours later they sat at Dajah's dining room table, sharing Kentucky Fried Chicken and icy cokes. And when the last bit of grease had been wiped from their fingers, a pall set in. It was time for everyone to go, and each person felt the impending separation on different levels.

Frieda, though somewhat relieved that her friend had gotten a place of her own, felt an unexpected absence in her heart. Martin and even Casey sensed the rising regret inside of Jeff as they dumped paper plates and made ready to leave.

Dajah was working in duality. A part of her was eager to spend time alone in her new place and a part of her enjoyed Jeff being around her all day.

She'd be a liar if she didn't admit that, for just a second, she imagined them climbing into her bed together for a first-night-in-her-new-place, last-night-together finale. The thought began the first time their bodies brushed. Kept going when she caught Jeff looking at her. Once, they were so close, she inhaled his exhale, his face inches from her as they hoisted a heavy box into the hall closet.

But she'd stepped back, hurrying downstairs and by the time she made the sixteen-step climb back up, it had become a memory. Most of it, anyway.

When she suggested that the hard work earned them some take out and asked Jeff to run out to KFC, she knew a piece of her was still holding on.

Frieda was the first to say good night. "I'll call you when I get home," she offered with a hug. Then Martin and Casey made their excuses, even though they had rode in with Jeff and would be going nowhere without him.

"Nice place Dajah," Martin's words.

"We'll be downstairs, Bro," Casey said.

Then it was Jeff and Dajah in the living room and un-expectantly, Jeff plopped on her couch. "Woo. You worked me hard today."

Despite herself, Dajah laughed. "You volunteered, remember?"

Jeff nodded. Looked at her a long time. So long, Dajah had to look away. "Never thought this would happen," he said after a while.

"But it did and your boys are waiting for you downstairs." Her voice held little strength.

"They can't go anywhere. I have the keys."

He looked so perfect sitting on her couch. Familiar. Right. Dajah found herself on an edge, seconds from falling. *I can't do this*, she thought. *I've walked away, got a new place. On my way to my new life—without him.*

That was the wrench in her plan, the *without him*. The *being alone* again. She didn't want to be. Never wanted to be. But she would be the moment Jeff left.

Would it be so terrible if, just for tonight, she'd let him stay? Would it be so terribly wrong if, just for tonight, she took what she wanted—Jeff for one last time?

Dajah had always been the good girl. Strived to be the upstanding woman. But it had been a hard boat to row, a long haul to carry and she wanted off the pedestal she'd placed her own self on.

Just for tonight. Just one more night and then Jeff can go away forever and I can get on with my life without him.

Her cell phone vibrated against her thigh. Dajah reached into her jean pocket, pushed the little green button, uttered 'hello' and headed for the kitchen.

"I made it home," Frieda told her.

Dajah exhaled. "Saved by the bell."

"Huh?"

"Nothing…listen, I was about to walk Jeff down. Let me call you back."

"Yeah, you do that," Frieda answered, hearing something in her friend's voice she needed to know more about.

Jeff was standing when she returned. "Guess I'll be heading home."

Dajah nodded. "Let me see you out."

"No need. I know the way," his smile too fragile to contain joy.

"I have to lock the door anyway."

"Oh yeah. Right."

She felt it then, his need to flee. Became confirmed when he was down the stairs and out of her front door before her foot reached the bottom landing; his "Take care" tossed over his shoulder like an afterthought.

He had felt it too. Felt the pull between them. Took off before it could go any further. Jeff, the gentleman, making an unexpected appearance.

Dajah sighed. Closed the door. Locked it. Looked up the long flight of stairs that led to her new life, a dull ache moving into the space that once anticipated a healing.

*

"I was so there," Dajah was confessing to Frieda by phone a few minutes later. "So damn close, it was scary."

"Because you still love him. This stuff between you two just happened what, less than a week ago? Just because you're gone doesn't mean the love is."

"But you know me Frieda. When I'm done, I'm done."

"We all change Dajah. What we did back then isn't what we always do now…if you had let him stay the night, I wouldn't have blamed you."

"But he cheated on me with that chick."

"Yeah, but where was he today? With *that chick?* Or helping you move. Up and down the stairs for eight hours. Bringing in your boxes and couches and tables and chairs. He didn't have to do that, but he did."

"Don't start Frieda."

"I'm not 'starting,' I'm just stating. Everybody's running around looking for the perfect person. There's no such thing. We are all flawed. And yeah, some flaws are bigger than others, but we all make mistakes."

"Did you forget that he slept with Jill and we were supposed to be married?"

"No, but I saw how he was looking at you. How he always looks at you. Hell, Barry hasn't looked at me like that in years."

"Yeah, but Barry didn't cheat on you, now did he?"

"But he's not perfect either. There's no such thing. And maybe you need to keep that in mind."

"I know that," Dajah said solemn.

"Well, good. Because the last perfect man ain't been around for a while and his name was Jesus."

Dajah laughed. Frieda joined her.

"Love you, girl."

"Love you back," Frieda's smile coming through the phone.

CHAPTER THREE

*D*ajah stood in front of the mirror on her closet door trying to decide on a pair of shoes. It wouldn't have been so bad if she had time to spare, but she didn't. She should have been out of the door five minutes ago, on her way to the McDonald's drive-thru for a cup of coffee and a ham and egg biscuit.

But she was stuck in front of her mirror, trying to decide if she should wear brown shoes or black, *because*...she couldn't finish the thought. Her emotions were all over the place. Thoughts of Jeff replaced by Rick.

A crazy woman had hijacked her emotions and was getting real comfortable in her head. The crazy woman was telling her that she had to look perfect just in case she ran into Rick. What the crazy woman inside her brain didn't mention was, even if she saw him, she'd be in her car, wouldn't stop, not even wave, and Rick wouldn't even see her shoes.

If Dajah was up to shaming the devil by telling the truth, she'd confess, if only to herself, that Rick had been floating around her brain every since she'd first seen the place she had come to call home.

But Dajah wasn't up to it this morning and so she blamed the crazy woman that was really just her feeling lost, alone, devastated and broken hearted. Blamed her for keeping her in front of her mirror trying to decide what color shoes went best with charcoal slacks and a crisp white military-style buttoned blouse.

Ten minutes past the time she was supposed to leave, Dajah snatched up the brown ones, hating her choice, but determined to shut the crazy woman down.

*

Bad idea.

Jeff knew that when he'd said yes. Jeff knew when his phone rang last night and it was Jill and he answered. Jeff knew that he should have ignored her call like he had been doing since the great big blow-up at his front door a few days ago.

Jeff knew all of that and still told Jill to come on over, letting her spend the night.

Sorrow sex. Mad sex. Hurting sex. Revenge sex. Last night it had been all kinds of sex with Jill except loving. He had pounded into her with a fury that made his bed frame quake and bruised her inner thighs. And though it had been good to her at the start, ten minutes later, pain replaced pleasure. She winced, tried to get away, but he wouldn't let her go.

The more he hurt her, the harder he got, the wilder it became and he when did come, his whole body exploded like he had stepped on a land mine; mind blowing for all the wrong reasons.

Afterwards, he should have told her that she couldn't stay, but something about the warmth of her would not let the words out. There was something about the way she nestled against him as if what he had just done was a good thing, or something that she'd let him do again.

There was a power in that and Jeff needed to be lifted up. So he'd let her stay. Let her snuggle against his spine as the long day and the rough sex thrust him into dreamland.

But it was morning now and whatever mojo Jill had on her side last night had vanished. He shook her shoulder. "Got to get up." She mumbled something against the pillow. Didn't move.

"Come on Jill, you have to get up. I got to get to work." She did too, but he didn't care what she had to do as long as she got gone.

Jeff snatched all the covers off her, pretty cinnamon-colored skin greeting him in the morning light as she curled into a ball and reached blindly for vanished covers.

His dick lifted once, twice.

A dick had no conscious. This morning, Jeff decided he would give it one. He reached over and pulled at Jill till she sat up.

"I'm getting in the shower. Please be gone by the time I'm finished."

As the hot water hit his skin, Jeff thought about Martin's words and Dajah's hurt, a deep pinch stinging his heart.

*

Time. It was going to take some time. That's what Jill told herself as she climbed into her car, her inner thighs tender.

She had been in the wrong, showing up and showing out like that to Jeff's fiancé, but Jeff had started it by calling her out of the blue, with lies about meeting for drinks to play catch up. Jeff had started it by going back to her place afterwards and laying it down to her good, the way he used to.

Jill hadn't known that he was engaged. She didn't even know that he was living with somebody. He didn't tell her until that second week. Telling her in such a way that it made Jill feel like he really cared for her, loved her maybe. That he was going to get married but wanted one last thing with her, because she'd always had a special place in his heart.

On paper it was ridiculous, but her heart didn't live in the black and white; it lived in her head and Jill believed him. Believed that Jeff almost loved her, so much so, he'd cheated on his fiancé to get one last taste.

The more she'd thought about it, the more she was convinced that he was about to make a mistake. That he shouldn't marry Dajah. That his heart wasn't one hundred percent; a part of it, still hers. The more Jill thought about it, the more obsessed she'd become and she took it upon herself to tell Dajah what was going on.

Jill wasn't sure that it was a smart thing to do when Jeff stopped taking her calls afterwards. But last night she'd called him on a whim and he had answered. Answered and invited her over. Let her stay the night.

He had been kind of cruel this morning and things got a bit rough last night, but he had some issues he had to settle inside himself and once he did, they would be fine. Better than fine. They would be together the way she'd always wanted.

This is what Jill told herself. This is what Jill struggled to believe.

*

The numbers that were always her friend became her enemy.

Dajah had run a set of reports three times and got three different answers. She had worked through lunch and still couldn't get them to gel. When one-thirty came around and she was no closer to the right answer, she did what she'd never done. Gave up.

She'd sooner cut off her arm than admit that she couldn't get the numbers to jibe. But she was stressed and the more she tried to find the solution, the farther away it ran.

So she went to her co-worker Diane and asked her to do it for her. When Diane asked if everything was okay, Dajah did something else she'd never done before—she cried at work in front of a co-worker.

Two minutes later she hid in the bathroom. Three minutes after that, she pulled herself together, went back to Diane's desk. Told Diane to give it to their supervisor Anthony when she got it right and then Dajah did a third thing she'd never done before, she left for the day.

*

Hank Moore thought he knew his daughter better than he'd known himself, but when Dajah let herself in with her key that Monday afternoon, unannounced, Hank Moore realized that maybe he didn't.

His only child had called off her wedding, but Hank didn't press for the details. When she was ready to tell the why, she would. He just didn't expect her to do it on a Monday afternoon when she should have still been at work.

It was all in her face, crumbling as she walked to him, her arms outstretched, in need of his hug. It was all there in her eyes, shiny, wet and red with tears. And it was in her soul as she clung to him, unable to speak, not even offer a hello to her own mother who came downstairs at the sound of the front door closing.

"Give us a minute," Hank told his wife Delia. And though Delia's daughter and her husband had had many such moments and she granted them privacy, it was quarter after two in the afternoon on a work day and whatever her daughter was in the grips of was too serious to give anybody a minute.

"Dajah, what is it honey?" Delia asked carefully.

Dajah sought her mother's eyes and could only shake her head from side to side. She couldn't say that she would tell it later, that she had to tell it to her daddy first. Her mouth wouldn't work.

"What's wrong?" Dajah's mother asked again.

"Mom, please...please?" Dajah managed.

Dajah's mother looked at Dajah, at her husband holding her tight and paused. Nothing in her wanted to leave the room, but the urgency in her daughter's plea made her. She went back up stairs, but stood on the landing just out of view.

Hank Moore eased his daughter away from him. "Come on, let's go sit."

The couch cushions molded around them as Dajah searched her pocketbook for a tissue. She had none. "I need tissue," she said apologetically.

"Delia, bring some tissue," her father called out over his shoulder. His eyes went to Dajah. "You ought to let her listen," he said softly. But nothing in Dajah wanted her mother there. Her father always handled her rights and wrongs without judgment. Her mother, well her mother was her mother and there wasn't much that could change that. "She loves you as much as I do Day and she's worried like I'm worried."

"I can't daddy. I just can't."

"Yeah you can." He lifted her chin. "And you will, right?"

Dajah looked at her father, not wanting to agree. Thirty-six years old and suddenly she felt five.

"Here you go." The box of tissue appeared under her face. Dajah grabbed three. Eyes down, she blew her nose.

"She's gonna tell us both," Dajah's father said softly.

And when she did, when she told the why, the how come and the where she was now, the simple words from her mother: "Sweetie, I'm so sorry," were the best medicine for her, sweeter than any her father had to add that day.

*

Dajah couldn't believe how much she missed the simple act of helping with dinner. An assigned duty growing up, she'd never enjoyed it until now.

Back then her mother was the authoritarian, doling out chores and punishment at will. Now, she was just her Mom, someone who knew her worst tribulation, didn't judge and had managed to put a smile on Dajah's face.

"Onion?" Dajah asked, reaching into the hanging basket.

"Of course. You know we love onion on our salads."

Out of the corner of her eye, Dajah watched her mother cut and clean the whole chicken, pat it dry and season it with such a flair, there was no doubt that it was a joy for her.

She looked around the kitchen that had grown so familiar over the years, seeing the space with new eyes. This was the place that the love and care you felt for someone came to life.

It was in making sure all the extra fat was stripped from a chicken thigh. It was in making sure the fried bacon had just the right amount of crunch for the sautéed corn. It was adding the perfect balance of seasoned salt, garlic and black pepper to a freshly cleaned chicken and making sure the hot oil was the right temp to fry it up perfectly.

It's what Dajah thought she had with Jeff.

"It's okay to miss him."

Dajah blinked coming out of her thoughts. "You say something?"

Her mother smiled. Shook her head no and began tossing the chicken into the Pillsbury All Purpose. The sound of meat pieces hitting the sides of the paper bag and the slight sizzle of the heating oil filled the void as Dajah peeled the last bit of skin off the onion.

"Is it really okay?" she said after a while.

"If you really love him, there's no other way to feel."

Dajah took that thought. Kept it.

*

Over golden crispy fried chicken, cucumber, tomato and onion salad and a heaping serving of fried corn, Dajah laughed. She laughed until her eyes watered; laughed until she choked on kernels of corn. Laughed until her side hurt. Became joyed up.

She'd never thought she'd feel so at home again inside her parent's house. Didn't realized how much she missed it until she had it again. Flakes of rusted sadness were showered away beneath long winded stories of her father; her dusty soul wiped clean by a mother's love.

At the meal's end, her father cleared the table and she and her mother cleaned the kitchen. Dajah invited them to her new place, the very walls anointed with the love and support they'd shown her this day; her apartment awash in new memories of brighter days and better times.

*

The Rib Shack on Linden Boulevard was renown for it ribs and sides. The scent of charcoal and smoked meat could be smelled for miles around.

Their slabs were to die for and their barbecue sauce was a perfect blend of sweetness and heat. Put those two aromas together and you had heaven on earth. Rick couldn't help but take a sniff towards the contents of the plastic bag riding shotgun in the passenger seat.

It was game night and the tradition of picking up a rib dinner from The Shack had started last year. Brea had balked at the idea of eating pork anything, but Rick indulged with abandonment.

The game started in under an hour and he was on his way home to both it and the take out. Solitude had taught him to appreciate the simple things in life, something he was reminded of as he finished up his call to his daughter.

"Yes Kanisha, Daddy's gonna pick you up this weekend…yes, we're gonna go see *Agent Cody Banks*…I know you want to see *Holes*, but you're not old enough…" Despite the PG rating, *Holes* dealt with a kid sent to prison. Rick had seen enough of the yard. "Yes, maybe next year. Now, let me speak to Mommy."

"Hey."

"Hey. So I'm going to try and get a two o'clock show in. Have to be to work Saturday night."

"You still on that shift, huh," Gina said with a slight laugh.

"Yeah. It suits me and the money's good."

"I hear you."

"I'll call you later on in the week with what time I'm gonna—," Rick was seeing things. Had to be. There was no way that Dajah, her mother and father was walking up to a house two blocks from his house.

"Rick?"

"Oh. Sorry. Got distracted…um, what was I saying?"

"You gonna call me and tell me what time you're gonna pick up?"

"Kanisha, yeah, right. Um, yeah. I'm gonna do that," at the corner, he made a quick left. "I'll get back to you."

"Alright." But Rick had already hung up.

By the time he circled the block, Dajah, her mother and her father were no where to be seen. But her car was. Parked right in front of 129-37.

Rick didn't know how to feel about it.

Go home Rick. He did. Ate his take out and watched the game, his mind on the house two blocks down. His mind on the car he'd seen parked out front.

CHAPTER FOUR

*D*ajah stood in the plant section of Home Depot, her heart saying yes, her mind saying no. She had already done in two ficus plants, it didn't seem right to get the chance to kill a third.

Her first had been four feet tall and she'd had it for five years before her relationship with Rick had killed it. Rick's life and Rick's needs didn't give her the time to tend to it properly and it went from being lush and green to stark, barren, stripped of all its leaves.

Her second ficus had been on its way to being what her first had been when she moved in with Jeff. There had been no place for it so Dajah put it out on the curb one morning. When she got back home from work, she didn't know if someone had rescued it, or if the garbage man had dumped it. Either way, she sensed it hadn't survived without her. Now here she was going for a third.

New life, remember? Plants had always been a part of her life. They'd stopped being when she let other people get in the way. Not today. Not anymore.

Dajah flagged an associate and had him put it in her car. It looked lovely between the two windows of her living room.

*

A gremlin had taken up residence in his apartment. That was the only explanation Jeff could come up with as to why Dajah's things started popping up.

He'd found a bobby pin on the coffee table, a fake pearl earring in his night stand. Her favorite cologne was in front of the extra toilet paper underneath the bathroom sink and one of her sleeping caps was tucked in the fold at the bottom of his bed.

Jeff found a flip flop sandal under the couch and a blouse in the hall closet. It wasn't enough to even fill a plastic bag, but he put everything inside of one and hung it with the blouse.

She might want them, might need them, especially her favorite perfume. He'd have it if she asked. Hold onto it for safe keeping.

Two weeks since her departure, her absence was the empty tomb he called home. Kelly missed her too, her dog bowl never finished of food and trips to the park, near lethargic.

Jeff comforted himself as he comforted Kelly, telling her that it was okay, that they'd be okay. But Kelly would simply look at him with big wet eyes and look away.

A dog knew the truth and every time Jeff felt Kelly looking at him, he sensed condemnation. "I'm sorry," he uttered one day, "I'm so sorry." But Kelly wasn't buying that either. She simply got up, trotted off to the bedroom, nestling on her dog bed, back to the door.

Telling his parents had been hard. The hurt in his mother's eyes and the disappointment in his father's had been thick, but what dug even deeper were the words his father spoke: "Two for two." That haunted him. No matter how hard Jeff tried to let those words go, they stayed.

"I know," all Jeff could say.

"Me and your momma, we're gonna be eighty this year. We're not gonna be around forever." That had hurt Jeff even more.

He went to his closet, reached down into the bottom, Dajah's blouse brushing his head, as he got his wooden box, and the sketch pad against the back. Right there on the floor, Jeff sketched a self-portrait, the wounded man drawn in charcoal, startling.

He looked at the image a long time. Studied the forsaken eyes, the lines in the furrowed brow. Was this really him? Was this how he truly saw himself?

He didn't roll it up and tuck it away like he'd done with other sketches. He laid it out on his drafting table as a reminder of who he had become.

The phone rang.

Jeff looked at the caller ID, saw it was Jill and ignored it. She'd call a few more times before the night was through. None of the calls would get answered. Her part in his madness was over. It was time to strike out in a new direction.

*

Jill was tired of hearing the recording. Tired of hearing Jeff say that he was sorry that he wasn't available, but leave a message and he'd get back to them as soon as he could. Jill had left a message. Three so far and Jeff hadn't gotten back to her.

She hadn't spoken to him in three days. Not a call, not a text, not a nothing. She was getting antsy and that was never a good thing. Antsy made her nutsy. Antsy had her thinking about doing things she was trying not to do. Like just go over there.

Just go over and ring his bell.

She'd done it before and sometimes he'd answer. Most time he wouldn't. Jill had a feeling this was a 'wouldn't' time. Despite her bright horizon view of who they would become, it was getting dimmer moment by moment.

She had not heard from him since that last time he'd banged her hard and had been down right rude in the morning. Jill needed to hear from Jeff. Needed Jeff period. But he was missing in action.

On purpose. And not because breaking up with his fiancé was traumatic either. The sensible part of her had been telling her that since the morning she'd left Jeff's bed. Jill, trying her best not to listen, went to go get her car keys.

She got as far the sidewalk before something came over her. Jill got as far as the sidewalk before she saw herself and what she was about to do—bum rush somebody who wasn't trying to bum rush her back.

She stopped dead in her tracks. Shook her head a bit, a layered bang sticking to her eyelash. She moved it out the way, surprised that her fingers came back wet. She was crying. Standing on the side walk crying.

She never even felt the tears well up.

Really, Jill? Really?

She wiped the corners of both eyes. Blinked a few times and looked around embarrassed. She didn't recognize herself. Didn't recognize who'd she'd become. The Jeff drama of the last two years came rolling in.

Two years of trying to be with someone who, in the end, the middle, and truth be told, the beginning, never just wanted to be with her. How did that happen? That was never her style. But Jeff had changed her. Made her this person she didn't know.

Jill recalled the days when dick didn't make her crazy. Recalled the days when no man could or would make her act like a fool. But that had been before Jeff.

They had started out fine. More than fine. Great. He had poured on the charm, doing all the right things, saying all the right things, laying out the bait that never felt like a trap. Jill had proceeded cautiously enough. Overly cautious, just to be on the safe side, and Jeff had bided his time.

When love entered her heart, she let go all of the restraints and the moment she did, Jeff changed. He stopped seeing her like he used to and made no bones about plans with someone else.

When she said she wouldn't see him if he saw other women, he told her that was up to her. Jill stayed away to prove her point. But as days turned to weeks and weeks turned into a month, she had to see him. Decided that she would be with him whatever way he'd have her.

Then he dropped her all together because he had fallen in love with someone else and Jill thought life would never be the same. She was right of course, life wasn't the same. But her world grew mega watt bright when Jeff had called her out of the blue a few weeks back.

Now that light was gone.

It's really over, she thought. Truth be told, it had never truly gotten started.

*

Jeff was running, his feet barely hitting the ground as he made his way around the track. Sweat flew from his skin in fast hot drops; the sun, just a hint of ecru on the midnight blue horizon.

It had been a while since he'd been out there. Muscles stung, his breath labored, but he kept pushing and found his rhythm. Jeff felt as if he were in flight as he conquered the six laps around the track.

Other people were out there, but he felt totally alone. He was trying to reconnect with who he had been, vexing the monster he'd become.

He upped the volume on his MP3, music taking him back to better days. When he was done, the beating he'd just given his soon-to-be forty year-old body made itself known. *No pain, no gain*, he told himself as he took painful steps back to his car.

He would have to soak in the tub tonight. But the pain he had inflicted on others couldn't be tended to with a dip in hot water. Karma was surely on its way.

He tried to prepare himself for what was up the road, but sensed that no matter how much he tried, his efforts would be inadequate.

CHAPTER FIVE

*B*een there, done that and she wasn't supposed to ever do it again, but Mya Angelique Williams Connor, forty years old but looking more like a sexy twenty-five year-old on her good days, was right back to the place she just knew she would never return to.

She was right back to that ugly game that had run her ragged from her teen age years straight through to her *let-me-see-if-he-could-be-the-one* thirty-something dating years. She had been blind-sided, and wronged too many times to count. She had given her trust, her heart, her soul, and everything else in between when she shouldn't have, to men who never really loved her.

Five years ago, she had managed to untie the knots, steam press all the wrinkles and gotten past it all. Mya had to learn to live life in a whole different way. She realized she had to learn to love herself first and foremost. And she had. The proof had been Alex coming into her life, like both he and God knew she was ready for a real grown up love.

He pushed her buttons in a good way, and his hand upon her skin had been the perfect union.

So she went with him, into him, around him, about him, and life was good and sweet and it was simple to say "I do," because she'd wanted a husband for a while and he was good for her.

But now, four years into their blessed union, that thing was coming back, rising up in her, making her think too much, question everything and trusting nothing. Not Alex, not his arms that reached for her, the words that came from his lips, nor the way he looked at her sometimes.

Initially life with him had been Jill Scott's *He Loves Me,* Lauren Hills's *The Sweetest Thing.* Life with Alex, perfect melodies. The bad times, over.

But they had come back, showing up every time Alex's cell phone rang and he'd hurriedly said 'let me call you back' like some side chick was calling. In the beginning he'd say: *"I'm with Mya. Let me hit you back later,"* or, *"I'm with my wife, so let me call you back."* These days Alex had stopped explaining. Worse, Alex had stop communicating, with her.

Mya wanted to talk about what was happening to them. Tried to, but Alex's world had become consumed by the not-for-profit organization he ran, taking up all his time as he struggled to keep its doors open.

The economy was taking a nose dive. So his days were spent at his center and his evenings were spent having dinner meetings with people who could offer much needed financial support.

It made their home a battlefield, minus guns and cannons. Made their home a war zone, minus bullets, blood and words. So they limped around each other, deeply wounded with no medic in sight. After months of the conflict, Alex didn't seem to have any incentive to bring it to an end.

Mya on the other hand was ready to wave her white flag. She was ready to surrender, concede and accept whatever came next. There was no point in keeping their marriage going if there was no marriage to keep. But she couldn't get Alex to even talk about what was wrong, much less if they should call it a day.

Yesterday she'd asked him about seeing a movie. It had been a while since they had and *Chronicles of Riddick* had just hit the big screen. Mya enjoyed *Pitch Black* and couldn't wait to see the sequel, but Alex talked about having a business dinner and maybe some other time.

He'd given her so many excuses in the past few months that they kept her company more than he did. This was the reason she was on the track, running like she used to. This was the reason she'd donned sweats and sneakers and got up before work and sunrise. This was the reason she ran into Jeff, the man she had betrayed so horribly; both stunned at each other's discovery.

"Mya?"

"Jeff?" They studied each other, looking for the changes the absence from each others lives had brought.

"Wow," Jeff said a beat later.

"Yeah, wow."

"What are you—,"

"Doing here?" She shrugged. "Running."

Before him was the woman who had so killed his spirit he turned into a relationship Boogey Man. Before him was his first attempt at 'I do.' Surprise gave way to pain and pain gave way to anger. "I have to go." Jeff said quickly. The words Mya spoke lost to the sound of his sneakers churning up the gravel track.

Jeff picked up his pace. When he ended up half a lap behind Mya, he slowed down. There was nothing good about the woman ahead of him. Nothing good at all.

*

Five Years Earlier

Running.

Mya felt her feet hit the ground, but little else. Everything above her ankles was weightless and heaven-bound. She sprinted. Caramel thighs kissing the morning sun. Sweat glistened on her skin, and she was one with the universe.

Her thoughts were cast in a hundred directions, riding the wind, making connections. Her mind, open and free, released itself. She urged her body forward, every muscle in her consigned to finishing the course she'd set. Twelve laps, three miles, her daily debt for the body that was firm and fit.

Sweat gathered, wetting her scalp, crawling into her eyes. Slid down her spine in hot little drops. Sweat, her earmark, the indicator that said she was on target, par for the course. Doing it.

Lap thirteen. She slowed, her body shifting gears. She let go of her last bit of energy until she was down to a stroll. Her body pulsed against the soft breeze, her runners high on its way.

She was in her own little world and liked it. Just her and her thoughts. No worry, no cares. She went on that way, semiconscious of the world around her, feeling good and competent, her three miles finished.

Then reality arrived, bringing her back into the here and now; her netherworld fading like smoke. Her eyes found her watch, confirming what she already knew. A few minutes were all she owned before she had to go home and get ready for work.

Mya sensed someone to the left of her and shifted to her right. Counted off seconds, waiting for them to pass. She walked, breathing hard, tense, catching a flicker of long brown thigh. *Was it him?*

For three days he had paced her mute and just out of sight. For three days, Mya had been aware of him, growing more anxious with each passing day. She needed him to say hello, break the ice, ask her name, put an end to what he had begun days ago.

Her chest began to hurt and she realized she was holding her breath. She released it, lowered her head. Looked up, a quick glance to the left, and there he was.

Their eyes met, locked and danced away. For three days he had lingered in her shadows. Now he was right by her side.

"Hi."

She nodded, reeling in her emotions. Took in air, determined not to be anxious; determined to be cool in the wake of his long-anticipated approach.

"Hello."

"I'm Jeff."

She took in more air, playing her hand. "Mya."

"You run often?"

"Often enough."

"You have a nice stride," Jeff went on to say.

"Thanks." She looked at her watch. Six forty-five. Time to go. There was a slight pause, a shifting of his energy and Mya knew this Jeff was going to get to his nitty-gritty.

"So, you married or anything?"

"Are you?" she asked, a certain humor in her voice. She knew her question had taken him by surprise. Years of dating had given her a slightly hardened edge and her tongue was known to bitter at the drop of a hat.

"Married? Me? Not yet."

"Kids then," she decided about the man with the nice runner's body and kind brown eyes who had followed her for three days around the track without so much as a 'hello.'

"No, not the last time I looked."

"Don't you know?"

He shrugged. "I'm as sure as sure can get."

This moment, anticipated for days, took a backseat as liability found her. She was on the clock and had a job to get to. She looked at him regretful. "I gotta go."

"Already?"

"Yeah…work."

"Can I get a number?"

She was surprised that he was asking. "You want a number?"

"Yeah."

She drew back then, two emotional paces from the man beside her. She denied her first instinct and opted for a second. She wouldn't give her number, just her mystery. "Seven."

Confusion clouded his face. "Seven what?"

She shrugged. "Just seven."

"Your phone number's one digit?"

Mya laughed, enjoying the moment, the puzzlement that danced on his face. "Hey, you wanted a number. I gave you one…really, I got to go." She gave a little wave and left off. Opened her car door and slid into the seat.

Mya lifted the water bottle to her lips and took a long sip. Watched him watch her, wonderment full in his eyes.

*

Jeff stood breathing deeply on the morning air. The Honda had disappeared seconds ago, but his eyes were fixed on the empty street.

Mya. Like a first breath, her name rushed him with wondrous ebullience, filling him, teasing him; playing hide and seek with his heart. It had been a while since he'd felt this way and the elation was so profound, so sweet, it felt like the first time he had experienced this joy.

Up-front, saucy. Sexy. Combinations too irresistible to ignore and too tantalizing to resist. There was an intensity to her; an excitement that was fire and ice. Getting too close could mean a serious burn, but that didn't deter Jeff. He liked his women spicy and getting close to the flame was half the attraction…

*

Present Day

Jeff had been wrong of course. Getting close to Mya's flame had gotten him burned and deeply wounded. And here she was popping up in his life years after those years. Jeff kept his eye on her until she became a speck on the horizon. Only then did he head back to his car—keeping distance between them, the best thing.

*

Alex had worked hard on becoming a person he could be proud of. He had gone deep into himself, examined the good and the bad and decided that from that moment on, he would strive to be his best self.

Practice made perfect and by the time he'd met Mya, he had discarding the head games, big ego, the BS, and all that other nonsense by the way side. Mya, having gone through her own metamorphosis, had been in the very same mindset. It was a no brainer that they connected the way that they did.

Like minded and soul-synchronized, the normal progression in their relationship had been a trip to the altar. And it was good, all good, really good, until the day-to-day matrimony began to dull.

Being around women, beautiful women, classy and smart was a part of Alex's job duties. He was always after funding and more times than not it was a female from some corporation he had to wine and dine.

Sometimes they would flirt and for a long time Alex didn't flirt back. But something happened a few months ago that changed the rules for him. Dawn Kessle happened.

In the middle of their business dinner, Alex found himself vibing on Ms. Kessle. Alex Connor, committed husband to Mya Angelique Connor, had gotten turned on at dinner as he sat across from a woman who was as fine as they came, smelling just as sweet, and sounding even sexier than the low cut dress she wore.

It had been his little secret until she had leaned over the table to straighten his tie.

Alex, the married man, began to feel anything but as Dawn took extra effort to fix his shirt collar, her hands jostling his shoulder-length black dreads.

She might as well have pushed him back in his chair, unbuckled his buckle, downed his zipper and reached into his Jockeys. Because that's how it left him feeling.

He should have made some excuse and left. But he didn't leave. Just sat there, emotionally sipping what Dawn was serving, convincing himself that his organization needed the funding and Dawn had the power to deliver.

But would he fuck her for it?

That was the question that slipped into his lap soon after. It floated over the table then settled in Dawn's smile as the main course was served. Soon her laughter and the sparkle in her eyes joined the party and the answer that filled Alex's mind made for a horrible choice.

Later, he would tell himself that he did it for Kwaleed House of Hope, the eighty-five thousand dollar check secured in his wallet. Later he would tell himself he did it for Morris, his assistant who hadn't gotten paid in two weeks. That he did it for little Kendall, a ten year-old who leaned on the center for the support and nurturing he couldn't get at home.

Alex would tell himself that he did it to keep the lights on, the center heated and the opportunity to get Mya a decent birthday gift. That's what Alex told himself, burying his mis-deed as if it never happened.

But it happened again a week later. The usual dinner meeting changed to a hotel out in Great Neck. Clean sheets instead of blackened fish. Hot sex instead of an after-meal coffee. A quick shower instead of a handshake goodbye and, no check.

That's when the truth of what he was doing hit home. He had slept with Dawn the first time for the sake of keeping his center open. But the second? Because he wanted to. Wanted to feel himself deep inside a woman who didn't know every inch of him like his wife of four years.

Alex told himself that that would be the last time. But the forbidden became like a drug and he began meeting up with Dawn on the regular. She had already bought and paid for him when she handed over the five-figure sum. He was just keeping up his end of the bargain.

That's what he told himself.

*

She had never planned a life-long career at Chelsea Data Processing. Mya had majored in marketing in college and had her dreams of starting her own firm. Chelsea Data was just supposed to be a pit stop on her way to the top. But when she marked her eleventh year at the company, six as an Executive Assistant, she understood that she would no doubt be there for the long haul.

In that time, she'd gone through three bosses, a ton of co-workers and three desk relocations. But the most impetus moment occurred when one Chloe Anderson had been hired several years before.

Until then Mya had been the only black woman on her floor and every day that she showed up to work, she made sure everybody knew it, out-dressing and out-styling the best of them.

Chloe Anderson's arrival changed all of that.

The tall, slim, smoky chocolate-brown Naomi Sims look alike had entered the hollowed halls of Chelsea Data and enraptured everyone she met. Classy, elegant, sophisticated and wise, Mya was certain Chloe had shown up just to steal her thunder.

Mya had been wrong of course but her own insecurities told her that it was the gospel. Chloe, understanding more than Mya could have at the time, took her aside, put both their cards on the table and made Mya see that she wasn't a threat to anyone; that Mya was a threat to her own self.

Chloe Anderson had gone from a co-worker Mya couldn't stand to a great friend, confidant and counselor in the years since. She'd helped Mya through rough times in the past and though it had been some time since Mya sought her out for advice, now was such a time.

"It only means something if you want it to mean something," Chloe's advice as they had lunch at an eatery on 8th Avenue. "So, do you want it to mean something?"

Mya was hesitant to answer. Alex's distance and Jeff reappearing in her life was all she could think about since running into him. She needed answers, not questions, but she knew Chloe would make her travel her own road of discovery.

"Tell the truth and shame the devil," Chloe said, serious.

"I love Alex." Chloe nodded. "I mean, I really love him. But it's like he stopped loving me back."

"So you think that running into Jeff after all that you two have been through and all the years that have passed and you being married to somebody else, really means something?"

"I do."

Chloe shrugged, annoyance dusting the shoulder of her jacket. "Okay."

"Don't do me like that Chloe. I'm confused."

"No, Mya, you're not confused. You just want some easy out. You want me to tell you that yes, it's a sign from God to divorce your husband and go back to Jeff, that man you cheated on right before you were supposed to marry. Welp, I'm not going to tell you that."

Mya loved Chloe. But sometimes she down right hated her.

"So tell me what I need to hear," she said after a while.

Chloe put down her fork. Considered her friend. "If you love Alex enough, you'll find a way to fix things. If you don't, you'll find a way to unfix them. So, you have to decide which one you really want." With that, Chloe picked up her fork, Mya got back to her salad, the arugula and crumbled feta tasteless in her mouth.

CHAPTER SIX

*T*uesday morning couldn't come fast enough for Rick.

He'd driven past that house the last few nights and Dajah's car had been parked outside in the same spot. Sometimes lights were on in the upstairs apartment. Most times they weren't, but her car was steady.

She had moved a few blocks from him.

Today, he was going to see her face-to-face.

He hadn't decided if he would drive by as she got in her car, honking his horn to get her attention; be out on her street on the pretense of walking, or just be waiting by her car when she headed out to work.

All of it sounded brazen. All of it sounded unsound. But he had to see her. Had to let her know that he knew where she was. Rick had to find out if she was living single or with somebody. Maybe he was beating a dead horse, but when you had nothing, it was simple to latch on to something.

She had to realize that she was in close proximity to him and must have been okay with it. So what was the harm in saying hello? They hadn't ended on the greatest of terms but maybe they could still be friends.

Absurd notions weren't new to Rick.

Buying a two-family house with his baby's mama and his child living upstairs while he lived down stairs and dated other people had been one of them. 'Forced' running into Dajah was making all the sense in the world to him.

He'd never wanted her gone from him.

Not even when it felt like he wanted to get back with Gina, his baby's momma. When Dajah broke up with him, he'd tried to get her back. She turned him down flat. Nothing about that last encounter said she'd change her mind, but Rick had to know for himself.

*

She wanted to believe she was seeing things.

Dajah wanted to believe that Rick standing outside his car across the street from her front door was a mirage. She knew running into Rick would happen, but she thought it would occur at the bodega around the corner, the Keyfood a few blocks up the street. Not him standing there, hands in his pockets, looking at her with uncertainty.

What she was supposed to do with that? What did he expect her to say besides "hey" and keep it moving? Dajah wasn't sure, but she acted as if he wasn't standing across the street as she turned and locked the door, keeping her eyes to the ground until she left out of the gate. Only then did she look up, words failing her as he headed her way.

"I've been seeing your car." Dajah nodded. "You live here now?"

She wanted to lie. Say she was just visiting, but he had confessed he'd seen her car. There was no sense in it. "Yeah. Long story." She hit the remote on her car.

"Well, welcome to the neighborhood."

"Yeah." She opened the car door, slipped inside. "Running late." She didn't wait to hear his response. Just turned on her car, closed the door and eased from the curb.

It took two blocks before she found her breath, another three before the dizzy swarm in her head ceased. She'd knew she'd run into Rick, but didn't think it would go down like that. What was she going to do about it? Did she want to do anything at all?

*

It took a few seconds for Rick to get moving. A few seconds to understand what had just happened, what didn't.

She saw you and wasn't happy about it. Saw you and bounced. So what does that tell you, Rick? Dajah may have been up the block from him, but she might as well have been on Pluto.

*

Her mind was soupy by the time she got to work. Once again, affairs of the heart had her off-balanced. She scalded her hand while pouring some coffee and put her pocketbook in the garbage instead of her desk drawer.

She misjudged the distance between her shoulder and the door frame when she went to the ladies room, and poked herself in the eye with a pencil. It wasn't until she was pressing a wet napkin to her injury did she understand that she was mad—with herself.

You mad? For real? You moved two blocks away from a man you left and now you gonna get pissed about it? Where was the anger when you pulled up to the apartment that first time and knew exactly what living there meant? Where was the anger when you smiled as you looked around and happily decided that that was where you wanted to stay?

Where were the self injuries when you turned over two months rent and a deposit? It was too late to be mad and self-sabotaging. She'd signed up for it. But what really had her annoyed was how much Rick scared her. How he had her acting like a Chicken Little.

Dajah wasn't up to asking herself why.

*

Saturday morning Rick came in from work, set the alarm for 12 noon and crawled into bed. He didn't feel too tired, but understood just how tired he was when the alarm went off in what seemed like only a few minutes after he lay down.

Bleary-eyed, he reached for the shut off, blinked a few times and tried to rationalize that he could get just fifteen more minutes. But he knew that fifteen minutes would become an hour and by the time he did wake up, it would be too late to catch the two o'clock showing of *Agent Cody*.

Rick wasn't looking forward to it.

He wasn't looking forward to some cheesy Disney movie as he struggled to stay awake through the hour and ten minute flick. But his daughter was, and that's all that really mattered, so he got up, got showered, got dressed and headed out.

He purposely went out of his way to avoid Dajah's street, feeling foolish for his attempted hi-jack of her attention. In the aftermath, he saw himself like she must of seen him and decided that she would be right if she tagged him a stalker—the last thing he wanted to be considered. But there was no doubt that what he wanted to be considered was a pipe dream, his and his alone.

*

"Daddy!" No matter how many times she said it, no matter how many teeth she lost and grew back in; no matter how much taller she seemed to grow since that last time he saw her, those words coming out of his daughter's mouth was Rick's whole world.

"Hi Honey," Rick answered, hugging her, the top of her head now reaching just below his chest. Just six and a half, Kanisha was taller than most kids her age. On her way to seven, her face was finally catching up with the size of her two front teeth.

He used to say: 'Hi Baby,' but some where within the last few months, Kanisha had decided that she wasn't a baby anymore, that she was going to second grade and he should stop calling her that.

"So, y'all be back, about what, five?" Gina asked.

Rick looked upon the woman he had loved too hard, then not at all, lost in the middle of the two for a minute, and nodded. "Yeah, about that time." He was happy to see that her weave-wearing, dragon claw nail days were behind her and her real hair, cut and layered to her shoulders softened everything about her.

"You feeding her before she get home?"

"Yeah, probably do a run through McDonalds."

"Wendy's," Kanisha said decidedly, slipping one arm through her pink jacket.

Gina laughed. "She don't do Em Dee's no more."

Rick wanted to ask *when did that happen?* but like many things, changes came into his daughter's life and he wasn't around to witness them. He accepted that fact and urged Kanisha down the stairs.

The movie wasn't half bad, but Rick dozed through the last twenty minutes, relieved when Kanisha shook him awake as the final credits rolled. "So, what did you think?" he asked.

"It was great!" All Rick wanted to hear.

He looked at his watch. It was just a little before four. "Wendy's, right?"

"Um hum. I want a chicken sandwich and a—,"

"Chicken sandwich?"

"Uh huh."

"But you were always the cheeseburger girl?"

"When I was a baby, Daddy. I keep telling you I'm grown up now. I'm going to second grade."

Rick smiled. "Yes, I know. Just never thought you'd give up the cheeseburgers."

"'Cause we all gotta change, Daddy, that's what Mommy say."

"Really?"

"Uh huh. 'Specially to Mr. Collin. She be telling him you got to change and he be telling her that he is changing and stuff."

Collin. The man in Gina's life.

Rick hadn't been particularly impressed with the young dude when they first met. Collin was a year older than Gina, but had a vibe about him that suggested a certain immaturity. Rick had run Collin's records through the Department Of Corrections and was happy that they came back clean, but Rick was holding out a final opinion.

Gina liked him and Kanisha was okay with him, but any man who was around his daughter would be suspect. Rick was always asking Kanisha how she felt about Collin and after a year, the reports were still good. As long as they were good, Rick tried to make peace with it.

"What else does he be saying?" Rick asked carefully.

Kanisha shrugged. "And French fries and a sprite." She looked up at Rick, mirror eyes looking back at him. "Can I get that?" Kanisha had turned the page. Rick knew it was time for him to do the same.

*

Jeff stood on the stoop, waiting for the door to open. He didn't call, decided to just show up un-announced. Two weeks since he saw Dajah, her blouse and other left behind items in the bag gave him reason enough to 'drop by.'

He wasn't sure if she would answer, but knew she was home. Her car parked in front told him so. But it felt like a lifetime since he had rang the bell three times, and as of yet, there was no answer.

He was about to ring it a forth when the door swung open. The person before him not Dajah, but Mr. Dent, the landlord who lived on the first floor.

"Can I help you?"

"Oh…sorry. I was looking for Dajah." Jeff said looking up.

"Hers is the bottom bell. Mines is the top."

That didn't make sense to Jeff, but he kept it to himself as his eyes settled to the stairs, wanting to slip past the old black man and run up them. "Try the bottom," final words as Mr. Dent stepped back and closed the door, wood meeting frame with a *swoosh.*

*

Just out of sight, Dajah had listened to the conversation between her landlord and Jeff. She had heard a car door slam, the sound of the gate creaking open and the sight of Jeff walking up the walkway.

Relieved that it wasn't Rick, she had been in deep debate about whether to go down and let him in. She had waited for her doorbell to ring, but it never did. She glanced out the window and saw Jeff's car still parked. A few seconds later she heard the downstairs front door open and voices. Easing her own door opened, she'd eavesdropped.

Then the door was closing again and soon after her doorbell was ringing. Dajah inhaled, exhaled and made her way down, despite herself, glad about Jeff's unexpected arrival. Truth was truth. She missed him.

*

Back in the eighties, Pat Benatar had sung *Love is a battlefield.* Dajah knew exactly what Pat meant as she sat on her couch, Jeff on the other end, laughing. She didn't even know what had struck her so funny, but there she was, mouth open, guffawing and struggled for air.

How they even got there, vague.

She'd opened the door. Jeff extended some things 'she'd left behind,' running down the inventory as Dajah dug in the plastic bag, her favorite perfume part of the bounty and the next thing she knew, they were upstairs sitting on her couch, laughing about something.

The ease he brought into her life returned full-force and the why of the whole messy affair faded. She was glad he was there. Glad that she could still laugh. Glad that he cared enough about her to make her laugh.

But then it was just her chuckles riding the breeze, Jeff going silent, his eyes on her full. That's when it struck her.

He still loves me.

There was no mystery in that. Of course he still loved her. Dajah had known that as she cursed him, packed her things and made arrangements to move out. But Love hadn't been enough to make her stay. She'd become a rock in that determination.

But now, she was feeling more like water flowing around the rock, getting past the block, the hump, the mountain, the thing that stopped their life together. Sitting there with Jeff, she felt everything in her flowing, drifting backward, toward what used to be.

"You want to go get something to eat?"

Food, good food was as good an aphrodisiac for Dajah as anything. In their initial days, he had treated her to the best hot chocolate in the world. Weeks later, at his place, he had hand fed her chocolate covered strawberries that made her want more.

He had tapped into what turned her on and recreated a manual that he studied like he was studying for his LSAT's. Jeff had infiltrated Dajah like no man had ever done before. How does anyone just say no to that?

"You want? We could go pick up Kelly…she misses you and head out to Jones. Get some seafood at the spot we like."

Dajah had never been into raw oysters until Jeff had opened her up to the perfect ones. A squirt of lemon juice, a dash of hot sauce and the sucking up of the uncooked morsels, just divine. And Kelly, that hug hairy ball of fur that loved her so unconditionally, was missed too. Where was a 'no' in any of that?

*

The smell of the sea air infused Dajah. The sun on her face, the sound of seagulls keening in the breeze, the feel of Kelly tugging at the Frisbee, sand beneath her feet, perfect. The sight of Jeff, ten yards away, watching her experience it all, overwhelming.

Had she acted too hastily? No one was perfect. Everyone made mistakes. And who else in the whole live world could give her this? What other man knew that playing with a dog on the beach in late April could be as potent as a night of dancing, a weekend getaway to the Bahamas? That being near the ocean was like worshippers going to a spirit-filled Sunday Service for her?

Nobody but Jeff.

Yes, he had slept with that woman, but fear was a crazy, dangerous thing. It made you do stupid things in a blink of an eye and she still had the power of forgiveness. Not for Jeff, but for herself.

There was that dress picked out. Wedding colors decided on. The church planned. Best man and maid of honor selected. The promise of life with someone who genuinely loved her. That ring on her left hand. Grandchildren for their parents.

Dajah tossed the Frisbee. Watched as Kelly raced toward it. Watched Jeff and his dog play, heart wide opened. Yes, she had the power to forgive. In that moment, that's where she was headed.

*

There was no more 'no' in her.

Whatever 'no' she had shored up to be used for such a time was gone. Dajah knew it and Jeff knew it as he let them into the place she, for a second, called home, and reached for her the moment he closed his front door.

'No' was gone from her vocabulary as his hands moved under her jacket, down into the tight fit of her jeans, cupping her behind like the warm soft half melons they were, and her body, so familiar with him, his hands, the way they molded and moved her skin, opened like a flower bloomed.

'No" didn't exist as he eased off clothing, hers, his and they were naked before each other, bodies responding in-kind to the snap back of their past, trying to mold a future with limbs and arms, and mouths and racing hearts and sighs and murmurs and whispers and entry and pleasure and pain that made her eyes shut and her mouth opened unable to keep his name out of her mouth. Jeff, a new/old sing song that her heart, in that moment, needed to be sung until there was no more breath, no more 'no,' inside of her.

*

At two in the morning, the 'light' came on inside her mind.

Right up until that second, Dajah, fast asleep, nestled and snug against Jeff, had been gone to the world. Suddenly her eyes snapped opened and she realized where she was, what she'd done.

The reasons why she'd left him came back like flood lights flicked on in a dark basement. Dajah blinked against the emotional brilliancy. Blinked again against the truth. She had slipped up, tripped up. Back-slid under the skillful talents of Jeff.

He had played a seductive concerto upon the violin of her shattered soul. With a nuance so subtle, she didn't even feel the snare. He had gotten her—hook, line and sinker. But there was still some strength in her and Dajah wiggled free.

Easing out of his bed, she snatched up her things, dressed in the bathroom and left, for the last time. That much she knew.

*

Dajah knew Jeff had set her up for a backslide. Forgave herself. But what she wasn't prepared for was the argument that ensued the next day.

"You can't tell me that yesterday didn't mean anything," he insisted over the phone.

"No, you're right, Yesterday was wonderful. Yesterday was perfect. Yesterday was the best damn day I'd had in a while. But that's the thing Jeff. What you did to me wasn't wonderful. It wasn't perfect. It wasn't the best damn thing and there's no getting around that."

"I saw you Dajah. I felt it. You still love me."

"Loving somebody and wanting to be with somebody is two different things."

"So, you're saying yesterday was a mistake?"

"Not a mistake, but not no ever-after either."

"I'm not asking for ever-after."

"You can't because you've lost that right."

"I messed up. I admit that. Have admitted that. All I'm asking for is a chance, to make it up to you."

She sighed, wearied. "There is no making up for it. None. You did what you did and I had to do what I did."

"So yesterday?"

"Just that…yesterday. What we had is over. Done."

"So, can I still see you?"

"Why? So you can get me to change my mind? I'm not changing my mind."

"You did last night."

Low blow. For a second, Dajah couldn't respond. But she knew she had to bring down the axe. Chop to bits what had happened just a few hours earlier. "Yes, I did. Why? Because I was hurt and lonely and confused and bewildered and for a few minutes, I just wanted all of it to go away. But the thing is, it didn't stay away. It came back on me like fire."

She took a breath, pain fresh in her. "It's over Jeff. Done. Don't call me. Don't come see me. Don't anything. You find something that's mine, dump it. If I didn't bring it with me, it means I don't need it…I gotta go."

Dajah hung up the phone.

*

An hour later Jeff was at the track.

He was running fast and hard, away from things, toward the unknown. He was trying to exorcise Dajah from his soul.

If he had any hope before, it was gone. Yesterday had been more than perfect. Yesterday, their life felt mended. When he'd fallen asleep, Dajah snuggled close, Jeff had been certain they would work things out.

But he'd forgotten how determined she could be. Realized too late that just because she'd gone with his flow in that moment, it didn't mean she'd be around in the aftermath.

He needed to get the whole attempt gone from him. So Jeff ran until his lungs felt ready to explode. Ran until his feet were minutes from blistering and went on and ran some more.

By the time he stopped, all he could do was collapse on the dead grass mesa, head down, lungs laboring, as tears mixed in with the sweat that dripped from his face.

He was in need of a healing, but had no clue how to begin.

*

Mya wanted to say her jeans had gotten a wee bit too tight. That the eighth of an inch of skin hanging over her bra strap needed attending to. But the truth was Mya was trying to get back to that place she'd been when she had been single and okay with it. Single and not afraid of it. Single and just fine with it. Loving it and herself.

So after Alex headed out to do whatever it was he did at his center, she had put on running clothes and headed for the track. It was on her sixth lap, that she'd notice the man sitting in the middle of the dead grass, head down.

He had looked up towards the sky and Mya recognized the profile, tripping over her own feet as the realization struck. She'd slowed to a walk, her overworked muscles glad, as she watched from a distance, relieved when he got up and headed for the bleachers.

It was her last lap and she would have to cross right in front of him. She couldn't bring herself to change direction. Couldn't make her feet go in any other direction than straight ahead. Chloe's words thrummed through her brain as she looked down at her ring finger, the silver glowing in the morning sun.

For better or worse.

The better was gone and there only seemed to be the 'worse.' Whatever was or wasn't going on between her and Alex, it had nothing to do with Jeff. Nothing.

Not about him, Mya reasoned, her eyes on the handball courts as she walked right by him; swallowing and swallowing again. *It's not,* she determined, her sight straight ahead until she reached her car, inhaling and exhaling as she applauded that tiny accomplishment.

But her heart felt it. Felt the forked road. Where it would lead, she didn't know, but it would change her world, forever.

*

Jeff watched Mya until she was gone from sight. She must not have seen him. Must have been deep into her runner's high.

He looked out on the track, memories of their past trying to rise up again. She had been the source of so much misery in his life. Long gone and her wounding was still causing him harm.

He had enough turmoil. There wasn't room for a drop more.

*

Sunday was the big meal day at Mya's house. She'd get in the kitchen around two in the afternoon and by five, a four course dinner would be ready to eat. But this Sunday was different and after coming back from the track to find the apartment empty, Mya decided she wasn't going to cook and went about making her some hot dogs.

The water was boiling on the stove and the package of Sabretts franks were on the counter as Mya searched the fridge for some relish. She didn't know what Alex would have and tried not to care. She hadn't heard from him since he'd left early this morning. If he couldn't be considerate, then neither would she.

The front door opened then closed. *At least he's back.* She didn't know where he had gone off to, even though he said he had some work at the center. It took everything Mya had not to go by there on the way home just to see.

A hand landed on her shoulder. "Hey."

She turned. Glanced at him. Looked away, glad that he smelled of nothing but Musk oil and his own sweat. "Hey."

"We have to talk."

"Talk?"

"Yeah, talk."

Mya forgot about relish, boiling water and franks on the counter. She forgot about being hungry, where he had gone off to and what he had possibly been up to. He wanted to talk now and she had wanted to talk forever.

Relief filled her. A tiny smile danced on her face. But that relief was short lived as he took her by the hand and led her to the living room. Vanished, as he ushered her toward the sofa.

Her gut knew. Whatever he wanted to 'talk' about would not be good.

CHAPTER SEVEN

*S*unday afternoon found Rick in his front yard, aerating the lawn. In the time since he'd moved in, the green grass had given way to broadleaf clover and dandelion weed. This year he wanted a lawn that made him feel welcomed when he pulled into his driveway.

The jerking of the machine hurt the muscles in his arms and the vibration made his wrist tingle. But there was something honest about working his 'land,' even though it was just a ten foot by twelve foot square.

Tomorrow, he would spread seed and water. As long as they didn't get a Nor'easter bringing a final snow, by May, his lawn would be nice and green.

Rick took a hot shower after his yard work was done then headed to a fast food place for some dinner. But half way there, he decided he'd wanted a home-made deli sandwich and went to the super market instead.

*

It wasn't that Dajah was a food snob, she just knew which grocery stores had the best and freshest food and Walbaums out in Long Island was a much better pick than the local grocery a few blocks from her house.

She only needed a few things and couldn't see driving out to Five Towns. So she headed over to the Keyfood to pick up some coffee, bananas and chicken breasts. By the time she got to the check out, her items also included sausage, ice cream, a two liter soda and fresh broccoli.

She thought about the television shows she would settle down to all by her lonesome and didn't feel too bad about it. Last night's adventure with Jeff demanded some real down time for her. She needed to settle things in both her head and her heart.

Even though she understood the why, it still had been a mistake. Jeff was her past. Without him was her future. It was time to truly start embracing that.

*

Rick looked down at his half a pound of turkey breast, quarter pound of Swiss cheese, the loaf of French bread and the six-pack of Arizona Ice Tea and felt like he was forgetting something. But he was already in the check out line.

The line was moving slower than he wanted and his stomach was growling and making percolating noises. Tomato. He needed a tomato and was out of Miracle Whip too.

He looked at the six people ahead of him and looked left and right to see how long the other lines were. All of them, full. If he got off the line, it would be a long wait. But his sandwich would be bland without the tomato and dressing.

He pulled back his cart. Said 'excuse me' to the person behind him, shocked to see Dajah. She had been right behind him and didn't utter a word.

*

She hadn't known it was Rick.

It wasn't until he turned did she realize it. Her mouth hung open for a second before "Oh. Sure," came out. Stepping back, she let him pass, not looking at him as he wheeled his cart away.

This was what living in the neighborhood meant—running into Rick. Running into a man she'd loved too much and he not enough.

That was the sticking point, she realized. That was the thing that made her quietly hostile in his presence. It was all the love she'd given him and how it felt like he'd barely returned the favor. It wasn't supposed to matter anymore, but as Dajah moved her shopping cart up four paces, she realized it did.

Being with Jeff had lifted her from the sludge pile that HAD been life with Rick, cleaned her off and allowed her to shine again.

But in the end, Jeff had dumped her in a brand new mess and once again she was trying to clean herself up, dust herself off, keep it moving. *Toward what?* A happy life. But that seemed easier said than done.

*

She didn't even say hello.

Dajah had just got out of his way as if they had never known each other, had liked each other, had history together. She had wheeled her cart, giving him wide passage without so much as a smile.

Rick could understand how the first time running into him had done her. But this was the second and her reception had been cold. He had apologized, hadn't he? Had tried to win her back? But she had turned him down flat and he let her be. So why the attitude?

He got his tomato, got his Miracle Whip and headed back to the check out. He got in a different line, spying Dajah three counters over. His line moved faster than hers and by the time he was exiting the store, so was she.

They might as well have been strangers as they turned blind eyes, grabbing up their items from their carts and heading to their cars. Strangers as they both pulled out of their parking spaces and headed for the exit.

Strangers as Dajah drove behind Rick until he pulled into his driveway. He heard her car go by as he opened his door. Listened absently as the smell of fresh turned earth filled his nose. Rick looked at the tilled soil, affirmed in what he did have. He still had life.

*

Dajah didn't plan on having any conversations about Rick ever, but seeing him had shut her down not once but twice and she needed to talk to someone about it.

Frieda knew the why. She knew from the moment Dajah told her. But her friend wasn't up to hearing it just yet and so she kept it to herself, taking Dajah off the hook. "It's going to be weird for a minute. You two had an intense kind of past. You can't expect that to just disappear over night."

"But you know me Frieda. Not much scares me, especially no man," which was a half truth at best.

"Running into him on the regular is all new. You'll get used to it."

"I hope so," Dajah said, meaning it.

*

Jeff was on the beach out at Far Rockaway when his cell phone rang. It was Jill. He didn't answer. When her text message came in a few seconds later, he read it. Debated.

It was Sunday afternoon. She'd made dinner. The idea of a home cooked meal didn't sound too bad. He'd take Kelly home and head over to her house. Get his grub on and split.

*

The piece of bread crumb was so tiny, most people wouldn't have noticed. But it caught Jill's eye like it was under a magnifying glass.

She'd wiped the dinette down twice. How in the world did she leave a crumb behind?

Jill had wiped, cleaned, swept and vacuum. She'd changed her blouse twice and checked her reflection in the mirror four times. She was being ridiculous, but she couldn't help it. Jeff was coming by for dinner and everything had to be correct.

She hadn't been sure if her invite would be accepted. Jill hadn't been sure of anything when she sent it. She hadn't seen or heard from Jeff in weeks, but Sunday found her needing one last thing from him. A confession.

She needed Jeff to say, out loud, that he never loved her, so her soul could be free of him. She needed to hear that it had been all in her head, so she could move on.

He arrived an hour later. He didn't reach for her and she didn't reach for him. She was a bit nervous as she closed the door and was glad he headed straight for the dinette table. This was about food and talk.

She fixed him a plate and didn't ask him what he wanted to drink because she knew he liked Orange crush. She came from the kitchen, carrying a plate. Put it before him.

"You're not eating?"

"I ate already."

Jeff shrugged, picked up a baked chicken leg.

"Did you ever love me?"

He looked at her, mid-chew. Looked away.

"I know you didn't Jeff. I just need for you to say it."

Jeff wiped his mouth. He'd come to eat and run. She had invited him to get the truth. So be it. "It wasn't that I didn't want to. But…"

"But, what?"

Truth left him. "I wasn't trying to love anybody."

"Not even me." The hurt in her voice, apparent.

"I really did like you."

"But not enough to count."

"I don't know how you define 'enough to count.'"

"Not enough to keep you from seeing Syreeta, Lisa and Joy." Jill was surprised at how calm she was. She was surprised that she was able to carry on the conversation without breaking down. Jeff was shocked that she knew all the names. Told her so. "You never tried to hide it," she responded. "You'd tell me, 'Well, I can't because I'm doing this and that with Joy.' Or, 'I'm going to the movies with Syreeta.' Not tonight. Lisa's coming over.' Remembering their names?" She chuckled, not a drop of joy in it. "You were always putting them in my face."

For the second time in less than a month, Jeff apologized to a woman he had wronged. "I'm sorry Jill for the way I treated you."

And for the second time, a woman found the apology hard to accept. "No, you aren't sorry, not when it mattered."

She had her answers. The first tear fell. She tried to reel in the second, but to no avail. Jeff resisted the urge to wipe them. He didn't feel comfortable touching her anywhere. Too much hurt was in her. Sympathy and regret was in him. The two coming together would be a bad combination. So he pushed his barely eaten plate away and asked if she could wrap it. "I think I better go."

Jill agreed and went off to get aluminum foil and a plastic bag. She wiped more tears as she waited for him to pack up his meal. Made herself look any-where but at him. Because even in the final moments, with truth shared and confessed to, a yearning remained. A yearning for the man called Jeff.

*

"Mya, it's late."

She heard his words, his voice; but the absence of light was soothing. Mya didn't want to leave it. She didn't want to exit the living room of deep shadows and enter any space where there was illumination. Alex's words had initially left her numb, but in the hours since, it had left her thinking.

She was still cocooned in her thoughts when he appeared, telling her the hour.

"You need to get to bed. You have work in the morning."

To bed? To bed, where? Their bed? There was no more 'their.' Her husband of four years had been sleeping with another woman for the last four months. Mya was trying to put that knowledge somewhere where it didn't hurt just to breathe. She was trying to stick it in some corner, a basement, far away from her so she could at least get up from the couch she'd found herself stuck on.

"I can take the couch," Alex told her.

The couch, the floor, the kitchen table. It wouldn't matter where he chose to lay his body this night, because his heart hadn't been with her for a while and Mya didn't know what her next move should be.

She did know that she'd been foolish enough to think that she would escape the fate of her own mother. She did know she'd been foolish to think that whatever man she married wouldn't be just like her daddy. That much she did know. But Alex *had* been different. He had been genuine. He had been true. He had been the real deal.

Had been. Here in the aftermath of 'had been,' Mya was trying to find out who she was supposed to become. Here in the aftermath, she was trying to find something inside of her that could keep her pushing forward.

"Mya?" His touch was unexpected. But she only jumped a little. She'd been shocked so much today, her surprise bank was empty. "Mya," he said again.

She looked up at him. Cried-out, dried-out eyes becoming wet. She'd thought she was done. Looking at Alex had made her a liar.

Being with Alex made her a liar, too. But he was right about one thing: it was late, she had work in the morning and she needed to go to bed.

Mya did. Sleep coming after a half hour of tossing. She didn't remember Alex coming into the bedroom in the middle of the night. All she knew was in the morning when she awoke, he was snuggled close to her.

She rolled away and looked at the clock. Shook him awake. "I thought you were taking the couch."

He peered at her through tired eyes. "It was too hard to sleep on. I asked you if I could get in. You told me yeah."

Mya didn't remember that, but there was no time to debate as the alarm went off. She went to the bathroom and was in the shower when he came in to use to the toilet.

For a few seconds, the familiarity of it blocked out the reality of it and she went about running the soapy bath scrubby over her arms and down her sides.

It wasn't until he'd asked if she wanted coffee did the truth come. Mya told him 'yes' as bits and pieces of yesterday flooded her. There had been talk of separating. Talk of him finding his own place, but the 'D' word hadn't entered the conversation.

Alex suggested that they take a few days to think about what happened next. Mya agreed. But as she stood in the shower, listening to the sound of the toilet flushing, her cheating husband on the other side of the curtain, she knew.

The 'D' word would have to come up. It would have to be spoken. To accept anything else would be condoning what he'd done. To consider anything else would be to deny herself real options.

*

Remnants of an April shower dripped from the green awning of the restaurant on 7th Avenue. Outside, the world was shedding its final bit of moisture as the sun battled its way through spent ash skies while inside vented heat made the damp day a memory.

Mya watched a raindrop dangle, fall then vanish from sight where condensation stained the window. She resisted the urge to write her initials on the steamed-up glass, as Chloe sat across from her, a worried look on her face.

"Do you love him?"

Mya sensed that would be the first question. Her answer "Yes," left her quickly.

"So, is there enough to that love to fight for it?"

"I left my battle gear behind a long time ago," Mya said decidedly. "You know that."

"No, you left bad and wrong relationships, including the one with yourself, a long time ago. Up until four months ago, your marriage was working."

"But it's not now. And he has gone where I'd never thought he'd go."

"Does he love her?"

"No." But him not loving the woman he was cheating with was apples and nails. They didn't mix.

"Does he still love you?"

"Yes," Mya answered, her hand lifting, leaving a single finger print on the fogged glass. "But he cheated."
She knew this would be a difficult conversation.

"And?"

"And I promised myself I wouldn't become what my mother became."

"Oh, so it's not about you. It's about your mother?"

"Chloe, you know my crazy family history. And for a long time I was going down that path. I got lucky; I got the chance to see the forest from the trees. I decided I wasn't going to become a Claudia Williams, taking crap from some no good husband and trying to act like it was okay."

"And you haven't, as far as I can see. But Mya, life isn't always so black and white. Gray areas pop up every now and then and you have to make your way through the muddle." Chloe reached out, touched Mya's hand. "All I'm saying is, don't rush to any final decision yet. I know what Alex did and it's major, but, sometimes forgiveness can be our true saving grace."

Mya took Chloe's words. Kept them.

Three days later, Alex moved out and Mya wasn't sad to see him go. Three weeks after that, him leaving didn't feel so good. A week after that, it hurt her in the worse way, but she had been in that valley before. She knew it wouldn't last forever.

*

Memorial Day found Dajah hanging with Frieda and Barry at Frieda's parent's house, Jeff manning the grill at his folks. Rick worked his regular shift at Rikers Island, Mya hanging with Chloe,

her Brooklyn roof-top a perfect get away from her loneliness, while
Alex had the doors to his center open, though no one came through.

Summer came, bringing heat, too much sun and no joy for
anyone in Mudsville. But up ahead laid the turning point, the forked
road for all them.

CHAPTER EIGHT

*T*he heat hit New York with a vengeance. Ninety-five degree days turned into ninety-nine degree nights. People sweated, and complained and got used to brown outs. They cursed Con Edison when the electric bills came in, but kept that portable air conditioning, that window fan, the circular one in the corner going non-stop.

People flocked to the beaches from sun up to sun down and Mister Softee did record business. Children attempted to fry eggs on the hot asphalt and the police department kept busy closing illegally opened fire hydrants.

It was such a day when Mya stepped into the cool comfort of Bretta Smith's office. The air conditioning was so soothing to her hot skin that she couldn't hold in the sigh that rushed her. "God, that feels good."

The receptionist smiled at her. "Hot day, right?'

"Hot doesn't begin to describe it." Mya looked at the wall clock. "I'm a little early."

"That's fine."

Mya picked up a magazine. Chose the seat by the back office door. Her eyes skimmed over glossy photos and bold prints of the fashion magazine, mindful of just how imperfect her world was.

Today was her sixth appointment with Bretta, a marriage counselor. Alex had been coming to see her on his own and today would be the first time they would have a session together. In the months since their trial separation, Mya had begun to feel a little better about Alex. But forgiveness wasn't on her menu just yet.

The door opened. Bretta ushered Mya in. "Alex is here already." That surprised Mya, but she didn't say anything. It was truth telling time and she knew she would need all her energy to get through it.

*

Dajah had planned her afternoon from early that morning. After work, she would change into shorts, flip flops and a tee shirt and head to the beach. Put her toes in the water, feel the ocean breeze. Eat a lemony icy, just exhale.

The sun bore into her as she left her car. Zeroed in on the top of her head as she made her way to the boardwalk. Sizzled against the back of her legs as she ordered an icy from the concession stand. Burned into her shoulders as she headed for the water.

Sea gulls flew away at her approach. The roar of high tide thundered the closer she got. Lumps of forgotten sand castles dissolved with each wave and the smell of brine filled the air like nature's best perfume.

Water rushed her ankles and the sensation closed her eyes. Cool water splashed her to her knees and the heat of the day seeped away. Dajah loved the ocean. Always had.

Right here on this beach, she had seen good times too numerous to count. Most of them with Jeff. But he was gone from her life and even though she'd been on dates, they weren't the type that counted.

Dajah had reached out to her ex boyfriend, but still-friend, David, and they had spent a few evenings hanging out. But that's all they did, sharing a hug at the evening's end then parting ways.

Dajah had run into Rick a few times, become more civil with each meeting. The last time she saw him at the gas station, she actually managed a smile. He stopped being the Boogey man when she realized he wasn't.

Jeff had sent her a birthday card and she called and thanked him, keeping the conversation brief and light. But life wasn't where she'd like it to be. No matter how hard she strove to get back to the 'Dajah' of before, it didn't appear to be happening.

*

It wasn't until Jeff was sitting inside of the subway car did he realize why there were so many seats during rush hour—there was no air conditioning. Sweating his way to the next stop he dashed out of the open doors and ran to the next car that was jammed packed.

Pushing his way in, he turned his body towards the platform zooming by until it became a blur. Kelly would need a walk when he got home, but the idea of going outside on such hot a day didn't suit him.

The idea of going out to the beach with ocean breezes did.

But he couldn't because he was taking Joy out for her birthday. Joy had been one of the four women he had been seeing when he met Dajah. In the months after Dajah left, Jeff starting reaching out to them again. Jill was done with him. Syreeta was seeing someone steady. Lisa had relocated to Arizona. That left Joy.

He had always appreciated how she'd been the least clingy. She never raised a funk about him not spending enough time with her and never tried to change his mind about anything. She was as familiar to him as a pair of old worn slippers and every now and then, it was nice to be able to slip her on and get that comfortable fit.

Jeff surprised himself when he mentioned that her birthday was coming up and that he would like to take her out for dinner. Joy was surprised too, but she played it cool, simply saying: 'Okay.' He'd just left the 169th Street subway station when she messaged him. She couldn't make dinner. Something came up, the word 'sorry' nowhere in her text.

*

"Mya, do you want to share with Alex what happened with Jeff?"

It had been going okay up till then. Bretta had carefully lead Mya and Alex through their history together, highlighting all the highs and getting them to discuss the lows. Twenty-three minutes in, Mya had actually sat back, relaxed in the sharing, eager to do more. The last thing she'd expected she would have to do was talk about Jeff in front of Alex.

"Jeff?" The sound of his name coming out her mouth, uncomfortable.

Bretta nodded. "I think in order for Alex to understand just how detrimental his infidelity was to you, he needs to know about your history with Jeff."

She could feel Alex's eyes on her. Felt anxiety rise up in him. If Mya didn't speak on it, Alex would think the worse. But if she did speak on it, he would still think the worse. She had been the good guy in this. Telling would change that.

"It's important," Bretta said carefully.

Mya looked down. Swallowed. Opened up her mouth and spoke.

*

"Wow," Alex's response to the Jeff tale. Even after Bretta encouraged him to say more, Alex couldn't. The most he could come up with was: "That's so deep."

Bretta took up the conversation, laying out some more tracks for them to follow, but Mya wasn't listening. She could only sit there feeling the silent judgment from her husband.

"Mya, you look like you have something on your mind." Mya looked at Bretta, brimming. Shook her head, looked away. "This session is about sharing. The idea is to release it here so that you don't have to tote it around all by yourself. The more you share, the better it will get. The less, well not so much."

"I feel like he's condemning me," she said after a while.

Bretta nodded. "Go on."

Mya looked at Alex. "It's like you're judging me and I didn't do anything wrong. You were the one that cheated."

"Alex?" Bretta said carefully.

"I don't know what to say."

"Why?"

"Because…"

"Because what?"

"It's like…it's like some kind of crazy karma."

"For?"

Alex swallowed. "Mya."

"And why do you think that is?" Alex said he didn't know. "What's going through your mind, right now?" No answer left him. "You're right there Alex. Right there. Just take that step."

"It's like she had this thing inside of her. This kind of twisted energy and it got inside of me."

"So, you're saying you did what you did because Mya had done what she'd done?"

Alex started to respond. Stopped himself, then spoke. "No, not like she made me do it, but it was a part of her."

"And not a part of you." It wasn't a question. "Because for you to suggest you stepped outside of your marriage for some past behavior that Mya had isn't fair, or true."

Silence. Then "I didn't want to be him." Alex said carefully.

"Be who?"

Alex swallowed. Sought out Mya's eyes. His voice arrived, bruised and tender. "My father…"

*

There was no escape in running away. Mya knew that, but she was up and out of the chair, the office and the front door before Bretta could wrap the session up. Mya went, her feet fast as she stepped out into the hot day. Then she was in her car, pulling out of the parking space, driving far away from Alex's history.

She managed two blocks before the first tear fell. Three blocks before she had to pull over. She'd never suspected that Alex was capable of infidelity. Never thought he even possessed the ability. But she had been fooled by him. His family history was as tarnished as her own.

Her father had cheated on her mother from day one. Even when a scorned lover had plunged a knife into him, Mya's father didn't stop cheating and Mya's mother chose to stay right by his side. It was only recently that Mya's mother had started demanding her husband do right, but in Mya's opinion, that putting down of her foot had come forty years too late.

Over the years, Mya had witness the light eaten right out of he mother's eyes. She'd seen the fake smile that had dotted her mother's mouth too many times to count, harden into a hurt that rarely allowed her to smile at all.

Bitterness crawled up the soles of her mother's feet, sprouting like weeds in an abandoned lot, every time her father shared her space; the joy just gone from her, leaving her hollowed, empty and *resigned*.

Cheaters and liars went hand in hand. Scotty Williams and Alex's father were both.

Today Alex had declared that's who he'd become, too.

Now, no matter what words came out of Alex's mouth, she wouldn't believe him. Couldn't trust him. And without trust, there wasn't much to hold onto.

Her cell phone rang. She knew it could only be two people and she didn't feel like talking to either of them. She let it roll over to voice mail and eased back into traffic. Ended up in Fresh Meadows.

She bought a movie ticket, a bucket of popcorn and a coke. Settled into the plush seats, eyes to the screen. *The Chronicles of Riddick* was a movie she had wanted to see for a while. Now seemed like as good as time as any.

*

Alex was waiting for her when she got home. He was sitting in his car, engine off, when she pulled up. The session with Bretta had drained her. The movie had tapped whatever little she had left. Mya didn't want to talk about anything. Just wanted to put on her pajamas and go to bed.

"Not now," she told him as he got out of his car.

"When?"

Mya looked at the man who she thought she'd known so well and saw only a wounded stranger. She considered the last five years of their life, four and a half of them pretty good, and tried to find an answer.

When? She didn't even know if that existed any more. "I don't know Alex."

"We have to talk about it Mya. Me and you. We have to talk."

She thought about all the weeks and months she'd wanted to do just that. "You're almost right. We *should* have talked, long time ago. But you didn't want to…it's late and I'm tired."

She headed inside her building, grateful that Alex didn't follow.

*

"I like the way you move…" Dajah sang along with Outkast, remembering the days when the dance floor claimed her Saturday nights. It had been a while, but she was singing and driving like she was back in the club.

Her legs were ashy and dried-out salt water streaked them. Sand clung to the bottom of her feet but the beach trip had done her good and she was feeling just fine as she made her way back home.

She saw Rick sitting on his stoop. Slowed a bit and tooted her horn. He waved. She waved back, giving her car some gas as she headed down the street.

It felt good to be a grown up again.

*

Rick watched until Dajah's car vanished from sight. She had finally stopped acting like she'd seen a ghost when they crossed paths. She actually gave him smiles and hellos. Tooted at him whenever he was outside of his house.

That was all good but what had him curious was how she was always alone. Where was her man? Her girl Frieda? Rick knew it wasn't really his concern, but that part of him that never let her go was curious…and hope filled.

*

The sun was low in the sky as Kelly raced along the shore chasing seagulls and retrieving the Frisbee. For the first time all day, Jeff felt as if he could breathe.

He was trying not to be bothered that Joy cancelled on him, but he was stuck on the irony that when he finally tried to do the right thing—she reneged.

Nothing had been really right in his world since Dajah left. These days he was play-acting a life. Martin had warned that if Jeff didn't get to the root, he would make the same mistakes again.

Even as he denied the source, he knew. Mya had messed him up. Turned his whole world one-eighty. Jacked up his life and went on and lived a great one. Where was the fairness in that?

He thought he was pass his anger with her, but standing on the beach, he knew he wasn't. There wasn't much he could do about it. Jeff couldn't prepare a Sunday dinner and invite her over and ask questions like Jill had. Even if she came, which she wouldn't because she was married, what could she tell him? What words could she speak that would undo the damage?

There was no going back to fix it. But that's all he wanted. He wanted to go back and change the past. Undo all the bad that had been done to him and he'd done to others.

*

A week later Mya and Alex were back in Bretta's office, the distance between them thick as a concrete wall. Mya barely glanced at Alex when he came in, but his gaze was on her like a fire, threatened to consume her.

Mya only had one thing she wanted to say and stayed mute through most of the session. When it was winding down, she shared it. "I want a divorce."

She had stored away the 'd' word for an 'in case of emergency' situation. Even as she stuck the idea in her back pocket, a part of her didn't want to have to use it. But the previous session showed her that staying married to Alex was no longer her option. "I do," she said again, looking at Bretta.

Bretta was shocked. So was Alex. He didn't say a word but Mya felt it.

"Divorce?" Bretta asked, concerned. "Five years isn't just a drop in the bucket, Mya."

"Four and a half," Mya corrected.

"Okay, four and a half. But you came to counseling to figure it out and you're only into your seventh session, the second with your husband."

Mya shook her head. "He's not my husband." She looked at Alex. "Hasn't been for a while. I don't know who he is, but I know who he's not," she looked back at Bretta, "and, I want a divorce."

Bretta spoke. "Alex, how do you feel about that?"

He swallowed, considered the woman three feet away from him. Wetness making his eyes glimmer. "If that's what she wants, I won't fight her."

Mya nodded, felt something loosen inside of her. Knew exactly what it was. It was freedom.

No more nights of wondering. No more days of pondering. No more reaching out to a man who refused to reach back. She wasn't young, but forty wasn't old. She had made a way for herself before. There was plenty of time to do it again.

Bretta started talking again, but Mya had stopped listening. She didn't know what would happen next, but she realized the only one who had that answer was herself.

*

"Are you sure?"

Mya expected that question from her mother. She even expected it from her girlfriend Gail, but she didn't expect it from Chloe. "How can I ever trust him? He comes from the same funky place I came from. It's always gonna be there inside of him."

"So, I guess it's always going to be inside of you, too?"

Was it? There had been a time in her life when she didn't even know she possessed the cheating gene. Not until Jeff.

Jeff. She didn't want to think about him. Mya didn't want to add him into her new stew of soon-to-be divorced.

"Does it?" Chloe asked again.

"Not for a long time."

"So it's completely gone, then?"

Hard ass questions, but she was trying to walk in truth. "It's like being an alkie or a drug addict, Chloe. It's never completely gone. You just learn to keep it under wraps."

"Oh, and you can, but Alex can't."

"He was the one that cheated."

"And I guess you never cheated on anybody?"

"You know what I mean."

"Yes, I know exactly what you mean. But what I'm trying to do is to get you to make sure you're not letting pride and ego mess up what could be the best thing for you Mya, that's all. I know you are all in the fire right now, and you're just hot and mad and,"

"I'm not mad," Mya defended.

"No? You could have fooled me."

Mya sat back. Reached for the cup of herbal tea Chloe had made her. Exhaled. "Okay, yes I'm mad and pissed and angry and hurt and all of that. But I know I can't be with him anymore."

Chloe picked up her tea. Took a sip. "Okay." Looked at Mya over the rim of the cup. "So, have you run into Jeff lately?"

"No."

"Do you want to?"

Chloe knew her well, too well sometimes. "No, I don't."

"Good."

But the insinuation stayed with her the rest of the afternoon, all through the night and into the next day. The insinuation picked at her and taunted her and she was forced to face up to it.

She'd be a liar if she said she hadn't at least thought about Jeff. Mya would be a liar if she didn't admit, at least to herself, that some part of her had wondered about what that would be like—be back with the type of man she'd thought Alex had been.

Up until she had done their relationship in, Jeff had been her real Prince Charming. He had been faithful, loving, supportive and kind. He had never so much as looked at another woman in all the time they were together.

She let the thought run wild and rampant and amuck, have its party including black confetti tossed in the air, and when the thought exhausted itself, she put it into a strong box, secured it with tape and tucked it away.

Leaving Alex wasn't about Jeff. It was about what was best for her.

CHAPTER NINE

*C*olumbus Day weekend was a big shopping time in New York. All the stores had super sales and doing the Mall Marathon was as much a part of Dajah's life as breathing. Dajah picked up Frieda early Monday morning and headed to Queens Boulevard. If they had enough energy and money left over, they'd try to get Green Acres in as well.

Life had become simple, uncomplicated and okay for Dajah. Six months after breaking up with Jeff, she still missed him but the missing grew less and less.

She filled her free time with solo ventures, outings with Frieda and occasional dinners with David. But at the end of evening, it was always Dajah going home alone.

"Ooh. These are nice," Dajah said, picking up a pair of brown leather boots.

"Yeah, they are." Frieda answered as she looked at her watch for the third time in the last five minutes. Dajah knew what it meant. Though they had planned a full shopping day, there was some other place Frieda wanted to be.

"Let me try these on. Then we can head home," Dajah offered.

"You sure?"

"Yeah, I'm sure. We've been out since nine. It's after two now."

"What about Green Acres?"

Word was bond with Frieda, but it was obvious that Frieda wanted to end the outing and go spend the rest of her day off with her boyfriend.

"We can do that another day," Dajah decided.

The boots were cute on her feet, but they pinched like hell. She put them back and the two headed home. She dropped Frieda off, spying Barry's car. "Tell Barry I said hey."

Frieda smiled. "Will do. I'll give you a call tomorrow."

Dajah nodded, pulled off, tingling with envy. She'd had three relationships in the time that Frieda had just one. Where was her Mister Right?

The late afternoon air hummed with the energy of people in the midst of special plans. The brilliant sunlight dappling through the oak trees emphasized how glorious Frieda's life was and how hers wasn't.

Dajah would love to pull up to her place and find her man waiting. Would love to go inside her apartment, find dinner on the stove and him chilling on her sofa.

She would love to spend the afternoon in bed, making love, napping, channel surfing, snuggled up close to him. But there was no him to do any of that, so she had to do it for herself. She'd start with Chinese for dinner.

She'd get some Mongolian beef, plain white rice and an egg roll. It was Monday and her favorite show *Girlfriends* was coming on at nine p.m. Getting lost in the world of *Joan, Mya, Lynn* and *Toni* sounded like a plan; getting lost in made up lives, better than her real one.

*

Five minutes. That's what the petite Asian woman behind the plexiglass window had told Rick when he placed his order for Shrimp Lo Mein, but it had already been ten. The smell of old cooking grease, fresh cut ginger and sautéed garlic was nudging at the hunger in his belly, and Rick just wanted to get his take out and head home.

He had gone back to the gym and had lost twenty pounds. He'd struggled his former six-pack back up to a four. In a few months it would be a six again. It would have been nice if there were someone to applaud his hard work.

Rick had never been much of a social person. Meeting women had never come natural for him. With the exception of Brea, all the other women he had dated had always hit on him first.

Except maybe Dajah.

Dajah hadn't hit on him, just needed his assistance one night. He had stopped at a diner on his way to take an empty bus back to Rikers Island and saw Dajah there. Even though he had sat next to her, his mind had been everywhere but on her. But when it was time for her to go, she'd looked scared.

It had been late, after midnight and she had two buses to take to get home. He had sensed her fear and offered to walk her to the bus stop and wait. But when the bus took too long, he had given her his can of mace for protection. Went by her house the next morning to pick it up.

Nothing had jumped off because he was still living with Gina. But meeting Dajah had made him see just how horrible his relationship with Gina was and Rick began to make moves to remove Gina from his life.

The best laid plans of mice and men often go astray and Rick's plan to live his life while still being close to his daughter had been a disastrous idea from the start. In the midst of that disaster, Rick had tried to have a relationship with Dajah, but his own heart tripped him up.

"Shimp Lo Mein? White Rice? Egg wholl?"

Rick jumped up. "That's me." He was heading to the counter when the cowbell over the door jangled. He didn't pay it any mind, just wanting to get his food and head home. He paid, took the plastic bag and turned. Ran smack into Dajah, his bag bumping her in her stomach.

"Oh…dang, sorry."

Dajah smiled. "It's okay Rick."

The sound of his name coming out of her mouth carried such a long ago melody, he smiled. He was glad to see she was returning the favor. "Getting your Chinese too, I see?"

"Yep. Gonna get my Mongolian Beef," pearly whites shining behind a big smile.

"Never had it," Rick confessed.

"Really? You have to try it."

"Guess I will." He looked down at his food, suddenly self-conscious. "Well, me and my Shrimp Lo Mein are going to head on home."

"Me and my Mongolian Beef is gonna be there soon, too."

Rick looked puzzled. "My house?"

Dajah caught the words she had spoken. Understood how Rick was confused. She laughed, looked away, suddenly embarrassed. "No, not *your* house. Mine's."

His smile left him. A tenderness deep enough to touch came over his face. "You're always welcome, to my house, I mean."

Dajah tried her best to not let his words touch any part of her. Failed. She could only look at him, the smile still full on her face and softly utter, "Okay." She pointed awkwardly behind him. "I better place my order."

"Yeah. Well, um, take care."

"You too," her voice, whisper soft.

*

Okay, the day brilliant with sunlight. *Okay,* the breeze blowing into the opened car window. *Okay,* Jo Jo and K-C singing from the radio about staying for a little while. *Okay,* so hope-filled and optimistic that the hunger that had Rick vanished by the time he got home.

Dajah's smile. That twinkle in her eye. Being so close to her he could smell Fendi perfume. A real conversation. Laughter. Goodness between them. Hostility gone. Closeness.

Rick forked up his lo mien, his mouth tasting nothing, his heart feeling everything and more.

*

The smile took a long time to leave.

It was with Dajah as she placed her order. With her as she waited eleven minutes for her food to be cooked. It blossomed, grew wider as she headed to her car and made her heart beat double as she drove past Rick's house.

You're always welcome...simple words that should not have mattered. But on that beautiful Columbus Day in New York, they did. And she made peace with it.

*

Rick picked up the receiver and put it down four times before he got the courage to actually dial the number. It rang five times before it went to voice mail. He wasn't sure if he should leave a message, but not leaving one seemed moot. A missed call notification would tell it. So he opened his mouth and spoke.

"Hey. I was just calling to say hi, I guess." He hung up, feeling lame. Rick hung up feeling lame, stupid and under the spot light. But it was done. There was no taking it back.

*

Early the next morning as Dajah headed to work, she turned on her cell. Thirty seconds after, she got a notice of a missed call. Listened to the message from Rick. There was no harm in 'hi.' No harm in saying 'hi' back.

Dajah hit redial, relieved when it rolled into voice mail. She kept it brief. "Calling to say hi back."

*

Later, she would try to figure out just how she ended up at Dante's on Astoria Boulevard in Astoria. Later she would try to piece together the hows and whys of her eating *Polla Anna Parmigana* across from Rick, enjoying it, enjoying him.

But for now, enjoying the moment was all Dajah wanted to do. She hadn't been to her favorite Italian restaurant in a while and it was good to be back.

"Second grade? Really?" Dajah was asking.

"Yep, second grade. And she's so excited about it."

"Wow. How tall is she now?" Rick put his hand midway his side. "She's growing up fast."

"Yeah, she is…" his voice trailed off. "I don't think I ever thanked you Dajah, I mean really thanked you for stepping in like you did to take care of her."

"It was the least I could do. Kanisha was the innocent in all of it. You needed someone to look after her." But the sting that came into Dajah's heart said otherwise. She had become so vested in Kanisha that when Gina came back reclaiming her stake in her child's life, it hurt Dajah, in the worse way.

"You didn't have to do it at all. And I know it wasn't easy. I just wanted you to know that I know that."

"It's the past Rick, right? All ancient history."

He nodded. "I guess you're right."

"And Gina? How is she?"

"Gina is doing fine. She's trying to get her GED. Failed it the first two times, but she said she was just going to keep taking it until she passes."

"Good for her."

"Yeah, good for her…got to admit I'm surprised you said yes."

Dajah laughed a little. "Kinda surprised I said yes too…I was so freaked about running into you in the beginning."

"Well, ya did kinda move into my neighborhood. What did you expect?"

"I just loved the apartment. I knew exactly how close it was to you, but when I walked inside, I just loved it. I wanted my old place, but it was already occupied and I just needed to get somewhere that I could call my own."

"How did you lose your old place?"

She hadn't told Rick about Jeff. She didn't feel up to it now. "Let's just say things changed and then changed again."

"Okay."

Dajah looked surprised. "Just okay? You don't want to know?"

"It's enough that you're even taking a meal with me. You tell me the whens and whys when you're up to it, okay?"

Dajah chuckled. "You know this is a not a date."

"Yes, you've already told me."

"Seriously Rick, it's not."

He shrugged. "Then it's not." He'd put no pressure on her. Wouldn't make her concede to anything. Like he told her, it was enough that she was sharing a meal with him. Enough that she'd answered her door when he rang her bell earlier that evening…

*

Rick had gotten her call back message just as he was rolling over the bridge at Rikers. He figured her schedule hadn't changed and she was at work. He would wait until after five to ring her back. He did and she answered.

He asked her how had she been and she told him. He asked her just how long had she been down the street from him and she told him. He'd asked her how she liked living there and she told him. He asked how was her Mongolian Beef and she told him that too.

That led to her opening up a bit, insisting that he needed to try it for himself, which led to him saying that he would, but if he didn't like it, could he give her the rest because he hated to waste food, which led to Dajah insisting that he would love it so much that he'd want to eat every bit of it.

That led to Rick inviting her to join him as he tried it, just in case. Dajah had balked, saying she had had her weekly quota and she wouldn't want anymore until the following week. Rick asked what would she like to have this week. "Something from Dante's," fell from her mouth without thought. Rick said that could be arranged.

"Really, how's that?"

"Well, tell me what you would like and I will go get you some, or, I could just take you to Dante's."

Silence. Dajah thinking, Rick hoping. Then…"You have a deal. But it's not a date," she said quickly.

"Okay, not a date. What time should I pick you up?"

"I don't need to be picked up. I have my own car."

"We live two blocks from each other. What's the sense in both of us driving?" Which was a truth Dajah couldn't argue with.

"Six thirty works for me," Dajah had offered.

"Great, I will see you at six thirty."

And when she opened her door to him, looking like the most beautiful woman he'd ever known in all the world, it took everything Rick possessed not to reach and touch her. It took everything he owned not to just hold her.

The drive started out quietly, each feeling, each thinking, each trying to put in perspective what this non-date moment was about. Then Dajah mentioned that he was not off the hook for Mongolian Beef and that was the ice breaker.

They argued the merits of what the best Chinese food was, heart beats up, voices high and lively by the time they were pulling in front of the restaurant. Then silence came back as Rick got out, ran around to her side and opened her car door.

"Gentleman," she muttered.

"I try to be."

She nodded. "Very true." Despite the madness, the craziness, Rick had always tried to be the good guy, and though he had failed miserably, it was enough that he tried.

But so had Jeff, always going that extra and beyond. Always making sure he was on the traffic side when they walked down the street, bringing her fresh brewed coffee in the morning. Opening doors, pulling back chairs. Taking her hand whenever they crossed the street.

Dajah let those thoughts go. 'Jeff' didn't belong at dinner with Rick.

After their meal was done, he asked about dessert. "You want to get something?"

Dajah, full as two ticks, said no. "No more room in this inn."

"I hear ya. The food was good, but I can feel it laying on my gut. Got to hit the gym tomorrow for sure."

"You work out?" Dajah asked as the waitress began clearing the table.

"Yeah. I had gotten real good about it and then fell off. Got back on that horse again." He flexed a bicep for her. "Check it out," a hoagie-roll size muscle straining the material of his dress shirt. Tentatively Dajah jabbed at it with two fingers. It was solid as a rock. Her fingers curled around the mound, gave it a squeeze.

"Nice," Dajah said, meaning it.

"Thanks," Rick said shyly, feeling her touch everywhere.

It wasn't in the cards, he told himself as the waitress came back with the check. Not in the cards, he told himself as he got out his wallet and laid a credit card on top of the bill. Not, he silently insisted as he looked at Dajah, surprised to see that she was looking at him in a way that was saying something different.

*

The island of Manhattan was a sparkling jewel across the water. Bigger than life, a million lights glowed in the tall buildings, casting its reflection along the onyx waters of the East River. Dajah sighed. "Like in the movies, but a thousand times better."

"Yeah, it is kind of cool."

The Grand Central Parkway was the closest way to get back home, but Dajah asked if Rick could take Vernon Boulevard to the

59th Street Bridge. "It's been a minute since I've seen New York at night." He willfully agreed and could taste Dajah's joy as his SUV sped down the avenue.

"It's funny how you can be around something your whole life, but you don't really appreciate it until later," Dajah said.

"Like?"

She smiled. Looked at him. "Like?" Looked out of her window. "Like this. I mean really, how many nights has this been here and I never really paid it much attention until now?"

"A lot."

"Exactly…we get so busy with the BS sometimes we forget to appreciate the simple things."

"Like Manhattan at night across the water from Vernon Boulevard."

"Yes! Exactly. I mean, when was the last time you drove this way just to see it?"

Rick shrugged. "Never."

"Exactly."

Rick laughed. "Okay Day, if you say 'exactly' one more time, I'm gonna have to charge you. Because you've said it at least ten times."

"No I didn't."

"Yeah, you did."

"I didn't say it ten times. Twice maybe, but not ten," she countered, having no real clue.

"Two. Ten. That's still too many."

"So, you're saying if I say the word one more time, you're gonna charge me?"

"Yep."

"Yeah? What?"

"Something."

"What? A dime? A dollar?"

"A kiss." The words left his mouth before he could even consider the implication.

"A kiss." It wasn't a question.

Out there, Rick stuck to his guns. "Yep, a kiss."

"What kind of a kiss?"

Rick laughed, relieved she hadn't taken offense. "What do you mean, what kind? A kiss."

It was Dajah's turn to chuckle. "You have to be specific. Do you mean a peck on the cheek, a dry closed one on the mouth?" She could kiss Rick tonight. It wasn't a date, but she was having fun. It wasn't a date, but she enjoyed his company. Him.

"Lip to lip and opened mouth," Rick offered.

"Like this?" She opened her mouth like a beached fish, leaned her face his way.

Rick glanced her dying-fish face. Laughed. "No."

Dajah eased back, comfortable with this new thing between them. "Then how?'

"How?"

"Yeah, how?"

Rick eased his car to the curb, slipped his hand around the back of her neck, slowly moved her head his way. Felt no resistance. Her eyes closed, her mouth parted as he pressed his lips to hers, a soft sweet tongue finding his, glad in the joining.

They kissed and kissed some more, not coming up for air, a need inside of them corralling them deeper into the moment, each other. It wasn't until Dajah realized she was inhaling his exhales did she find her way back.

That had been more than just a kiss. That had been a wide-opened door into what they'd had before.

"Wow," she managed. Looked at him. "What are," she tried to ask. But Rick placed a finger to her lips.

"Just a kiss."

"Rick, that was…,"

He quieted her again. "Just a kiss, Dajah."

But Dajah could tell he didn't believe that either. It was all in his eyes. Those Allen Iverson big, round, baby brown back-lit wonders, were churning full of love—for her. But she nodded. "Okay." Willing to let it go, refusing to ask herself if she loved him back.

Rick put the car in drive, headed down Vernon Boulevard.

Dajah, eyes wide to the view that was Manhattan at night, saw none of it.

*

In front of her house.

Rick's words—*just a kiss*—still heavy in her head. It was no longer necessary to ask what the evening was about. It was about who they were and who they could be.

"Thank you," Rick said carefully.

"For?"

"For agreeing to let me take you to dinner. It was one of the best times I've had in a while."

"You're welcome," she said tentatively.

"I'm not expecting anything Dajah. I'd be lying if I said I didn't want anything, but whatever happens next will be your call, okay?"

Dajah let out a breath, relieved. "It's a lot Rick."

"I know that and there's not a thing I can ask of you. So, you decide the next move. No pressure. Promise."

She smiled. Nodded. Uttered "thanks" and got out his car.

Rick waited until she was inside and then eased from the curb, the evening more than he had hoped for. The evening, more than enough.

CHAPTER TEN

*S*ometimes, if the world is going right and your mind isn't fuzzied up with problems, you experience a deep appreciation for everything outside your window.

That's how Dajah was feeling as she did sixty-five miles an hour down the Southern State Parkway, the trees along the Interstate painted in the hues of fall, dappling and sparkling like newly discovered treasures.

Her driver's window was down and the breeze held the faint smell of burning wood. Somewhere, someone was burning leaves.

It was Indian summer and Dajah was in love with it. She loved how the world seemed to slow down and the earth showed out. Last year she'd taken a trip upstate with Jeff just to enjoy the scenery. It was something Dajah wanted to do again.

She wanted to take a road trip to the land of trees and mountains. Find a little turn off and get out of her car. Stand on a high peak and survey the wonder of nature; drink in the bright yellows, wine reds and startling orange of the maples, elms and oaks.

But there was no trip on her horizon, so she yielded to the next best thing—the cornucopia of trees along the parkway as she drove from work.

She'd stop by and see Rick, hang for a little while and then head home. Life, better for her. Life, taking a good turn.

True to his word, he was giving her all the space she needed. There was little surprise that she didn't need much.

In the time since their non-date, they'd gone to the movies and he had agreed to accompany her to Alvin Ailey's Dance Theatre's fall series. Men in tights didn't scare him. Dajah liked that.

Twenty minutes later, she drove down his street. Pulled up to his house where he was stoop-sitting. The outdoor cushion next to him made her smile.

He stood as she came through the gate. "I figured a day as nice as today, you might of wanted to enjoy it for a few minutes."

"Yeah," she answered, delighted. "I would."

"Thirsty?"

"No. I'm good. I am a bit hungry though."

"I was going to hit the Rib Shack. You're welcome to come along."

"A man after my own stomach."

Words jumped Rick's tongue. He made them stay there. "So, is that a yes?"

"Sure. Why not?" She paused, studied the houses across the street, the rays of sunlight slicing along the driveways. Closed her eyes. Heard the faint chirps of birds. "But can we just sit here a little while?"

"Sure."

"I used to do this all the time when I was young," her voice dreamy.

"What?"

"Stoop sit. Especially this time of year. I would stay out until the street lights came on. Cold, shivering, but I just didn't want to leave it. Leave outside, y'know? Especially this time of year." She looked at him. "You know why?"

Rick didn't even pretend he did. "No, why?"

"Because it's fall and after that was winter and, even though I played in the snow, it was like I was trying to drink in all of Indian summer to keep me warm through the long winter."

"I hear ya."

Dajah laughed. "No. You don't." Leaned her head against his shoulder. "But that's okay." Pulled back. Studied him. "So how was your day?"

"Went to Home Depot and got some annuals. I know they'll be dead in a month." He stood up. "But I figure for the month I have, I'd plant them along the front. Want to see?"

Dajah told him yes, trekking across the lawn, heels sinking into the thick dying grass. Along the side of the house half a dozen planters of orange marigolds sat.

She looked at him, seeing him through brand new eyes. "They're beautiful Rick."

Rick smiled. "Yeah, I thought so."

*

November 2nd.

Jeff used to love that date. He used to play around with the numbers—one, one, zero, two—when he was a kid. Because they added up to 'three,' a perfect trinity, he felt that that date was better than any other day of the year.

For a long time it had been. No matter what else was going on around him, Jeff could look to the second day of November as a happy one, where he'd celebrate another year and there was always someone special around him to join him.

This year was different.

Beyond turning the big four-o, and a solemn cake cutting at his folks, there was nothing else planned. No dinner with a gorgeous lady, good seats at a Knicks game. Nothing. The impromptu sing song his office had given him right after lunch didn't count. Even though they had given him a huge birthday card (too big, too cumbersome and too embarrassing to try and take home on the subway), and a really nice drafting set (which he didn't need either), there was not a drop of gladness in him.

Martin had texted him happy birthday but nobody had actually called. Not even his parents. He wanted to tell himself that they were waiting until he came over for dinner, but it felt like a punishment for messing up his life.

On a whim, he dialed Jill.

Jeff knew it was a desperate move, but he was feeling mighty low. She loved him, or at least she used to. Maybe enough of it remained that she'd be willing to meet him for a drink, or something.

He shouldn't have been surprised when he discovered it rolled to voice mail and a man with a thick East Indian accent asked him to leave a message. Jill had changed her number. He shouldn't have been surprised. But he was.

His cell rang.

His eyes lit up when the caller ID said: *Jill.* "Hey," he uttered softer than he'd ever said to her before.

"You called me?"

It took a moment to realize that it was the new owner of the number—the man with the thick East Indian accent.

"Oh, yeah. I'm,"

"Who is this?"

Jeff quickly disconnected. In that short time he had completely forgotten that Jill's number was no longer Jill's. But worse was the question the man had asked him: *Who is this?* Who was he? Jeff didn't know, and that was the saddest part of his whole 'special' day that had been anything but.

His shoe string popped when he retied his shoe. The store had run out of his favorite Mentos and a lady rolled her baby carriage over his foot when he was getting on the train.

Something sticky and wet was on the pole he grabbed and the man next to him had the worst case of halitosis Jeff had ever smelled.

He'd tripped up the steps coming out of the subway and the bus to his parent's house pulled off even though the driver saw him flagging him down.

A group of York College kids laughing made Jeff feel like they were laughing at him.

He felt small.

The thought of pretending to be happy when he got to his parent's house, too much to bear.

He called them, made an excuse and then called up Casey. But even as Casey said he was good to go, the sadness clung to Jeff. If he hadn't done what he'd done, it would be Dajah he'd be spending his birthday with. Dajah—younger, smart, pretty, funny. Attractive. Loving.

She'd put him through the paces to win her heart, but once he'd won it, she'd been all his. *But you blew that, didn't you?*

Jeff went home, changed his clothes, didn't walk Kelly and headed out the door. He picked up his partner, the two of them heading to Ruth's Chris Steak House in Garden City, where he drowned his sorrows in thick steak and scotch on the rocks.

By the end of the meal, Jeff was full to the brim and a bit tipsy. But the reality of all the day wasn't, was never too far away.

The pile of dog poop that greeted him inside his door seemed to sum it up quite nicely. His birthday had been crap.

He cleaned it up, got the leash and took Kelly for a walk. The night had turned cold, and the world seemed darker. Tomorrow was another day, something said. But in that moment, it seemed a million miles away.

*

Dajah knew the date, too.

She would never forget it. It was a thing with her— remembering every birthday of every man she'd dated since she was in her mid twenties. She wondered how Jeff spent his—alone or with someone. *With someone* she decided. There had never been a shortage of women in his life, so Dajah didn't see how that would change.

She wanted to mentally wish him a happy one, but a part of her still was holding a grudge. They had such a good thing and he ruined it.

She and Rick were going along platonically and smoothly. They laughed, did things together and talked. But they both seemed to be holding back, unwilling to cross the final line. Sometimes it was a simple thing to do. Sometimes not.

But she'd seen the growth in Rick and the drama that was Gina had gone away. So Dajah was going with it, flowing with it, a part of Rick's life again and he hers. But moments came when she missed what she had with Jeff. Moments came when she was blatantly reminded that, while Rick was a wonderful guy, in some respects, he wasn't Jeff.

She was smart enough to understand it. Smart enough to respect it. But she was still working on making peace with it. Working on how Jeff had messed up what had been one of the best relationships she'd ever had.

*

Rick didn't know that Dajah was watching him, but she was.

They were seated in the orchestra section of City Center on Fifty-fifth and Sixth, watching the Alvin Ailey dance concert. The first number had the male dancers in pants. For the second number, they were wearing nude colored briefs.

Dajah was watching Rick to see if he really meant men in tights didn't bother him. From the expression on his face, they didn't. That allowed her to sit back and enjoy the performance. She clapped loudly when she felt compelled, her hand going to her chest when a step was executed with such grace and beauty it made her heart thump.

By the end of the performance, Rick was on his feet giving a standing ovation. Dajah smiled. He had just one-upped Jeff. Jeff had been a bit mugged face when he had taken her last year. Rick had gotten into the full swing.

She squeezed his waist. Uttered 'thank you' in his ear.

Rick nodded absently, never stopping his clapping, eyes fast on the stage. When he brought his fingers to his mouth and whistled, Dajah knew it was all good. That there were things about Rick that Jeff would never possess.

CHAPTER ELEVEN

*T*hanksgiving arrived with Mya and Alex on their way to being legally single, so it was surprising that they spent the holiday together.

They had a few more joint counseling sessions and it was there that Mya got a clearer picture of who Alex was, versus who he had tried to be. That helped her understand that it wasn't anything she'd done. It was simply about whom Alex had tried not be.

They'd become civil with each other in the last few months. They weren't quite easy breezy, but were in a better place, which allowed Mya to extend him an invitation to join her at her aunt's Thanksgiving table.

It was by no means an easy decision. But Mya knew enough of Alex's life. Knew that his mother had died years ago, he was still estranged from his father and his sister lived in California.

His circle of friends was near non-existent and though no doubt he could have gone to Morris', his assistant's house, but that relationship was work-based. They'd never gone to a game together, shot hoops or any of those things.

She knew he wouldn't spend the day with Dawn, because it was revealed in session that Alex had stopped seeing Dawn right after he'd told Mya about her. Alex didn't love her. Just used her to play out the drama. Once her part was done, Alex was done.

So Mya invited him to go with her to her Aunt Martha's. She still loved Alex. But hope of a reconciliation didn't exist. Alex knew that and respected that, grateful that she still wanted to have him in her life. A lesser woman wouldn't even have considered it.

*

"Son-in-law!" Scotty Williams bellowed, getting up off the sofa to give Alex a hand shake.

"Scotty," Alex said back, cautiously. Mya's father had always tried to intimidate him, but until recently Alex had the footing to stand his ground.

"So, guess I'm gonna have to go back to calling you Alex, huh?"

Mya cut her eyes at her father. "Daddy. Stop it."

Scotty chuckled. "It's the truth. I mean…"

"Scot, I need you in the kitchen to cut the turkey," Mya's aunt interjected.

Scotty looked towards the kitchen, looked back at Alex. "Best turkey carver around," he declared heading out.

Mya let go her breath, glad to see her father gone. That had been round one. Round two would come when they were all seated around the dinner table. It was just her father's way.

She spied her cousin Little Man sitting on the love seat playing a hand held video game. "James!" she said quickly. "Boy, you hear me?"

He looked up, those Williams eyes sparkling her way. His smile rose up as he did. He hugged her, the top of his head to her stomach.

"You're getting tall."

He stepped back, grinned. Two front teeth missing. "I'm six."

"Six? Already? My goodness…you remember your cousin Alex."

He looked up at Alex. "Hey."

"How you doing?"

"Goo-ud."

"How's school?"

"Goo-ud."

"What grade are you in now?"

"Kindergarten."

"You getting good grades?" James Jr. nodded emphatically. "Well, keep up the good work, okay."

"Okay," and then James Jr. went back to his seat and his game.

"Where's your daddy and your brother?" Mya asked him.

"They down stairs."

"Your momma coming today?"

James Jr. shook his head no. Kay-Kay was a phantom in both of her children's lives. Mya resisted asking when was the last time he'd seen her.

Dysfunctional at it's worst, Mya's uncle had stepped out on his wife Martha, took up with a woman young enough to be his grand daughter; had a child with her, a second one coming that wasn't his, but he claimed nonetheless and Mya's Aunt Martha was taking care of both children.

Mya applauded her aunt and the kids seemed to be doing just fine, but that was a heavy burden to take on as far as she was concerned.

"Mya?"

Mya looked towards the kitchen. Smiled. "Hey Mom."

"Good to see you Alex," Mya's mother said gently.

Alex smiled his first genuine one since he'd arrived. "Good to see you too, Miss Claudia."

*

"Amen."

Jeff lifted his head, looked at the holiday spread, his mother and father seated on opposite ends of the table and felt an old envy. An only child born to parents up in age, he felt the weight of never having brothers or sisters as his mother passed the platter of turkey.

All of his father's family had died or moved away long ago and his mother's family had stayed south. There was one aunt in upstate New York, but family meals at her house, though great, were a rarity.

There had been too many moments like this for him and sadness slipped into his heart as he realized that one day, their numbers would be just two.

He had wanted to come with a date, but it seemed no one wanted to be bothered with him. Not the women of his past and he couldn't seem to attract anyone in his present. The Jeff who could grab attention with just a look had disappeared. He was becoming some one else and wasn't comfortable with who.

"Gravy?"

Jeff snapped out of his thoughts, the sound of the television drifting into the room. He looked around the table, seeing what his future could have been. He saw the empty chairs filled with a wife and children. Imagined the laughter and free flowing talk that could have spilled around the room.

He imagined Christmases with too many toys, his wife helping his mother baste the turkey. Saw family joy off in a distance he could not reach.

"Jeff? You want gravy?"

Jeff looked at the extended gravy bowl, the gnarly brown hand that held it. Sought his father's eyes, nodded and looked away.

*

Dajah put the last bit of pumpkin pie into her mouth, filled to the gills before it even reached her mouth. Her jeans were unsnapped beneath her top and her stomach was still digging into the waist band, but it was Thanksgiving, a time for over-eating and getting the *itis',* so she chewed, swallowed and suffered.

"Man, that was good."

"Glad you enjoyed it," Delia Moore said, her smile careful on her daughter. Delia liked Jeff. Up until what had happened happen, she considered him the perfect choice for her daughter. Delia couldn't help but miss him at the holiday table.

"Delia, you want me to start taking things to the kitchen?" Marilyn, Dajah's aunt asked.

"Yeah. We might as well get started."

Dajah wanted to help, but she was too full, too stuffed to move just yet. "I'll be there in a minute," she said, leaning back in her chair. A smile full on her face.

"Look at her," her Uncle Rob, declared. "She know she's not telling the truth. The girl is so stuffed, she can't even move."

Dajah laughed. "That is not true Uncle Rob."

"Ain't it?" He addressed Dajah's father. "Hank, your little girl over there looking like one of them Macy's Day Parade floats and she's talking about she gonna help in the kitchen."

Dajah's father chuckled. "I know. But her intentions are good." He reached out and touched Dajah's face. "Right baby? You mean well." Dajah smiled. Nodded. "See Rob?" He let his eyes remain on her, glad for a new kind of joy that had come into her as of late. He wasn't sure of the source, but knew that Dajah would share when she was ready. He was just happy that today she was in a good place.

Dajah's cell vibrated against her thigh. She reached in her pocket, pulled it out. A text message. Dajah excused herself and left the room. Her father watched her go, happy for her.

Movies? – was what it said.

Dajah quickly texted back her answer. Slipped the phone back into her pocket and headed towards the kitchen. She'd help out a bit and then head home. She had a date. With Rick.

*

Everyone was concentrating on the plate of food before them. Compliments to the 'chef' coming and going as stuffing was tasted, mac and cheese sampled and collard greens were dived into.

Aunt Martha was seated next to her estranged husband James. James' son Little James was seated next to him and Kay-Kay's son Daniel was seated next to Martha. Mya looked at the four of them, knowing the dynamics, affirmed that family was who you made family to be.

Was Alex still family? By next year she would have her name back and legally all ties to him would be severed. Would this be the last time he joined her at a family gathering?

It hadn't felt as crazy as she thought it would feel. They had laughed together, genuine and freely. A few times it felt like old times between them. But Mya wasn't sure if it was just the final wrap up of who they had been to each other, or a pathway to who they could become.

"I just need something explained," Mya's father declared. "Now, I'm no learned man, never went to college or none of that. Hell, barely got out high school, but," he cast his eyes on Mya and Alex, "somebody need to explain to me how two people in the middle of a divorce are still together?"

"Scotty!" Mya's mother said quickly. "You are not going to do that, not now, not today." The force in her voice vibrated the whole table. The look in her eye said she meant business.

"Claudy, I…"

"Claudy, I nothing. Don't you dare start with none of that foolishness, you hear me? Because if you do, I swear I will go home right now, pack my bags and you will never ever see me again."

She meant it. Everyone at the table knew she meant it. She had left her husband twice in the past four years. The first time she was gone for a few months. The last time she'd left for a whole year. When she returned, she told her no good, cheating, selfish husband that if she left one more time, she was not coming back. And her no good, cheating, selfish husband had looked into the eyes of the woman he had known for over forty years and knew she wasn't playing.

Things had changed for Mya's mother and father. Where once Scotty Williams had run his roost anyway he wanted, anyhow he wanted, those days had come to an end. He was home every night and on those nights he wasn't, his wife was out with him.

His days of philandering with other women were over. Getting stabbed in the chest by one of them hadn't stopped him, but Claudia's new-found will had.

"So you go ahead and try me, hear?" Claudia added, her eyes full of fire on her husband. "Go ahead. Try. Me."

Mya's fathered blinked once, twice. Forked up some collard green. Put them in his mouth and chewed. The rest of the table went back to their meal, too.

All except Mya, who could only look at her mother being the type of woman she'd never thought she could be. Mya, looking at her mother with new eyes, silently applauding her, praying for the same resolve.

Because when this evening was through, when she left out of her aunt's house, it would be just her and Alex on the ride home. And despite what she thought she knew, her mother showing a real backbone and changing up a wrong marriage into a better one, had Mya thinking; had Mya going from being a rock in the water to becoming the water itself.

Her decision was dissolving from a solid thing toward one that flowed with the current. Maybe what she'd felt was her future, in that moment, maybe wasn't her future at all.

*

She had been so nervous.

Despite her best friend Tarika coming over early that morning and helping her in the kitchen; despite being on the phone with her mother getting step-by-step instructions on how to make candied yams; despite the kitchen table laid out with a real table cloth, matching silverware and a little autumn centerpiece in the middle, Gina was nervous.

It was her first Thanksgiving dinner ever.

She had invited Tarika and her boyfriend Justin, Collin and Collin's son, and her mother. She wasn't so concerned about what Tarika, Justin or Collin would think. She was concerned about what her mother would think of her cooking, her decorating. Her effort.

Gina didn't realize she was holding her breath as her mother put a piece of turkey in her mouth. She didn't realize that she was watching her mother's face closely, until Collin leaned over and asked if she was okay.

"You got a funny look on your face," he whispered in her ear.

"Oh, no, I'm good." she answered but her eyes never left her mother's face. Her mother rarely complimented her for anything. Gina could never recall her mother ever saying she was proud of her.

"Umm," she heard her mother say, but her mother's face was screwed up a bit. Gina watched her chew some more. Let her breath go as her mother nodded her head. Wanted to cry a little as her mother said. "This is good."

"I made it," Gina said quickly.

Doreen looked at her daughter. "Did you?"

"Yeah Momma, all by myself." Which was the truth. Tarika had offered to help her, but Gina was determined to do the turkey alone.

"Well, it's good. Tender. Not dry. Seasoned good."

Gina waited for her mother to say more, but Doreen was done talking. She was about eating and she did with gusto. This had been the first home cooked meal that she hadn't had to make herself in a long time. And she was going to enjoy it for all it's worth.

"The food is the bizness, Gina," Justin said.

"Well, I tried."

"Really good, Babe. Really good," Collin added.

"Yeah," Collin Junior piped in, a sliver of collards clinging to the corner of his mouth.

"It's good Mommy, real good," Kanisha told her.

Filled to the brim with compliments, Gina could barely taste what she put in her mouth. The looks on the faces around her table filling her more than any food ever could.

After the meal they played Taboo. It had been Tarika's idea. "Give us something else to do beside sit around watching football." So while the game was muted, everyone partook, including Gina's mother.

Gina didn't think her mother would want to play, no less hang around after dinner. But Doreen did, laughing and enjoying herself in a way Gina never thought her mother could. At the evening's end, Doreen actually hugged her. Told her she had a good time. That she was doing good with her life and to keep it up.

What Doreen Alexander didn't say was 'thank you,' though she'd felt gratitude all in her bones. If Gina hadn't invited her to Thanksgiving, she would have been resigned to go to one of her friend's house, which would have been okay, but it wouldn't be family. Though Doreen and her daughter had rarely seen eye-to-eye, this day Doreen had been extremely grateful that Gina had invited her. She was even more surprised that she had had a good time.

*

The movie started at nine p.m. By eight-fifteen, it was all Dajah could do to keep her eyes open. She called Rick and asked for a rain check. "I'm so sleepy. I'll fall asleep half way through."

Rick had been looking forward to seeing Dajah all day. He had even taken the night off to be with her, but he had promised her no pressure, so he said it was cool.

"You sure?"

"Yeah. No problem. No sense in going to see a movie if you aren't going to be awake for it."

"How was your day?"

"It was okay. Went to my moms."

"So, you had the day off?"

"Day? No. Night. I took the night off. I figured we'd be going to the movies and all…"

"Oh. Damn…you took the night off for me. I'm sorry Rick."

"Not a big deal Dajah. I have plenty of personal business days."

"Yeah, but still. Now I feel bad."

"No, don't."

She looked at the time. It was a little after eight. Not early, but not late. She was tired, exhausted even, but he only lived down the street. She had some wine in the fridge. Inviting him over for a drink was the least she could do. "I'm not up to the movies, but if you want to come on by, you're more than welcome."

"No, that's alright."

His answer surprised her. "No?"

"Nah, I'm good."

"Really?"

"Yeah, really?"

"Why?" She didn't mean to ask that, but it came out of her mouth anyway. They had been out three times already and talked to each every day but he'd never been to her place and she found it hard to believe he refused her invite.

"I got reasons," all he offered.

"What kind of reasons."

"Reasons. Let's just leave it at that."

He was turning her down. She wanted to know why. "No, I want to know."

"No you don't."

"Yeah. I do."

"You're not going to like it."

"How do you know?" she snapped, anger slipping into her mix.

"Because I know you, that's why."

That shot straight to her core and shut her up for a second. But what it inferred wouldn't let her stay quiet. "You know me…really?"

"Yeah Dajah. Look, I'm not trying to blow it out of proportion. So just let it go."

But that was like telling her to stop breathing. Impossible. "No Rick. You started this."

"No Day, *you* started this. You won't take no for an answer."

He was absolutely right, but she wouldn't back down. "Because I need to know."

"No you don't."

"Why not?"

"Because you aren't going to like it."

"Try me."

Rick sighed. "Let it go, okay. Just let it go."

"Since you 'know' me so well, then you know I can't."

"You can, but you don't want to," he said with a chuckle, a much needed relief breaker.

She chuckled too, anger fading. "I can if I want to."

"Then do it."

"No."

"See? I told you you can't let it go."

"Seriously, Rick. Why?"

"Let it go, Dajah. Things were going nice between us. I'm not trying to mess it up."

"So telling me would mess it up?"

"Probably."

Infuriation snuck up to her toes. "So you playing word games now?"

"No Dajah. I'm trying to get you to believe me."

"How can I believe you when you won't tell me?"

He sighed again. "You gonna let it go?"

"I don't know, am I?"

Silence. Rick thinking, the truth on the tip of his tongue and Dajah waiting for his response. "Okay, but when you get all mad, don't blame me."

"I'm not going to get mad."

"Alright. Like I said, things are going good between us and I'm not trying to mess that up. Coming down there, this time of night? Well, that might mess it up."

"How?"

"Because if I come down there, I might not want to leave."

Dajah blinked. "Oh."

"Yeah, 'Oh.'"

She smiled. Tickled. Did he really think? *Didn't you?*

Dajah had been trying to ignore what was behind the curtain of her and Rick's re-discovered connection. She had to decide if she wanted what she thought she'd never want again in life—Rick. But he was already in her life. Him coming over was just that final destination. Did she want that? Go back to what she'd left? Step back into what she had emotionally clawed her way out of?

The fact that she hadn't mentioned anything to Frieda spoke of her fear. The fact that she had been chatting him up on the phone and had gone out with him a few times spoke of her desire. So was this the night she'd let that final segment play out?

"We're grown ups, right?" she said quickly.

"Of course we are."

"Okay, so I think we can both handle you coming down here for a little while."

"Just a little while?"

It took a moment for her to answer. "Yeah, just a little."

*

Dajah wished things.

She wished he hadn't worn that tight knit top that clung to him like cellophane, showing off his muscled chest and that thinly veiled six-pack. She wished his jeans had been looser around his waist, instead of fitted, emphasizing that fine rise of his behind.

She wished he had lost that swagger of a walk, wished he hadn't put on cologne. Wished he had shown up in a hoodie and some sweats, instead of arriving so fresh and so clean.

"Tour?" she asked as they stood in her living room.

"Looks just like my upstairs."

"Yeah, it is, but come take a look see anyway."

He followed her to the kitchen, peeked his head into the bathroom. Rick stepped into the second bedroom and stood out in the hall from her main one. He mentioned her ficus by the front window and said something about still having the same couch.

Then the tour was over and Dajah went to get some wine. She came back with two glasses, giving him one and sitting opposite him on the couch.

"Nice place Dajah."

"Thanks."

"But your other place was nice."

Dajah took a sip. Her eyes drifting. "Yeah, I loved that place."

"So, what happened?"

At some point she would have to tell. She just wasn't sure if it was now. "Life happened, I guess."

"You don't have to talk about it."

She nodded, whispered 'thank you.'

"But I have to admit that I've been thinking about it."

"Really?"

"Yeah. I mean, the last time I saw you, you were at the restaurant with some dude. And then, a year later, you're living on my street."

"Yes, I am," she said with a slight chuckle.

"So," Rick said carefully, "As far as I can gather, something happened between you two that made you either lose or leave your place. And whatever that something was, it must have been major because he's not here."

Dajah sipped more wine. "Right again."

"So?"

She felt him looking at her. Wished she could return the favor. But she couldn't bring her eyes to do that, so she studied her ficus. "That's number three, you know."

"What?"

She indicated her house tree. "The ficus. Number three."

"Oh, okay."

She chuckled, knowing Rick didn't know where she was headed, she unsure herself. But something in her felt compelled to talk about it. Talk about her tree and how there had been two before it. "The first one, well that died while I was taking care of Kanisha. The second?" she shook her head. "I had to abandon it. I couldn't take it with me, so I had to leave it on the curb. I didn't have a choice."

She put the glass to her lips. Finished half her wine. Made a face as the wine stung her throat. "Now this one, this one is the third one...I wasn't even sure I wanted it. Wasn't sure I deserved a third go. I mean I had killed off two. What right did I have to a third?"

She was looking at him, her eyes wide and searching, a little buzz in her. Rick was looking back, his eyes just as wide, just as searching.

Dajah looked away, shook her head a bit. Got up. "You want more wine?' her glass nearly empty.

Rick reached out and stopped her as she headed towards the kitchen. "You don't have to get drunk Dajah."

She reeled back. "I'm not trying to get drunk."

"You downed that glass like it was water. All I'm saying is, you don't have to…get drunk to be comfortable with me here. And, if you have to get wasted for me to be here, then maybe I should go."

Dajah blinked. Blinked again. Saw herself tossing that glass back. Knew Rick was right. She sat. Considered him. "When did you get so wise?"

Rick shrugged, not knowing the answer, only that he wanted truth between them. Their past had been filled with enough lies. "I don't know. But if this is too much for you, I can go."

She looked at him, feeling it. Feeling that opened window shift into a cracked door. "I can't fully trust this Rick. Can't fully trust you here with me. I know you said no pressure and you've been true to your word. But what we went through before, what I went through…" she looked away, looked back at him. "It was brutal, emotionally, I mean. And you wanted to come back, and I couldn't take you back and I was glad and sad about it all in the same breath. I walked away forever, but here I am again, with you."

"If you want me to go…"

Dajah shook her head. "No, I don't want you to go…don't you see, that's the problem," her voice went painful. "I want you to stay."

He reached for her. Kissed her. Simple pecks on her lips. Once, twice. Four times before she parted her lips, allowed his tongue in. Wetness filled the corner of her eyes. A single trail slipped down her cheek.

He pulled back. Studied her. Sadness, reluctance and future regret filled her eyes. "You okay?"

She shook her head no. "No, I'm not. You're not supposed to be here, but you are. I'm not supposed to want you here, but I do…but what I went through…" She was out of words.

"Never stopped loving you Dajah, not once."

"I know."

"Are you afraid?"

"Yes," she managed.

"Me too."

She looked at the man who wasn't suppose to be there, who was just as afraid as she was. Love wasn't supposed to make you fearful, but it did sometimes. She wasn't supposed to love him any more, but she did.

"What are you gonna do?" she needed answering.

"About?" he said carefully.

"Us."

"I don't know. But I do know being back here with you feels like I was never gone. And I know that I did you wrong. I don't want to do that to you ever again."

She put her forehead against his. "Promise?"

"Promise."

She kissed him. He kissed her back. It was familiar and brand new, daunting and wonderful. The smell of Rick, the touch of Rick, tucked away in a box in the basement of her heart, buried beneath a life with Jeff, re-emerging.

For better or worse, Rick was reclaiming his space inside of her heart.

He pulled away suddenly. His eyes, thoughtful. "I have to make a run."

Dajah was confused. "A run?" A run where?"

He looked sheepish. "Condoms."

"Condoms?" Was that really how this night was going to end?

"Yeah," he said cautiously, waiting for a yay, or nay.

But there was magic in the moment and Dajah was afraid that if he left, what she was feeling and how she was feeling would go back into hiding. Dajah wasn't sure that when he returned, she'd still want him.

Rick got up. "Be back." He wasn't waiting for her answer. He decided for the both of them as he headed out of her front door. The sound of it closing, jarring. The absence of Rick, bringing the reality of it all in full focus.

*

He was back in less than ten minutes. Her smile was forced, her mood changed.

He sensed it, understood it. Spoke on it. "I don't have to stay Dajah. I can go."

Such kindness. Such consideration. But his naïveté had high-jacked them from time to time. "No, it's fine."

"You sure?"

She wasn't. "No. I'm not sure about any of this. But stay." She patted her couch. "Come. I'll get us something else to drink." She got up, "I have soda, juice." Made her way to the kitchen. "I know you drink Sprite, but I don't have—," arms slipped around her waist; the contact startling. Dajah, in front of the opened fridge, felt Rick's warmth against her spine and cool air against her chest. Provocative. She leaned into him.

His mouth moved close to her ear. Tickled it with his words. "You feel so good." She murmured a response, eyes closed. Juice, soda, something to drink, forgotten. They stayed that way, want a powerful thing, and she let the power of it fly. Gates flung wide open, it was easy to turn around, lean into the heat of him, the smell of him, the warmth of him. Easy to slip her hands around his neck, possession, nine-tenth of her law.

Easy to nibble his top lip, his bottom, feeling him throb against her just so. His desire had her name all over it. His desire, her own, dismissing who was who to when and where, shedding the bitter past between them.

She closed the fridge door with her foot, took his hand, led him to her bedroom. They did not turn away from each other as they undressed, eyes upon each other, like the first time.

"I've missed you," Rick said from across the room.

"Missed you to," Dajah answered back, closing the distance.

CHAPTER TWELVE

*F*rieda knew.

She never told Dajah that she did, but she could see it in Dajah's face, hear it Dajah's voice and realized it when reported Rick sightings disappeared. So when Dajah decided to spill the beans, Frieda's response was "Wondering when you were going to say it...you told it without telling. You got really happy right after we went shopping for shoes. Just stayed happy for weeks after. I'd see you and knew something was up. Since you didn't mention you had met anybody, I realized it was because you had been seeing Rick."

"So, you're not surprised?"

"Nope."

"I am," Dajah said softly.

"How? You moved two blocks from the man, loved him so much you turned your life up-side down. And besides, you are in the middle of a rebound from Jeff. How can you be surprised?"

"It's not like I planned it."

Frieda laughed. "Didn't you though? You might as well have moved into his house, acting all shell shocked when you ran into him. But I knew. I knew it from the moment you moved on his block."

"That's not how it went down Frieda," Dajah said, not liking what her friend was saying.

"It's cool Dajah. Rick had his flaws, but we all learn and grow. His crazy baby momma is giving him space to live and breath and you've given him the goody-goody. I know Jeff happened after Rick, but there's no shame in going back for a go-see."

"It's more than a go-see."

"Dajah, lighten up. I'm happy for you. I'm just tickled that you didn't see it coming."

Dajah laughed. Gave it some thought. "I did, didn't I?"

"Yep. But you did what you've always done. Saw what you wanted and went after it."

"I didn't go after Rick."

"No, you didn't. You just put yourself out there to be caught."

*

"The rest of the soup is on the stove. You have plenty of crackers and ginger ale, so you should be set until tomorrow."

Alex looked up from the bed, nodded. Grateful. "Thanks."

"No biggy," Mya said quickly. "I'll check on you tomorrow, okay?"

"Yeah, that would be great."

She leaned down, kissed his fevered forehead. Tucked the comforter up to his chin. "Feel better."

"I'll try."

Then she was leaving Alex's apartment, boxes unpacked in corners. Just a few pieces of furniture. Nothing about his apartment said: lived-in. *His choice*, that much Mya knew as she stepped into the early evening.

Dusk stained the horizon. Stars sprinkled the early night sky. Apartment windows spilled honey-colored light from their confines. The last of the rush hour commute brushed the streets in the sporadic sounds of buses breaking, horns honking, and slips of brief silence.

It was the time of day when the 'rush' to rush hour had faded. The time of day when cars were parked for the night, dinner simmered on stoves and a home's comfort was appreciated. Adults settled down to the last bit of evening news and youngsters, sprawled across comforter-covered beds finished homework, internet surfed or engaged in giddy phone conversations.

There was something definitive and complete about early evening; something comforting, fixed and felt long over due. But Mya was feeling anything but as she headed to her car, chilled air nipping her ears; her breath misting from her nose. Tonight the temps were going to drop to the thirties. Winter, well on its way.

Playing nurse maid to Alex had not been a part of her soon-to-be-divorced plans, but when he had called her and asked her to bring him by some things, it was simple to say yes. There was still consideration between them.

When her car got a flat, he came and changed her tire. And when he went to Chicago for a convention, she checked on his place and got his mail.

Mya had stopped seeing Bretta, but Alex was still going. At Bretta's suggestion, Alex had called his father for the first time in fifteen years. It had not been an easy conversation for either man, but they both agreed that they had been apart for far too long.

In a few weeks, Alex would be joining his father on a road trip to South Carolina to spend Christmas with family he had never met. Mya was proud of him for that.

Alex's life was on the road to healing, but Mya's was feeling a tiny bit stuck. A part of her just wanted the papers signed and her old name back.

She'd been going to the track on the regular in the evenings after work, but as the fall moved closer to winter, there were less and less people out that time of evening. She'd switched to early mornings. Eventually winter would shut it down for her, but until then, Mya ran.

*

Morning arrived shivery cold. So cold, it took her a full lap and a half before her body felt okay with it. Dark, sunrise was still a few minutes away. The royal blue sky was clinging stubbornly to the night.

The darkness didn't help one bit but she made her way through, experiencing the other side as the world around her came into focus.

There was something spiritual about being out there that time of morning. Something profound, separate yet attached about the day not yet arrived. Reverence filled her. Peace surrounded her. Hope infused her soul.

With others out, Mya was able to run with ease. The comfort would stay with her for a while before the reality of life would slip back in. *But I'm still here*, she would tell herself. Still here, still standing. Still loved?

Mya wanted things as her divorce proceedings moved along. She'd wanted Alex to keep the betrayal going. Hoped he'd start seeing other women.

She needed him to be that man who had deceived her so that she could step away from him forever. But he hadn't. Alex wasn't seeing anyone. Just dedicating his time to his center, and when moments called for it, her.

He'd stopped telling her that he loved her, missed her. But it was there every time they shared the same space. She didn't need that. Mya needed him to let her go.

She thought about Christmas coming in a few weeks. Considered New Year's Eve that came a week later. Who would she be ringing it in with? *Myself?* She'd done it before and survived it. There was no doubt she could do it again, but did she want to?

Of course not.

*

Odd man out.

Jeff dropped a dollar into the tip jar, Seven and Seven in hand and headed back to the corner that had claimed him most of the evening. He'd watched co-workers talk too loud, drink too much and danced badly with each other for the time he had spent holding up the wall.

Jeff was only at the Lucent Design Associates holiday party because it was required. With his mandatory one hour coming to an end, Jeff would finish his last drink, head over to O'Brien's on 46th, get a corn beef on rye, wash it down with a Heineken and head on home.

"Surprised to see you flying solo."

Jeff looked to his left, saw Allison standing there. Smiled. "How it goes sometimes." He took a sip of his drink.

She cocked her head, curious. "A first."

Allison was his co-worker. She lived in Brooklyn, was in her mid thirties and friendly. She wore her hair natural, this day pushed back off her forehead, with her mandatory brightly- colored beaded earrings hanging from her earlobes.

She was Afro-centric as far as corporate would allow and had worked in Jeff's department for three years. Their conversations had never gone further than 'hello.' But it was almost Christmas, almost the New Year, and rules were primed to be broken.

"You want to show them how it's done?" she asked him.

"How what's done?"

"Dancing." She indicated the make--shift dance floor, filled with fifty-year-old managers trying to find the beat and twenty some-thing'ers owning it.

Jeff shook his head no. "I'll pass."

Allison considered him for a moment. Understood she wasn't going to score. Made peace with her self. "Well, maybe Grant will assist me."

"Help you show them how it's done?" Jeff said with a free smile.

"Exactly," Allison declared, a finger pointing his way to emphasis the point. Jeff watched her leave. Silently applauded her. He knew what it was like to go after what you wanted and how sometimes what you wanted wasn't always what you got.

*

Jeff took a seat in the near-empty F train, the orange plastic seat hard and unyielding. There was no heat, but he was too tired, too full and just a tiny too buzzed to care. He closed his eyes as the train rolled out the station, opening them forty-eight minutes later when it pulled into 169th Street. Not up to taking the bus, Jeff took a cab, eyes closing again on that final ride home.

Gone all day, there was no surprise at the pile of doggy poop by the front door. He sprayed it with a shot of anti-bacterial 409, got it up with paper towels and got Kelly's leash. Tired as he was, his dog needed walking.

The night had him huddling inside of his North Pole jacket, but Kelly didn't seem to notice as she walked, sniffed and heeded nature's call.

Christmas lights twinkled everywhere Jeff looked. Snatches of Nat King Coles "The Christmas Song" drifted from a car window. A metallic smell drifted in the air and Jeff knew the first snow was on its way.

He hoped it would be a blizzard; the need to hibernate deep inside of him. He needed a break, tune out the world. A heavy snow would give him that.

Morning arrived bright and sunny and not a snow cloud in sight. What was present was solitude of the day—December eleventh. The twenty-fifth was but a stone's throw away and it was looking like another solemn holiday.

He checked the day temps – low thirties – and debated if he'd get to the track. Nothing in him wanted to get out there, but he made himself go.

He stepped onto the gravel behind a chatting older couple. He couldn't hear much of the conversation, but their laughter was consistent.

Jeff envied them.

He wanted to intrude on their space and ask questions. How long had they been together? How'd they made it work? But the need to pick up the pace hit and he jogged past.

He was on his third lap when he spotted Mya, bundled up but moving swiftly around the track. He didn't realize he was watching her until he almost ran into another jogger. *Get it together Jeff.*

But his life was a mess and the reason why was an eighth of a mile away. There was nothing she could do or say to take back what had been done. But something in Jeff made him pick up speed until he was by her side.

She seemed surprised to see him. Her face going through various metamorphoses before it managed a tight smile.

"I need to talk to you," came out of his mouth.

"About?" Mya managed, never slowing her pace.

"Us."

Those words tripped her. Made her loose her rhythm and stumble over her own feet. "Us?" Because there hadn't been any 'us' to them in years.

"Yeah. Us. You fucked my head up real bad, did you know that?"

Mya didn't. She slowed down to a walk. "I'm sorry."

"Sorry? Is that all you have to say?" After all those years, Jeff was still hurt and angry, carrying around what she'd done inside his heart.

"What else do you want me to say?"

Jeff stared. Grappled for his truth. Found only confusion. "I don't know."

"I don't know either," Mya replied, nonplussed. "All I can say is I'm sorry. Truly sorry. That was so long ago and you're still hurting...I'm sorry," she said a final time.

Jeff saw in her eyes that she was and those words were all she had for him. She didn't have answers, solutions, none of that. Just her apology. He pulled back. Shook his head. "I'm sorry."

"For?"

"Coming at you like that...my world is just so fucked up right now and I..."

A tiny chuckle escaped her. "Yours too."

"Yours too?"

Mya nodded. Smiled a careful smile. "Yep. Blown to smithereens."

"You want to go get some coffee?"

"I have to finish my run," Mya said tentatively, unsure.

"After. Get some breakfast or something?"

Mya looked at the man she had loved, then didn't, then did and then made it not matter. She thought about the pain she had caused him, a hurt he was still toting five years after the fact and knew there was no way she could tell him no.

*

He watched her as she unzipped her down vest, exposed cleavage above the coral-colored top, a visual delight. Mya caught him staring. Placed a hand on her shoulder, blocking the view.

Jeff blinked, sat back. "Sorry."

"No biggie." But everything about it was. Mya Williams Connor, soon to be just Mya Williams, was sitting in the diner on the Queens/Long Island border with Jeff Gingham, five years after they broke up and a few months from divorcing another man.

She was sitting there, trying to stay out of their past and keep herself firm in the present, a present that included a sick soon-to-be ex-husband who was waiting that very minute for her to come and check on him.

She dug in her pocket and got a rubber band. Slipped it around the gather of shoulder length hair, air finding her too-hot neck, making her sigh. "Whoo."

"Still warm?"

"Yeah. Seems like the older I get, the more hot I get."

"There's a word for that. It starts with an 'M.'"

"Don't you dare say it," she said with a laugh. "So," she was unsure of what was supposed to happen next. "You said you needed to talk about us, but Jeff, there hasn't been any us in a long time."

"I know...just that...my life," he shook his head, "it's just...fucked. And when I look at when it all went wrong, it comes back to you."

"Funny you should say that because my life?" her hand went to her chest. "My life is effed too and when I look back, it seems to point to what happened between me and you."

"Seriously?" Mya nodded. "How so?"

She didn't want to tell it, but knew that there was no healing in hiding the truth. "I met Alex a few months after we broke up. And for the record, our break up, Jeff, was one of the best things that could have happened to me." She saw his surprised expression. "I know, sounds crazy and I'm truly sorry for what I did. It was so wrong on so many levels, but in a crazy kind of twisted way, it was the only way I could begin *my* healing."

She shared meeting Alex, how they both seemed in the same place and the marriage that followed. "It was good. Better than good. Just the best relationship I'd ever had. It was healthy, loving, supportive, true, kind, all of that. But a few months ago, he had an affair." Mya looked off, the words making her eyes damp.

Jeff plucked a napkin. Handed it to her. She waved it off. "No, I'm okay." He sat it by her coffee cup just in case. "I didn't know at first. But he finally came out and told me. Turns out we both came from families where infidelity was the norm and though we both tried real hard to not make that our history, well, we failed. Me with you and him with me."

"So how was that your doing?"

"You know about energy? Everything is energy. Your conscious is energy, sub-conscious—all energy. So how we perceive the world is what our world becomes."

"Okay."

"And even though I thought I had gotten myself together, in truth, that infidelity thing was still inside of me, but it was hiding. Alex came into my life because that's what I was attracting. Does that make sense?"

It didn't. "I'm trying to follow you."

Mya realized Jeff wasn't where she was, where she'd been. Tried a different approach. "Okay. Think of all of us like individual magnets. We are attracted to certain types of personalities based on our magnets. Well, my magnet is infidelity."

"Did you ever cheat on him?" Jeff asked.

"No. Never."

"Did you ever want to?"

"No."

"Then I'd say that your 'infidelity' magnet has been wiped clean. You can't take blame for what he did. No more than I could be blamed for what you did."

Mya sat back, thought about it.

"Guilt is a powerful thing," Jeff said softly, the impact of his own words finding a home.

"Yes it is…I did feel guilty. I felt very guilty."

"Why do you think that was?"

She was quiet for a while. "Maybe it was because of what I had done to you. After what happened, you changed so much. Became somebody I didn't know, didn't like…"

"Yeah, I did."

"Did I ever say sorry?" She asked carefully.

"Before today? I think once. Right after you told me, but it didn't feel genuine."

Mya remembered that night. The night she confessed she'd slept with Vincent. A bunch of words and emotions flowing out of her, not necessarily the truth, just instinct.

She reached out. Took his hand. Looked at him until he was looking back. Tears welling in her eyes. "I am so sorry Jeff. I really am."

And there in the diner, he believed her. Open wounds on their way to a healing.

*

Their goodbye was awkward.

Old history and new discoveries swathed them. The end of this special time together, daunting.

"Maybe I'll see you around," Jeff offered.

Mya smiled. "Yeah."

"Well, you take care."

"You too."

And then he was getting in his car, she was getting in hers, both heading off in the same direction before he made a right turn and she made a left.

CHAPTER THIRTEEN

We're friends again, just friends. That's what Mya told herself as she stood in Alex's kitchen, stirring up chicken noodle soup. The early part of the day had her feeling things she wasn't comfortable with feeling. Since leaving Jeff, his presence had been hanging around her like a shawl, shoulder draped and warming.

"Ridiculous," she muttered as she got a bowl from the cabinet. In the distance she heard the shower going, grateful that Alex felt well enough to get cleaned up. In a day or two he'd be back to his old self and Mya was glad. She was tired of playing nurse, but could not *not* do it.

A part of her wanted life without Alex, but the part that didn't, that was tethered to what bound them, wasn't quite ready to let go. Running into Jeff, having coffee with him, only made the war in her heart harder.

"Mya?"

She faintly heard him call. Putting down the bowl, cutting the flame from beneath the pot, she went to him.

He was standing outside his bedroom. "Think we can change the sheets?" which translated to: *can you change my bed?* Because there was hardly enough strength in him to toss a pillow.

"Yeah, sure…go in the living room while I get it done."

Alex, grateful, did what he was told.

*

"I'm starting to feel like I can't breathe," she was confessing half an hour later to Chloe on her drive home, the blue tooth fixed in her ear. "I didn't mind in the beginning. But now? It's getting old, quick."

"So, how is he?"

"This is day five, so he's better, but he's still weak."

"Has he gone to the doctor?"

"No. He says it's just the flu."

"Probably. No doubt the stress of what you two have gone through has knocked down his immune system."

Mya's phone beeped. She looked at the screen. Saw it was Gail. "Chloe, I got another call. I'll call you back later." Mya clicked over.

"Hey."

"Hey back."

"What are you up to?"

"Just left Alex's…feel like some company?"

*

Friends since high school, the history between Mya and Gail was rich, something Mya appreciated as she flopped down on micro suede couch. "Whew. What a day."

"What's up?"

"Where do I begin?"

"The beginning?"

Mya considered her friend, about to tell what she hadn't told anyone. "I literally ran into Jeff today."

"Again?"

"Yes, again. At the track. Didn't even know he was there until he popped up beside me, pissed."

"Pissed? For?"

Mya shook her head. "He's still angry with me."

"Why?"

"Because of what happened a long time ago."

"Are you serious?"

"Yep…I'm out there running, doing my thing and the next thing I know, he's beside me talking about we have to talk about us."

Gail frowned. "I'm confused."

"You? Imagine how I felt. I didn't know what the heck he was talking about. But later, we went to that diner on the border and—,"

"I'm sorry, you did what?"

"Went to the diner, to talk." Mya raised a hand. "Don't ask. We go. We talk and he's still messed up from what I did. I had no clue. I mean, after all this time, I figured he was straight. But he wasn't. Isn't."

"So what did you do?"

"What could I do but apologize?"

"And?"

"No and," Mya said quickly.

"Does he know about you and Alex?"

"Yeah."

"Were y'all cool afterward?"

Mya thought about it. "Yeah."

"Okay."

Mya didn't know what the 'okay' meant, but she wasn't up to asking. Right now the sleeping dogs were sleeping. No need in stirring them up. "I'm fine with it, really."

"Well, good."

"I just want to get out of my life with Alex."

Gail gave her a careful look. She had been there through most of Mya's beginnings, middle and ends. Had sat quietly next to her when she cried. And did the happy dance in her head when her friend was jubilant. But she never ever thought that Mya's marriage would come down to this. "I know you do. I know a big part of you just wants to close the door on all of that," she paused, careful with her words. "But inviting him to the holiday table and taking care of him when he's sick isn't helping. You have to start letting go, for real."

"I'm trying. Really I am."

"Maybe you have to try harder. I know it's not easy, but it's like you're on the fence. And sooner than later you have to pick a side."

"He still loves me Gail."

Gail pursed her lips. "Now you know there's all kinds of love out there, right, wrong, real, fake. And sometimes even the truest love isn't the right kind."

Mya looked towards the kitchen. "You got something to drink?"

"I have half a bottle of some Zinfandel?"

"Sounds good." Mya watched her friend go to the kitchen, admiring the full glossy hair that bounced at shoulders the color of smooth cocoa. Some days Gail looked more East Indian than black. Today was one of those days.

A grandfather by way of Bombay had given Gail her rich mocha look and Mya recalled days that she'd envied that. But it wasn't about what a person looked like, rather what was inside their heart. Dimly she wondered what was inside her own self as Gail handed her the wine glass.

She downed half in a single gulp. Sighed. Blinked a few times. "Just what the doctor ordered…thank you."

"For?"

Mya looked at her friend, heart wide opened. "…for being my friend."

"Who else am I supposed to be?"

Mya shrugged, fragile. "I don't know. But you're my friend, my best one, and that means a lot to me."

Gail saw the tear in Mya's eye, touched. There had been quite a few times when it seemed Mya needed Chloe more than she needed Gail. Times when what Gail said didn't seem to matter, but what Chloe spouted was gospel. "Means a lot to me too," Gail told her back.

*

Mya's reason for going to the track changed. Determined to walk in truth, she accepted the fact that running had become about Jeff.

That accidental first meeting and coffee afterwards became meeting him every morning since. Smiles instead of frowns. Laughter instead of tears, the two of them ran their course together for six laps before the cool-down walk, where they chatted like happy little campers about everything except what was before them.

It became the highlight of their day and, though they had yet to exchange phone numbers, it had become vital.

She and Jeff had history, one that they were in the process of re-mending. Being friends was okay. And it was until that fifth morning when Jeff was a no show.

They normally arrived within five minutes of each other, but Thursday morning came and Jeff was a nowhere to be found. It pinched Mya's heart but she kept the routine. She tried not to take it personal, but that was like telling her not to breathe—an impossible feat.

*

Jeff looked at the clock, knew where he should have been and told himself it was okay to miss a day. It wasn't that he was too tired to get up, it was fear. Fear of being hurt. Fear of being betrayed. Fear of Mya snatching the rug from under him and sending him tumbling, again.

Yes, it had been all good and all gravy between them the last four days, but this morning he hesitated. Didn't go meet up with her.

The 'run' was no longer about running.

Yesterday as he'd watched her pull up in her car and head towards the graveled track, his heart filled with their time of before.

In an instant she'd gone from a potential friend to possibly the keeper of his heart. The closer she got, the more he felt it. The closer she got, the more he'd felt *her*. He'd tried to shake it during their paces, but the imprint remained.

It unnerved him. He wasn't supposed to feel that way about her ever again. They ran. That was all. But for the rest of the day and all through the night, his heart told him different.

Jeff couldn't risk going there with her again, so he backed off. Stayed home.

The next morning arrived with a cold rain. Saturday came without a cloud in the sky. Jeff donned his running gear and headed to the other track by the airport. There was no chance of seeing Mya there and, for him, that was a good thing.

*

Saturday, heart beating fast, Mya got out of her car and looked around. Third day in a row that Jeff was a no-show. *What are you gonna do?* She wanted to turn around, go home and lick the wounds for things she didn't even know could still be injured.

But that was the old Mya. She was working hard on becoming the new one. And the new one said being at the track wasn't supposed to be about Jeff; that that was a choice she'd made and she had the power to 'un-make' it.

So Mya ran. She ran like she was being hunted. She ran until there was no more in her and to prove that she was fine, ran one more lap after that.

And when she was done, when all the air had left her lungs and her feet, ankles, and thighs protested the fierce beating she'd just given them, she went to the bleachers and caught her breath, sorrow slipping in with every beat of her heart.

*

Jeff finished his run, haunted. He had tried to escape what plagued him, but it was still there. *You still love her.* He didn't want to. She didn't deserve to be after what'd she done, but he did. Still loved the woman who had screwed up his world.

She screwed up, or you did?

She didn't put a gun to your head and make you treat those women as badly as you did. She didn't force you to become a true hound dog, sleeping around and caring about none of the ones you were sleeping around with.

What she did, nobody deserved and it was wrong all the way around, but you always had a choice and what you chose to do with your life after Mya was on you.

Responsibility.

Jeff realized he had been ducking and weaving it for years. But life was playing catch-up with him now; his own doings were out in the light of day.

All those years he'd blamed Mya. All those years of behaving badly and never taking personal accountability. Always Mya's fault. Never his.

A different truth was before him. The real one.

Mya may have crushed his spirit, but it had always been his call to heal and be a better man for it.

*

Mya could barely walk. Everything from her hips down ached, throbbed. She had pushed herself too hard yesterday and had hurt herself in the process. *For the wrong reasons.*

An old pattern returning and she didn't like it. She'd worked too hard to get out of that sticky trap and here she was sliding back. She had planned to go to the track this morning, but her body needed rest. So, she didn't go. Got back into bed and fell into a fitful slumber; sleep coming, begrudgingly so.

*

The next morning Jeff was back at the old track, but Mya wasn't. He went through his paces, every quarter mile completed arriving with the hope that she would show up.

He wondered where she was before he realized she'd probably changed her routine because he had changed his. Without uttering a single word, his actions told her that she didn't matter to him much.

She wasn't the same 'Mya.' She *had* changed. The old Mya would have been in his bed by the second day. The new Mya, even though in the midst of her divorce, was keeping their friendship just that—a friendship. And that's what he needed in his life about now – a friendship.

Jeff abandoned his run and got back in his car. Eight minutes later he was entering Mya's lobby and ringing her intercom. He wasn't sure what he would say, only that he needed to speak to her.

*

Fast asleep, Mya didn't hear the buzzer the first time Jeff rang. She barely heard it the second. But by the third buzz, she work up, yelled "Coming" from her bedroom, headed to her intercom. "Yes?"

"It's me, Jeff."

Whatever bit of sleep she had vanished. Mya stared at the intercom as if it possessed all of her secrets. Jeff. Downstairs. Wanting to come up. Did she dare?

Buzz. She pressed the white button. Muttered. "Give me a sec," because she needed some time to decide if she was going to let him in. Mya needed some time to figure out what was the best move.

She looked around her apartment, down at the short tee shirt she had on and nothing else. Came up with her answer. "I'll be down in a few."

She wouldn't let him in. Better to meet him in the lobby. Better to meet him fully dressed.

The lobby felt just like what it was – a transitional space designed to get people from outside to the elevators. It wasn't a place to have a real conversation, and it certainly wasn't a place to talk with an old ex while you were still legally married.

Still, Mya indulged Jeff. She didn't ask anything, just needed him to have his say and be gone, but in the five seconds she stood before him, arms wrapped protectively across her breasts, he hadn't spoken.

"What's going on?" she had to ask.

"You weren't at the track today."

"And you weren't there a few days ago," she shot back. It took her a second to realize what *was* going on: *Absence*. He'd felt it like she had.

Regret dusted his eyes. "I needed to get my head straight."

She felt compelled to explain too. "I ran hard the other day. Too hard. Needed to give myself a break, that's all."

Jeff smiled.

She felt it then, the crazy tango they were in the middle of. Eventually the music would stop and when it did? Would they stand tall or fall?

"So, you're okay?" Jeff wanted to know.

"A little sore, but okay."

"You'll be back out there tomorrow?"

"Weather permitting."

He seemed glad and relieved. "Guess I'll see you tomorrow?"

Mya nodded a yes.

*

"You're coming, right?"

Mya wasn't expecting the phone call. In the days since Alex had gotten back on his feet, his need of her had began to fade. They were no longer a couple, no longer an anything and the idea of helping with his annual holiday party at the center stopped existing in her universe.

For a minute she was stymied, then pulled, but ultimately conflicted. "I..,"

"You always come."

Freedom rode words she'd wanted to speak for a long time. "Alex, that was before. This is now and what was, no longer is."

"I could really use your help," he said softly.

She'd spent so much of her life in pursuit of what other people wanted and it was hard to say no. But divorce papers and all that she'd done for Alex since flashed in her mind. Like Gail said, she was fence walking. It was time to pick a side and stay.

"I can't Alex. Sorry, but I can't."

CHAPTER FOURTEEN

*T*oys *R Us* stores were the Las Vegas casinos at Christmas time. Parents entered with a set amount of money to spend but always wound up spending more.

Dajah looked at the bright red shopping cart filled to the brim with boxes and bit her tongue. It was way too much.

She wanted to tell Rick that Kanisha didn't need the extra package of fake food because the kitchen came with more than enough. She also wanted to tell him that it would be cheaper to buy cake mix from Keyfood rather then the Easy Bake Oven brands Toys R Us was selling.

The accountant in her wanted to say that more than likely both the Easy Bake Oven and the play kitchen would be abandoned for the Wii game system Gina was getting his daughter.

Kanisha was closer to eight than she would ever be five again and the money he was spending on the kitchen and cooking things would go to waste.

But she didn't because every time Rick hefted up a box and stuck it in that cart, his whole being lit up.

Dajah couldn't say the same. The boots with the five inch heel were cute for getting in and out of cars, but they were not designed for the trillion mile marathon they had been doing inside the store. Her feet hurt.

"Is that everything?" Rick asked her.

She quickly looked down at the paper she'd been holding, check marks next to each of the written items. Smiled. "Yep, that's it."

"Hungry?"

"Absolutely."

"Chinese? West Indian?"

Dajah looked around the crowded store. Thought about the Italian restaurant in Astoria. "Dante's."

"Dante's it is."

With just a few days until Christmas, traffic was horrific. Stop and go was the way from the North Conduit right up until they got on the Grand Central Parkway. Finding parking on a Saturday in Astoria was just as maddening, but after circling the block seven times, they found a spot.

Dajah had lobster ravioli and Rick enjoyed the shrimp scampi. A glass of wine, confessions of having the *itis'* then they were heading back to Rick's place for gift wrapping, complete with Christmas songs on the CD player.

Later as they snuggled in Rick's bed, he asked about going to church. "So, you've decided if you're going tomorrow?"

"Where?"

"To my mom's church. They're having their Christmas program tomorrow. I haven't been in a minute, but I told her I would come."

"Where?"

"Emanuel Fellowship right off of Foch."

Church. Dajah hadn't been in years herself. "What time is the service?"

"Eleven."

"What time do they get out?"

Rick laughed. "You know black folks don't know how to get out of church."

"So, kinda all day?"

"Yeah."

Dajah thought about it. She thought about what the year had brought her. There were definitely some thanks to be given. She told him yes.

*

She didn't know, Dajah's first thought as Mrs. Trimmons headed her way, surprise and shock on her face. *She didn't know me and Rick are back together*. Dajah hardly knew it herself, moments coming when the idea caught her off guard, stunned her a bit.

She accepted the embracing arms, the faint scent of Joy perfume and the Pentecostal-brown colored lips pressed against her cheek. Dajah readied for the question, for it was as sure to come as the chorus hitting the final notes on the exit music.

"Dajah? What a surprise?" Rick's mother eyed him. "Rick?"

"Mom. Long story, but isn't it enough that I'm here?"

A smile replaced surprise. For the first time in a long time, Rick had come to a service and beside him was the one woman Mrs. Trimmons always thought suited her middle son the best. Rick was right, it was enough.

*

The IHOP on Rockaway Boulevard was jammed full of after-service churchgoers and Christmas shoppers. It took a while to get a table, even longer for the ordered food to arrive, and in those between points, Mrs. Trimmons asked questions as only a mother could – straight, no chaser.

"So, you two," she began, the metal spoon spinning inside of the tiny ceramic cup, giving an off kilter melody. "Since when?"

Dajah left it up to Rick to reply.

"Since a few months ago."

Mrs. Trimmons shook a package of Sweet and Low. "How many?" Rick shrugged. She tapped sweetener into her coffee. "One? Two? Six?" Stirred.

Rick touched her arm. "We're here, together, all that matters."

Mrs. Trimmons considered her son, Dajah next to him. Nodded.

*

Later, the conversation that Dajah held onto since meeting up with Rick's mother spilled out as they headed back to his house. "You didn't tell her, did you?"

"I was going to," Rick defended.

"When?"

He shrugged. Didn't want to think about the real answer. Certainly didn't want to share it.

"When, Rick?"

"When, the time was right."

"Right? Really? Really? Well, when is this right time, Rick?" Because there was something low down about him trying to keep it a secret. That's how Dajah felt in that moment, anyway.

"I just wanted to make sure," he said reluctantly.

"Made sure of what?"

He looked at her plainly. "Of us."

That surprised her. Hurt a bit. They were 'sure.' *As 'sure' as before? Because you two were a certainty back then and look what happened.* Fingers could be pointed at Gina, at themselves, but no matter the reason, they had fallen apart.

Even as this realization came to Dajah, she pressed him. Because if he couldn't tell his mother, what did that say about them as a couple? "Meaning?"

"Look. Life has changed a lot for me, and I mean a whole lot. Those crazy choices I made back then I know I'll never make them again. But life has a way of pulling the rug sometimes, y'know? And yeah, it's good between us now. Real good. But I didn't want to say anything to anybody until I was sure."

Dajah frowned a bit. "There isn't any 'sure' in life Rick. It's what it is and what you make of it. But I'm here with you…you need to be here with me, too."

"I am, Dajah."

For the first time in a while, she felt reluctance in him. "What's really going on Rick?"

He studied the road for a few seconds. Swallowed, the words hard. "I'm scared."

"Of what?"

He looked at her. Those Allen Iverson eyes, piercing. "Of us, not making it."

"Why wouldn't we?"

"It don't feel real sometimes. Just like some kind of dream, y'know?" She didn't. Told him so. "Well, that's how it feels for me…I wake in the middle of the night, asking myself, is she really back, with me? Why would she even want to after all I put her through?"

Clueless. Rick was clueless. She had accused him of being just that before, but the new, improved grown-up Rick wasn't supposed to be. The clueless Rick was supposed to have been long gone. In the wind.

But he wasn't.

Dajah knew what she had to do. But didn't feel up to the challenge—try and convince him that they would be just fine.

So she just kept quiet. The ride home silent, stunted and without joy.

*

Gina pulled back the receiver, stared at the hard plastic then put the phone back to her ear. "You serious?"

"Yeah. I'm sorry."

Damn, but wasn't he though? Always sorry. Always not keeping his promises. Like now. His promise to go with her and Kanisha to the Mall to see Santa, broken. "But you promised Collin, not just me, but Kanisha."

"I know, I know. But my uncle got me over here helping with the boiler and I thought—"

"Yeah, you always thinking, way damn too much." She pushed the disconnect button. Leaned against the wall, caught her breath, the tear that filled the corner of her eye. Swallowed, stood straight and called out to Kanisha to go and get dressed.

Next, she called her friend Tarika. It was Sunday. She was off. Maybe she'd want to go with them to 34th Street. Some company was always better than none.

*

The F train was crowded, but the two women and the little girl had gotten seats. Kanisha had her face pressed against the window. She liked the way the lights flickered and sparks shot up.

She also liked the way the train lurched and squealed and the fact that she was going to see Santa. Christmas was two weeks away and she needed to get him her list.

What Kanisha didn't like was how Mr. Collin wasn't going to meet them or how her mother's face looked mashed up, even when she greeted Aunt Tarika, who showed her her new boots and the recently done manicure with the sparkly things on the tips.

Kanisha didn't quite understand just how Mr. Collin helped make her mother's world brighter. But she did know that lately, he just seemed to make her sad.

She wished Mr. Collin could be more like her daddy who rarely made her mother sad. Maybe she could call her daddy later and have him call Mr. Collin and tell him how not to.

"Kanisha, our stop."

Kanisha snapped out of her thoughts and reached for her mother and her auntie's hand. She skipped a little between the both of them when they got on the platform, glad that her mother didn't tell her to quit it. She was off to see Santa and nothing else mattered more in the world.

CHAPTER FIFTEEN

*O*ut of words and stuck in fear. That's what Monday yielded
Dajah and Rick as one headed off to work and the other, a day off.
Neither were comfortable with the uncertainty. Neither strong
enough to break the ties that separated. So that's where they
remained. Stuck.

*

Rick closed his cell phone for the seventh time that day.

He had been opening and closing it since he arose a little before
eleven that morning. It was now a little after six in the evening and
he hadn't heard from Dajah. Hadn't spoken a word to her since he'd
dropped her home Sunday afternoon. Rick knew he had messed up,
but he wasn't sure how.

He had told the truth. How could anyone fault him for that? But
Dajah had. She'd gotten real quiet, barely saying goodnight as she
got of his car. No hug. No kiss. Not even a look.

Rick dialed her number, nonsense leaving him with every
unanswered ring; what was important, filling the void.

*

Slack.

That's what Dajah had become in regards to her hair. She was
supposed to shampoo and condition her braids every week, but
being with Rick had her going into a third without benefit of either.

Always some sacrifice with him, wasn't it? Always some part of
herself that she'd abandon, leave behind, in her quest to be with
him.

Quest. Was that it? Some long arduous journey to reach the
place where he was? From the beginning, she had pursued him, not
so subtly suggesting that if he ever got out of his relationship with
Gina to look her up. And hadn't she done the same thing, moving a
mere two blocks away from him?

Her head hurt.

She headed to the bathroom to wash her hair. Didn't hear her phone ring under the shower as she closed her eyes. The water, warm and soothing, eased the troubles, if only temporarily, from her head. And for those few moments, she was at peace.

*

No answer.

Rick threw on a jacket, untied sneakers and headed out of his house. The cold air felt good on his warm skin. Felt good around his mind full of thoughts. By the time he came onto Dajah's block, his pace picked up.

He needed to break the silence between them. Needed a way back into what had been.

*

The conditioner smelled of mango, pineapple and something else fruity. Dajah inhaled the scent as she worked it the length of her braids. She'd had them for six years and knew it was time for a change, but giving up their convenience was hard.

Maybe in the New Year, which was right around the corner.

Time had flown, sprouted wings. Just yesterday had been summer. Now it was less than two weeks to New Year's Eve.

What would it bring? she wondered as she turned on the faucet and stuck her head under the rush. *What will the New Year bring me?* Something better, a whispered prayer.

*

Rick stood on the stoop and rang the bell. Counted to ten and rang again. Stepped back and looked up to the second floor window. The lay of curtains, still. He rang a third time, a fourth, each pause feeling like a lifetime come and gone.

He got hot under his collar and unzipped his hoodie. Stepped back and looked up at the window. *She ain't answering. Just like that time you went to Gina's and she didn't answer, pretending like she wasn't home and no doubt laughing at you while she did. Why? Because you're acting like a fool just like you were back then. She don't want to see you, hear from you, nothing. So you might as well take your sorry ass back home.*

But Rick didn't. He stood and rang and window-watched until the front door opened, Dajah with her head in a towel, robe wrapped tight.

"Everything okay?" she asked, surprised.

"I've been out here ringing your bell for like five minutes."

"I was in the shower...you okay?"

Tension left him. Rick sighed, spoke from his heart. "No."

Dajah frowned, remembering her hair, only half rinsed. She frowned because Rick had shown up at her door, needy.

That was all she could see in the moment. Not love, not connection, the fun times. Just the interruption of what she needed to do for herself because he needed her to do something else.

"I was in the middle of doing my hair." Talking through the screen door, she made no move to open it.

"I called and you didn't answer."

"I was doing my hair, Rick." Testy.

"I see that now, but then I come down here and I'm ringing and," he stopped himself. Looked at her, nodded in some private defeat. Took a step back, hands up in surrender. "It's all good." With that, he turned and jogged down the steps.

Nothing in Dajah wanted to call him back, so she didn't. Just closed the door, locked it and headed back up to her apartment. Shivering as she took off her robe, she turned on the faucet, waiting for the hot water to reach the pipes. She needed it's warmth to sooth her.

*

"For real?" Frieda was asking an hour later, Dajah on the other end of the phone.

"Yeah Frieda, for real."

"Okay. Let me get this straight. This all started because Rick didn't tell his mother that he was seeing you again and he confessed that he was scared and you got pissed and when he came down to your house and wanted to talk, you couldn't cause you hadn't washed your hair in like three weeks because of him and you had conditioner in your head that needed to be rinsed out and so, you wouldn't let the brother in. Is that correct?"

It sounded foolish to Dajah's own ears, but she refused surrender. "It wasn't like that."

"No? Cause I could have sworn that's what you just told me."

"I'm always giving something up for him."

"No, you stopped doing things for yourself because you chose to, Dajah. You can not sit there and tell me that three weeks ago if you told Rick – hey, I have to wash my hair tonight – that that man wouldn't have been right there in the tub with you trying to give your head a good lather." Rick would have. Whether he knew what he was doing or not, he would have tried his hardest to do it. "You need to get over yourself, Dajah."

"What?"

"You heard me. You need to get over yourself. You are a grown ass woman making decisions about your life every single day. Since when was taking an evening to wash your hair or not Rick's fault?"

"Okay, well maybe not now, but before. When Gina was gone I had to take care of Kanisha and my plant died and—,"

"Did Rick hold a gun to your head?'

"No."

Frieda sighed. "You're just looking for excuses as to why it won't work and you need to figure out why."

Dajah felt the answer as soon as Frieda called her out. She was scared, too…

*

Dajah was gone from Rick, again. But if there was one thing Rick knew, it was that life kept on moving. Christmas was coming. It was still the holiday. Rick was determined to celebrate it.

He went to Home Depot and purchased outdoor lights. Spent the day and a part of the early evening stringing them along his gutters, around his windows and up the black wrought iron railing on his steps.

He purchased a real tree, some ornaments and with WBLS playing at a nice volume, he commenced to decorating. He sipped egg nog, sung along when the mood hit him and then went back outside to study his handiwork.

It looked good. Real good.

Next up was finalizing his Christmas plans. He had a ton of toys for Kanisha and would call Gina about getting them over to her place. He'd get there early, hang out long enough for Kanisha to open her gifts then head to his mother's for the Christmas meal.

Head up, despite Dajah, Rick kept moving forward. He'd learned a while back that it was the only way to go.

*

It didn't surprise but it did hurt that Collin would be spending most of Christmas in the Bronx with his son and his son's mother. He said he would come by Christmas night. Gina told him "Don't bother."

"What do you mean?"

"Just like I said Collin. You ain't got to come here. You can stay your ass right up there in the Bronx."

"You mean that?"

"I do," Gina said hotly. "This has been tired a long time ago. Now it's really fucking tired. You have a nice fucking life, hear?" She slammed the receiver down and stared out her kitchen window.

Out, she wanted out. Out of her life, what had been with Collin, but mostly out of the sadness that claimed her.

She thought things. Wild things. Scary things. Foolish things. Gina thought about her old days of self medication, how a joint would make everything better. She thought about old smoking buddies, the taste of burnt weed in her mouth.

She thought about the mellowness that would come right after her second toke. Nearly smiled. She couldn't remember the last she'd had a joint, but knew it had been over a year.

Over a year of no weed. She couldn't remember how she stopped, didn't even care that she had.

Only that she wanted to break that record. Gina set her mind about doing just that.

*

Less than two blocks from her momma's house and about fifteen from the place she called home, Gina didn't start to feel conspicuous standing on the street corner until the *po-po* did a second drive by.

There was no law against standing on a corner and had there been a bus stop, she could have faked it real good. But there was no bus stop, just the mail box, gummed-stain sidewalk and the bodega behind her.

Where the hell was Ce-lo? He was suppose to have met her ten minutes ago. She called him on her cell, no answer. She thought about just going over to his house, even though he said it wasn't cool cause his moms was home; that he'd meet her on the corner of Farmers and Liberty and they'd go to the school and smoke.

The longer Gina waited, the less it felt like that was going to happen. She saw herself, standing on the corner waiting to get high. Thought about where'd she left (her own apartment) and who'd she'd left (her seven-year-old daughter all alone). Recalled the last time she'd done such a thing and had ended up in jail, losing her fly apartment and her child.

Gina stepped to the curb. Flagged a gypsy cab and headed home.

*

Her phone was ringing as she let herself in, Kanisha bounding out of her bedroom, throwing her arms around her mother tight. "You was gone a long time. I was scared."

"You ain't got to be scared, ever," Gina said absently, prying Kanisha loose, going to the answer the phone. "Hello?"

"Hey Gina."

"Hey."

"I was calling about Christmas morning."

Christmas morning. Just her and Kanisha with probably just two gifts under the tree for her—one from Tarika and one from Rick. Collin...she tried to smash the thought but it latched on tight. "We gotta do this now?"

"I was just trying to see what time I could come by."

"Whenever...it don't matter no way."

"You alright?"

"Fucking Collin." Curse words and the man Gina was seeing in the same sentence. Trouble. What affected Gina affected Kanisha. What affected Kanisha affected him. "You all eat yet?" the words out of his mouth before he could check them.

"Nah. I was gonna make something in a minute."

"How bout I take you and Kanisha to our old favorite spot…Red Lobster."

For the first time in a while, Gina smiled.

*

It was crowded, full of holiday shoppers, but they got a table after a twenty-minute, Kanisha picking up the menu that was nearly as big as she was, happy to be with her momma and her daddy and getting the chance to eat shrimp.

She hoped that her daddy would talk to Mr. Collin about not always making her momma sad, but her momma's mood had already gotten happier, so maybe that happiness would stay around for a while.

"That is his child," Rick was saying, as he looked over the menu.

"I ain't saying he ain't. All I'm saying is you make plans with me and you keep on breaking them? You ain't really trying to be with me then."

"So you think he's cheating?"

Gina shook her head, unwilling to acknowledge that that was exactly what she was thinking. "I don't know. All I know is the nig—, dude ain't with me as much as he used to be. Every time we make some kinda plan, he ends up cancelling and I'm tired of the bull—, BS." She looked down for a minute. Softly said, "Sorry."

"Well, you can't let him stop you, Gina. You're doing good, real good. You've come too far to let anybody stop you."

"But this ain't no regular time, you know what I'm saying? This Christmas time. Christmas and he supposed to be with me if I'm his woman."

"Didn't he say he would?"

"That night? That ain't no Christmas nothing. That's just some bullshit." She didn't apologize over that curse word. Rick let her slide.

"Look. I'll come over early, like eight or so. Kanisha will open her presents, then we can go get some breakfast or something and you all can hang with me over my mom's." Even as Rick said it, he couldn't imagine it, but he knew what it was like to spend Christmas alone.

Her face turned ugly. "Your Mom's? For real, Rick?" Gina shook her head. "That woman don't even like me."

"But she loves Kanisha. Besides, you know how my mom throws down. You don't have to cook or nothing."

Gina thought about spending all day with Rick. Didn't settle too well. "What time is dinner?"

"Probably around three."

"Well, I'm down for the breakfast part, but I got to think about the rest."

Rick sat back. Surprised that he had been leaning forward. It was no longer like that for him and Gina. Hadn't been in a while. He realized it was because he genuinely cared about her. And from what she was saying, Collin was up to something and nothing good.

Rick would never come out and say it. A part of him knew he didn't have to. Gina was always on top of things.

*

Big girl panties.

Dajah was wearing them again. She thought about what Frieda said, what her own heart had told her and decided to call Rick and confess as soon as she got home from work. It was his day off and so it was sort of surprising when he didn't pick up.

She tried a second time. It went straight to voice mail. *Third times the charm?* Dajah called Rick as she headed to her kitchen to make some dinner. If he answered, she'd make enough for the two of them. Problem was, Rick didn't answer.

*

Laughing, Gina was laughing and digging up old memories as they made their way home. He got out of the car, escorted them into the house and upstairs to where Gina stayed. Gave Kanisha a big hug and kiss and gave Gina a hug.

It made her sheepish. She awkwardly stepped back. "Damn, am I that sad a case? You giving me a hug and shit—I mean, stuff?"

"No, just giving credit where credit is due."

"Ain't nothing special."

He touched her face, lifting it. "Yeah, you are."

"You always know how to make me feel better, well I mean some of the time anyway…" she titled her head a bit. "What about you? You found that special lady yet?"

"Still working on it."

"Well, don't you give up. She out there…" Gina looked off, suddenly uncomfortable with it all. "Kanisha got school tomorrow. Got to get her to bed. Next week she gonna be with my moms, cause she out and I got to work."

"So, you still like working at the library?"

"It's alright. But I want to get into an office, y'know? With a real desk and phone and a secretary I can boss around all damn day."

"It can happen for you."

Gina smiled. "Hope so." Got that sheepish look again. "Got to lock the door."

Rick headed down the stairs, Gina behind him. Tenderness was between them, genuine, true and without any physical involvement. Rick understood just how much they both had grown.

He was in his car when he realized he had turned his cell off. No sense in turning it on tonight. The only people who ever really called him was Gina and Dajah. He'd just left Gina and Dajah had stopped calling, so he saw no need to. Didn't.

*

A few hours later, Rick was opening his closet door, pulling out the blue corrections shirt still encased in the dry cleaning plastic. He had never been fond of ironing and with his job demanding a clean shirt every day, he had resorted to the dry cleaners.

It was his last clean one, which meant he had to go to the cleaners tomorrow to pick up his next set. He made a mental note and slipped on his shirt. Putting on his slacks, he checked for his mace, his flashlight and hand cuffs. Rick put on his black socks, black shoes and brushed his hair.

Reaching into the front closet, he retrieved his heavy Dept. of Corrections jacket and checked the pockets for his gloves. Glanced at the clock and saw it was ten after eleven. He'd get to Rikers about twenty to twelve, plenty of time to clock in and get to his assigned cell block.

He turned on his cell and saw three calls from Dajah. Started dialing.

*

Sleep left her because she hadn't spoken to Rick in over twenty-hours. Sleep got whisked away as she heard him say, "You called me."

"Yeah, I did. I was trying to reach you to apologize. Just stupid stuff and being scared."

"You too?"

"Yeah, me too." She paused. "Silly."

"Glad you called…I truly missed you."

"Missed you too. So, okay. We're both scared, but that's okay and I want us to be…"

"Be what?"

"Okay."

Rick started his engine. "Can you just run down and meet me at your front door?"

"Now?"

"Yeah. Just put on a robe and come downstairs."

Dajah didn't ask another thing. Stood in her front doorway until the headlights of his car brushed her dark street. She waited not knowing why she was there, but trusting him enough to know it was important.

"I just had to see you," his first words as he stepped into her foyer.

"I wanted to see you too," she answered, slipping her arms around him tight.

CHAPTER SIXTEEN

Jeff looked out his office window, the building across the street—identical boxes of glass surrounded by slate-colored stone—all that he got for his perusing. The skyscraper gave no light, reflected no light, just consumed the grey of the sky above.

Winter had stripped New York of its finery. Strategically planted trees were bare of any leaves and the occasional window planter gave root to nothing but air. The city had become a bone yard of asphalt, concrete and steel.

The sun had been in hiding since yesterday and its absence suffocated Manhattan like heavy wool.

Jeff looked down from his perch on the 59th floor. Pebbled-sized people moved down Madison Avenue cloaked in the shades of winter. No yellows, no pale blues. Just dark colors that drearied the world and made him long for summer.

He longed for heat, brilliance and humidity. Jeff longed for the smell of barbeque and the sound of open air jazz. But the cold air pressed against the thick insulated glass told him that winter was here to stay and like everyone else, he would have to bear it till spring time, a season that seemed a million miles away.

He turned from the window. Sat in his executive chair. Tapped some keys on his keyboard, eyes to the monitor. But even as he got back to work, as his eyes swept numbers and blue prints and mathematical calculations of required BTUs for a seven-thousand-foot office space, the part of him that longed for warmth, sought other alternatives.

He couldn't go to a warmer climate, but maybe he could bring a bit of the warmer climate to him. Lately all of the dinners he prepared had been heavy—stewed beefs, roasted chickens and thick deep fried pork chops.

Summer meals were lighter. Summer meals were yellow squash, corn on the cob and salads. It was grilled chicken and fresh fried fish…fish. Jeff couldn't remember the last time a perfectly fried Porgy fish had graced his mouth.

The more he thought of it, the more of a plan it became.

After work, he'd make a bee-line for the fish market on Linden Boulevard. Get some fresh porgy then head over to Keyfood and pick up some yellow squash. Dinner would be the fish, fried yellow squash and maybe some jiffy cornbread.

Jeff knew it was a plan when he imagined taking that first bite. A nice dinner tonight and a meet-up with Mya tomorrow. Life was on its way to being okay again.

It wasn't where he hoped it to be, but he was beginning to see how his marriage to Dajah may not have worked. The unresolved issues with Mya would have reared its head sooner than later. *Better sooner.*

He'd thought about Dajah more times than he wanted to admit, a part of him hoping that he would get so lost in his next relationship that the tainted one he'd had with her would vanish from memory.

But it hadn't. And every now and then just how deeply he'd hurt her visited him. He had loved her enough to marry her, but Mya was proof that having enough love to marry someone wasn't enough to sustain it.

Mya—there was no denying the charge between them every time they met up. Still she wouldn't commit to more than running because legally, she was still married. So he didn't call her unless he couldn't make it to the track. Hadn't gone to see her since that first time. Hadn't asked her out, over and anything.

Just the way it should be, something told him. This together-but-not-together time was giving him a chance to clear his own heart and mind, come to pertinent conclusions and think with the head above the waist.

Jeff's dog days were behind him.

He hadn't slept with anyone in months. But he wanted to. Lord knew he did. No crime goes unpunished and Jeff looked upon this time in his life as penance for his past sins. In the process he was renewing his body and spirit, getting rid of the bad and making way for the better.

*

Mya Angelique Williams Connor was not staying.

She would drop off the pan of baked shells she made and leave. She would not check to make sure that the buffet table looked nice or have a five minute chat with Alex's clients.

She would not have a cup of apple cider, hang around for the lighting of the Kwanzaa candle or the reciting of what each day's principle meant.

This is what she told herself as she pulled around the corner from Kwaleed House of Hope. This is what she reminded herself as she got out of her car, took the pan of baked shells out of the trunk and locked it with a *beep* of her remote.

She didn't even want to make the pasta for the event. Planned to stay away from it and Alex. But Alex had gone on about how her shells had become a part of the traditional food and the entire premises of his organization was based on tradition.

So she relented. Ultimately she saw no harm in bringing it. She just hoped that same mindset would remain when she entered the store front. Hoped that her path to freedom would remain opened and uncluttered from the man who, in truth, she still loved.

*

Fried sweet Porgies, sautéed yellow squash and jiffy corn bread was on Jeff's mind as he drove down Linden Boulevard to the fish market. Jeff began looking for a parking space when he got two blocks away.

Everything on the boulevard appeared to be taken but he spotted a spot on the side street. He made an illegal U-turn then sped up a block before he made a right. Easing into the space, he was turning off his engine when the sound of a trunk closing reached him.

And there, directly across the street, was Mya, hoisting a big aluminum pan as she headed toward the boulevard.

Jeff rolled down his window, quickly shouted, "Mya!"

Startled, turning awkwardly, the pan she was carrying did a teeter-totter before it fell to the concrete, rich tomato sauce, and bits of creamy filling splattering her ankles, her legs and the bottom of her coat.

She looked down the street at Jeff who was looking back at her, 'sorry' written all over his face.

*

"You're just making it worse," but Jeff didn't seem to hear her as he applied paper towels he'd had in his car, dampened with water, which he also had in his car, to the tops of her ankle. Bent down literally at her feet, it was a scene so abstract from any reality she'd ever perceived, she laughed.

"I'm so sorry," he went on to say a third time

The laughter faded. She shrugged her shoulders. "Just pasta." She realized that while she had forced herself into helping Alex, God, once again, had other plans.

She lifted the hem of her coat, saw bright red on the soft cocoa brown wool. It was an old coat but it was her favorite. *Let it go.* If the cleaners could not get it out, she would trash it. She looked at Jeff still trying to clean up a mess that she'd made, unable to let that go. He was sorry. Said so three times. Mya stood there, touched and affected.

*

Jeff insisted things and she'd insisted things right back, like she couldn't just leave. That she had to at least go and tell Alex that there would be no hot pan of food from her. That she appreciated Jeff wanting to take her coat right that minute to his cleaners and have it dried clean and she could use a sweat shirt he had in his car until she got home, but she couldn't leave Alex hanging like that.

"I'll wait."

"Why?"

Jeff pointed to her splattered coat. But his whole being said it was about more than that.

*

Alex was disappointed, shocked and a bit stunned as Mya shared what had happened around the corner, her coat and the empty dented foil pan, proof. As she offered her 'sorry' and her goodbye, she understood just how much as his palm curled around her arm.

"Stay."

"I can't Alex. I have to see about my coat and I told you before that I wouldn't be staying."

"But Eric is about to recite a poem and he's worked so hard on it. You know how tough things have been for him. He needs all the support he can get."

Eric Beltry was a fifteen-year-old headed for serious trouble until the courts had mandated him to Alex's program. He had gone from the road of soon-to-be-drug-slinger to being back in school and a discoverer of the spoken word.

Mya knew this because Alex had shared his progress with her over the last year, but Mya had only met Eric once and she doubted if Eric even knew she was there.

"He'll do just fine without me."

Alex looked away. Released her arm and Mya let go her breath. As she headed out of the busy, noisy celebration, she realized that Alex would always have some need of her. It was up to her not to make it hers.

Jeff was waiting by her car. Leaned against it, arms folded, nothing about him anxious. *So different from Alex.*

"You're gonna follow me?" Jeff's question. "To my cleaners? He's up on Merrick." Jeff glanced at his watch. "Might still be open."

Mya looked at hers too. She wanted to but shouldn't be doing anything with Jeff besides running.

"He'll be closed by the time we get there," she decided.

"Well, I can follow you home, get the coat and drop it tomorrow."

She looked down at her coat. Looked at the red and silver tinseled Christmas star affixed to the power lines of the traffic light. Thought about the man who had promised her so much and broke that promise. Thought about the one before her who had promised her much and kept it.

Conceded. "Sure, we can do that."

*

There was nothing surprising about the arms reaching for her the moment she closed her front door. But what surprised them both was how Mya pushed back, standing her ground with the simple word 'no.'

I'm still married, could have been her response, or even *what do you think you're doing?* But she chose the most basic answer, and that was simply, "No."

Still, it warmed her that Jeff even tried. Warmed her that he backed off without confrontation. It warmed Mya that he took her coat, said he'd do his best to get it cleaned, apologized a fourth time before asking if she'd be at the track tomorrow.

Mya looked at him, tentative. "Gotta run, right?"

*

Mya wanted music. No TV. No images rolling across the screen, just lyrics and melody. She needed to feel connected to something in a real way, because she was feeling adrift.

Jeff...you still love him? In a world where she had, hadn't, had again and then made herself stop, she was almost too scared to answer. She had stopped loving Jeff through force. There was no way she could've toted it around and became free. So she'd pushed those feelings deep inside a box, dug a hole in the basement of her soul and buried it.

But the ground was being disturbed, shook loose. Mya didn't trust it. She didn't trust what would happen once it was finally set free. Wasn't sure if she wanted it to be freed at all.

The grown-up in her knew she needed to get the business with Alex finished before she could entertain anyone else. But that part of her that loved hard, deep and forever wanted to dash head first.

It was a battle for sure, but Mya knew which one she'd have to succumb to. No matter what her heart was saying, this time around, she had to go with her head.

*

Jeff was a no show the next morning. He'd texted her and said he was taking her coat to the cleaners so he wouldn't be at the track. She was trying to wrap her head around things, so it was fine with her.

But he invaded her world when he called her at work. Their life was supposed to be about the track and nothing else. No phone calls, no visits, just running. "You get my text?"

"You're calling me here?"

"Yeah. Is that a problem?"

"Jeff, look. I don't know…no, that's not right, I do know…"
Mya paused. "Can I call you back later, after I leave work?"

"Yeah. Sure. Everything okay?"

"Yeah. Let me call you later, okay?" She needed some space.
She would tell him just that.

*

Mya knew better.

She knew better than to try and navigate the subway steps, slick
with an icy rain, and dial Jeff on her cell at the same time. She
knew it but did it anyway, slipping on a patch of ice, her Kyocera
leaving her hand, bouncing down the steps, landing in a puddle.

She dashed after it, her heel hitting a patch of ice. She ended in
a cut-split right there at the 50th Street subway entrance; one leg in
front of her, the other behind. The people behind her stepped
around her in typical NY fashion. Those coming up hardly gave her
a glance.

Mya laughed. She laughed because she couldn't believe she
ended up in this predicament; laughed because no one seemed to
care, people avoiding her like she had the plague as icy water
soaked into her pants.

She was still chuckling when hands grabbed her arm pits and
hoisted her up. When she turned to utter thank you, her cell and
crazy predicament were forgotten at the sound of her own name
coming out of *his* mouth.

She was looking into the eyes of Vincent, the man she had
cheated on Jeff with; the man she'd once swore up, down and
sideways, had loved her like no one ever had.

He hadn't of course, but Mya didn't realize it until after the
cheating.

*

Five Years Earlier

Mya had dated Vincent off and on for two years before Vincent
had broken things off. She'd always believed that Vincent had been
'the one', but Vincent had other plans. When he left, Mya had been
devastated. She'd given him her all and still it hadn't been enough

to keep him. Months after his departure, she still longed for him, but he never came back.

When she met Jeff, she made it unimportant. When Jeff asked her to marry him, she pushed Vincent further into her past. Mya thought she had succeeded until one day, in the midst of planning her wedding, she ran into him up on the Avenue.

She had no intentions of having a long conversation or anything with him. She quickly told him that she was getting married, hoping that would shoo him away. But it didn't shoo him away. It only made him more interested in getting back into her Kool-aid.

He convinced her that they should at least have lunch together one more time since she was getting married and all.

The brief lunch stirred up feelings Mya thought were gone. The deep kiss he gave her at the meal's end stirred it up even more.

For days after, Vincent plagued her mind and body. She thought that if they had a sit down talk about why he left her, she could get over him and get on with her life. So she called him up. Asked if they could meet somewhere to talk.

He'd stated that he was in between pay checks and couldn't go to a restaurant, but she was welcome to come to his place if she liked. Mya told him she'd be there in ten minutes, feeling certain that it would be okay. Certain that it was what she needed to have that happy life with Jeff.

*

Her first word, "Hi" was lost as Vincent wrapped his arms around her the moment he opened the door. He snatched her against him and had her in a body lock before she could think.

Her body responded to the motion and all those questions, answers and explanations were lost, faded as his hands slipped up the back of her blouse, his palms warm upon her spine.

She'd tried to pull away, half-attempt as it was, but some part of her needed to know she still mattered and her reason for coming left her and logic jumped ship as old hunger found her and there was nothing else in the world she wanted but satisfaction, from Vincent.

For two weeks, after she told herself that she loved Jeff; that she wanted to be his wife. For two weeks Mya did the mad dance, overwhelming Jeff with love every chance she got, determined to hang in there, keep them together; love him with all her heart.

But no matter how hard she tried, she couldn't shake Vincent.

She made herself not call him again, pulling up all the resolve she had not to. But he was a drug in her veins and, like a junkie straight out of rehab, the Jones was too profound. For two weeks, she tried to stay away from him and in the end, failed.

*

She lay in Vincent's arms, physically satisfied but plagued with doubt. "You love me?" Her voice, thick.

"*Love's* a strong word."

"So, you wouldn't marry me?"

"That's so far down the road Mya, I can't even see the signpost."

"I wasn't asking when," she intoned.

"And if you were listening, you heard my answer."

A truth found her, ugly and biting. She needed Vincent to tell her that he loved her; that she mattered. Mya had felt if he told her, just once, she could walk away and be with Jeff and go on with her life. But that quest didn't hold the slightest probability of being achieved. *Can't give what you never had...* she sat up, swung her legs out the bed.

Mya got up, looked around, found her panties, her bra, only one sock. She got dressed, did not say good-bye. Neither did Vincent.

She went home, took a long hot shower, wanting to wash away the unwashable; take back the past month of her life. But she couldn't and knew there was only one thing left to do.

*

Jeff's first words, "You okay?" broke her heart.

Mya felt unworthy of his concern, his love. She hugged him quickly, knowing what would come; knowing that what she was about to say would rip them apart.

"You know I love you right?" she asked, her voice whispery, fragile.

"Yeah, and I love you, too," Jeff answered, heart wide open.

"And it was never my intention to hurt you."

He pulled back, taking his arms with him. "No," he said adamantly.

She reached for him, her last chance to show him how much she loved him before the news arrived. Mya reached for him, to brace him against it; soothe what would be unsoothable, but Jeff refused her.

Mya made herself go on. "Vincent." Not that it mattered. It could have been anybody and the results would have been the same. "A guy...I knew...before you," she made herself say.

"Why, Mya?"

She shook her head. "I don't know."

"What do you mean, you don't know?"

"I don't know, Jeff..." She implored him with her eyes. "But I didn't want any secrets. I don't want to start out with lies. I didn't want that for us."

He looked at her like she'd lost her mind. "No secrets, Mya? No lies? You slept with another man. What the fuck is that then, huh?"

"I really don't know," she whispered, because in the aftermath, it made no sense at all.

Jeff was done with her after that, rightfully so. And Mya began her journey of self discovery and healing. The truth was uncovered months after the fact. A philandering father and a blind-eyed mother had been her template on love and relationships. Even though Jeff had been a good thing, her inner workings could only love a cheater.

So she'd set herself up for failure. Made it impossible for her marriage to Jeff to go on. Mya had self sabotaged, but in the process, became someone who learned to love and be loved the right way.

Her lesson? Learning to love herself, *first*...

*

The Present

Her cell phone was dead and Vincent was way too close up on her.

Mya kept pushing him back but Vincent took it as some game he would win by the train ride's end.

"You act like you don't know me?"

"No, I'm acting like I am—," she waved her ringed finger in his face. "Married." Except there was no ring. Just a faint line of what had been.

"Where's the ring?" Vincent wanted to know and all Mya could think *was how did I ever think I loved him? How did this crude, rude man ever claim my heart?*

The subway doors opened. White letters against black tile said *Fifth Avenue*. Twelve more stops to go before Vincent got off. Twelve stops too many. She'd ditch him at Jackson Heights and catch the F train, which was express. His stop was a local and so he wouldn't be able to follow.

But of course, Vincent had other plans.

Vincent got on the F train right along with her. "Just ride down to Parsons Boulevard," he told her. "Besides, it'll give me a chance to spend a little more time with you."

"Why?" Mya knew her voice was indignant, that the people crowded around her stared, but she didn't care.

"What you mean, 'why?' Girl, as much as you loved me?"

He went *there*. So Mya created a new route. "Love-*da*. As in the past, like long time ago, you mean?"

"Oh, so, it's like that now?"

Mya looked directly at the man who had been so wrong for her. "It should have always been 'like that,' but like you said, I loved you." With that, Mya managed her way through the crowded subway car that smelled of wet wool, cooked food and Hugo Boss. She moved, forcing herself through leather backpacks, bent elbows and feet turned out at every angle.

Vincent didn't follow, just gave her a last look before he got off at Parsons. For the briefest second, she saw that thing she'd never seen in him before—regret. *Too bad, too sad*, final thoughts as the train whisked her toward 169th Street.

She pulled out her phone. The display was shattered and the insides, wet. She needed to get a new phone because, more than ever, she needed to call Jeff.

*

"You've reached Mya Connor. Sorry I'm not available. But leave a message and I promise to ca—," Jeff disconnected. Wait, all he could do.

She said she'd call him after work. It was almost six-thirty. She should have been home by now. Should have called.

Ice pelts hit his living room windows. The weatherman said the freezing rain was becoming an ice storm. He looked out onto the streets, huge white Sanitation trucks salting the boulevard. Dialing her number again, he got no answer. For the first time in decades, Jeff closed his eyes. Prayed.

*

An hour and new cell phone later, Mya got off her bus, shoulders hunched against falling ice pellets and made her way home. Slush was gathering at the curbs and just crossing the street meant stepping into piles that came past her ankle.

Power lines were already glistening in a crystal coating and traffic lights sported icicles. A nasty evening, it was one for getting home and staying there. Snuggle under two comforters with the thermostat set high.

Mya was looking forward to taking off her cold wet boots, damp pants and slipping into some fuzzy warm pajamas. She was looking forward to the heat coming from the vents and something warm in her belly.

What she wasn't looking forward to as she crossed the street, was telling Jeff what she didn't even want to tell herself.

She didn't want to come out and say *despite me still not quite being divorced and the horrible thing I did to you that I don't see how you could ever forgive me, I want to try again.*

She didn't want to say *despite me marrying someone else who I truly and genuinely loved, I still love you and only a crazy person would even consider taking me back.* So, she'd set herself up where she didn't have to make the phone call at all by trying to do so going down icy subway steps.

Inside her apartment. She leaned against the door, toes stinging, heat arriving. She slipped off one boot, the other and got her new phone out. She turned it on and saw Jeff had called her five times.

Stripping as she headed to her bedroom, she changed out of work clothes into comfy ones. Called Jeff back.

He answered on the second ring. "Hello?"

"Hey," a soft hurt in her voice.

"You okay?"

"Yeah," but she didn't believe her own words.

"You didn't answer my calls."

"Because I killed my phone."

"What?"

"I said I killed my phone." Humor, she needed it.

"How? Why?"

"Well, *how* was because instead of waiting to try to call you, I decided the best place to do it was on some iced up subway steps as I was walking down them. I slipped. The phone fell out of my hand, ending up in a puddle. I went to go after it, slipped again, ended up doing a cut-split and someone helps me up and it's Vincent and by the time I go get my phone, somebody had stepped on it. Thus, it got killed."

"Sounds like an accident."

"It wasn't...not much in life is...like running into Vincent. You know, it was almost like God was trying to show me that I've come real far; that my past mistakes don't have to define who I am today. I mean, I'm standing there in front of him—"

"Who him?"

"Vincent."

"Who's Vincent?"

Mya inhaled. Let her breath and the truth go. "The guy I cheated on you with." Silence. Mya didn't expect a response. "I'm standing in front of him today and he is literally making my skin crawl. I'm stuck in a subway car with no way out until the next stop at least and I was embarrassed that I even thought I loved him."

More silence. Mya pressed on. "It was me, Jeff. Not you. It was never you. It was all about me and being so damn twisted. Seeing Vincent today reminded me of just how twisted I was and how when we met, I wasn't ready. I thought I was. *You* thought I was, but I wasn't. I had a ton of growing and maturing and just painful moments to work through, but I made it through. Then Alex..." she stopped.

"Did what he did. It wasn't about you."

"Yeah, but it didn't feel like it and sometimes it still doesn't feel like it. It's like this great big loop, going around and around in my head and I want to stop it but it just keeps going round and round—"

"Breathe," he said softly.

"What?"

"I said breathe. Take a breath."

She did. Felt better. "I'm still married."

"I know that."

"And even though me and Alex aren't together, legally we are."

"I know that too."

"But the bigger part is why. Why would you even want to talk to me?"

"Because before it got all bad, it was good for me. You were good for me."

"Must not have been too good if years after the fact you were still hurting," Mya said carefully.

"Were. That's the key word here. Were, as in the past."

"So you've forgiven me?"

"I think the fact we're even having this conversation says I have."

"...sometimes I just feel so damaged," she confessed.

"We all have our issues, Mya."

She shook her head. "No, not like mine. Mine are wow. Major."

"You've changed. You said so. I've seen so."

"Thirty minutes at the track every day doesn't count."

"Thirty minutes at the track, the best part of my day," Jeff stated.

Quiet for a second, confession left her. "Mine too."

"So, there you have it."

"You serious about this Jeff? Us? Are you serious?"

"What do you mean?"

"I mean do you really want us back together?"

Jeff thought about the woman she'd been, the one she'd turned into and the one she was today. Felt doubt. She'd shared her truth. It was only fair he shared his. "I'm a bit unsure."

"Thank you for saying it."

"But life isn't about guarantees. We try, all we can do."

"April," she said softly. "Divorce becomes final then."

"He's not protesting it, is he?"

"No."

"And you're not, so it's just a matter of the judge's signature, right?"

"I guess so."

"So, if technically the marriage is over and you two agree it's over, what's to stop you from going out with me?"

"I'm just trying to do this right."

"By binding yourself to a piece of paper that in four months won't matter anymore? You got to start trusting yourself again, Mya. You've got to start trusting who you are today. Don't let the past be a chain or a decider for you."

Silence. An intake of air. Another. Jeff knew she was crying.

She didn't want to. Didn't want the tears that streamed down her face. Mya just wanted the whole thing with Alex to be over. She felt trapped by the new sense of honor. "I just want to do the right thing. For so long I was doing all the wrong things, y'know?"

"I know. But in the midst of all that, what does Mya want?"

"To be happy."

"Being all honorable, is that making you happy?"

A chuckle left her. "No. It's just making me crazy."

"So stop. Stop being unhappy and crazy."

Jeff was right. She'd held the torch of virtue long enough. It was time to lay it to rest. "Okay."

"Okay?"

She smiled a bit. "Yeah. Okay."

"Weather permitting, can I take you out tomorrow night?"

"Yeah, I'd like that, a lot."

CHAPTER SEVENTEEN

"*B*oston!"

Those words felt so good coming out of Dajah's mouth, she wanted to say it again. Light danced in her eyes as she jumped up from the table, did a little spin and raised her hand in the air.

"Sit your butt down," Frieda insisted with a chuckle, gathering up the playing cards. Barry headed to the kitchen, while Rick sat quietly, a smile on his face.

He had warned Dajah that Bid Whist was not his game, that he was much better at Spades, but Dajah insisted that he'd do just fine and he didn't have a choice because they were invited over Barry's house for the card game.

"We have to go because we haven't hung out with them in years," Dajah had gone on to add. What she didn't say was that it would be her formal announcement that he was back in her life.

Rick obviously knew what he was talking about because they lost seven games in a row. He wasn't sure about what to bid, how to count cards or how to pull jokers from the opposing team. In truth, Rick sucked.

Dajah tried not to get annoyed with him, but with each mounting loss, her composure slipped.

So when she'd been dealt that phenomenal no bid hand, complete with two aces, the deuce, three, five, six and eight of Hearts, she knew that their terrible luck had changed.

When she was able to slap that last card on the table, with nothing in front of Frieda and Barry, she couldn't contain herself.

"*Choo choo*!" she sang, tugging on an invisible horn cord. "Y'all smell those beans?" She leaned over the table. "High five, Rick." She slapped his palm so hard it stung. "Good game, Partner."

"Who wants more wine?" Barry asked, bringing a bottle of Pinot back to the table.

Dajah raised her glass. "Me."

Barry poured. Turned to Rick. "Some more?"

Rick begged off. "No, I'm good. But I would like some more of those slammin' wings though."

Barry indicated the kitchen. "Plenty on the stove. Help yourself." Rick did.

In his absence, Frieda gave Dajah a careful look. "I'm so glad you got that hand."

"Why?"

"If you could have seen your face, Day...I felt so sorry for Rick."

Dajah frowned. "What do you mean?"

"You were looking like you wanted to jump across the table and beat him."

"I did not."

Barry piped in. "Yeah, you did. I was like: *damn Day, it's just a game.*"

"I was?" Dajah wanted to know.

"Yeah, you was."

"Was what?" Rick asked, coming back with a small plate of hot wings.

Lie or tell the truth? Dajah went with the truth. "Taking the game a little too serious."

"Oh, so you caught that?" Rick took his seat. "For a minute there I thought I was gonna have to mace you, giving me the gas face and all," he said with a chuckle.

"I'm sorry, but Bid Whist is my game."

Rick picked up a wing. "So I see." Took a bite.

"No, seriously. The calculations. Counting cards. Strategy."

Frieda leaned into Rick. Half whispered. "You know she got a thing for numbers. They're like her first love."

Rick laughed. Shook his head.

"She serious," Barry added.

Rick looked at Barry then Dajah. "For real?"

Dajah nodded, embarrassed. "Yeah. Always loved math and numbers. From the time I learned what two plus two was."

"So, you been cheating on me?" his smile easy.

Dajah laughed. "No, but me and numbers..."

Frieda's eyebrow rose. "See, I told you." She looked at Rick's plate. "Those wings do look good. Think I'll get some."

"Bring me some, too?" Dajah asked.

Barry reached for the cards. "Guess we're done," gathered them up. "Y'all up for a game of Taboo?"

Rick killed them.

He was able to figure out the clues faster than anybody. "Damn Brother, how in the heck did you get that?" Barry asked after Rick got an answer with just two clues.

Rick shrugged. "I just have a good memory. I guess working in the prison did that."

"What do you mean?"

"You have to always be on top of stuff. Always have to be watching, observing. Have to know how to connect the dots with what you see and what you don't see to keep safe."

"I hear you man. I tell you though, I thought my job was dangerous, climbing those utility poles, but being a C.O.? God bless you man."

Rick's face grew serious. "He does, every day."

"I hear you." Barry picked up the remote. Turn on the TV. "Knicks fan?"

Rick laughed. "Is my name Rick?"

Frieda got up. "My clue to the clean kitchen." Dajah got up too.

Elbow-deep in hot soapy water, Frieda scrubbed the Pyrex dish. "You got a good man."

Dajah put some plastic wrap over the bowl of celery sticks. "I do, don't I."

"And he loves the hell out of you." Dajah felt a warning in her friend's tone. "Don't mess it up, okay?"

"Mess it up? Why would I do that?"

"You know how you can get sometimes."

"Meaning?"

"Taking the tiny things and making it bigger than what it is."

Dajah wanted to call Frieda a liar, but there was proof to what her friend was saying. "I've been through so much, too much in these last few years. It's hard not to always be on guard about something."

"I know you have and that's why I'm just saying, be cool. You got him. He's not going anywhere. Relax and enjoy what you have."

"I'm trying," Dajah said softly. Her voice dropped to a whisper. "But sometimes I miss those things I had with Jeff."

Frieda nodded. "I know."

"I mean I know what I have with Rick is good, great even, but Rick's not Jeff."

Frieda paused her dish washing. Considered her friend. "But Jeff was far from perfect. If he was, you'd still be with him. You got that second chance with Rick. All I'm saying is, appreciate that."

Dajah nodded. Went and got more plastic wrap.

*

Mya stood before her dressing mirror, looking at herself from head to toe. Her hair settled in soft waves just above her shoulders. Her top was a silky shiny print that looked more like a negligee than a blouse. It fell off one shoulder and felt a tad too sexy for her taste. But it went so nice with her boot-cut chocolate slacks she wanted to wear it.

The ice storm from the day before had been brutal, so no cute boots tonight. She'd have to wear the ones with the wedge and grip rubber on the bottom.

The third finger of her left hand caught her eye; the faint line, still visible. *Just a date,* she told herself as she put on lipstick and perfume. *Just,* last thoughts as her intercom rang and she buzzed Jeff up.

*

Mya didn't realized how much she missed the smell of CK cologne until she was sitting in Jeff's Jeep. After years of knowing only the musk oil that Alex wore, it was refreshing. "CK?"

"Yeah. Why?"

"No reason," but she was smiling.

"Does it smell okay?"

"Yes," her answer, more sigh than word.

"Good." His hand went around hers, squeezed.

Just a date she reminded herself as she squeezed his hand back.

*

The live jazz combo band was delightful. The food, still great. Manhattan Proper was where Jeff had taken her on their first date years ago. It was nice to be back. Nice to see that the place hadn't lost its charm. Neither had Jeff.

Mya hadn't laughed this hard in years. Every other thing Jeff said had her chuckling to tears. It was a good thing she hadn't worn mascara because she would've looked like a raccoon before their main course was served.

"You got to stop," she insisted, trying to catch her breath in between her laughter.

"It's good, you know," he said carefully.

"What?"

He studied her as if she was all brand new.

"You. Laughing. Happy. It's good."

Mya blushed. Searched for an ice breaker. "You look the same."

"So do you," but even as he spoke, his eyes were still looking at her as if she was a new great find.

"Jeff, you're staring."

"I know."

Butterflies filled her belly. Stayed for the rest of the evening.

*

Three in the morning saw them at her front door. So many thoughts in her head, she grew dizzy from just breathing. She couldn't look at him. Studied the floor, shy.

Jeff sighed. "Track's jacked up. It'll probably be that way for a few days."

"Yeah."

"But we can do brunch, if you'd like."

"Brunch sounds good."

He leaned in, kissed her forehead. Pulled back. "Call when you wake up, okay?"

"Yeah. Okay."

"Good night, Mya."

She gave him a final smile. "Goodnight Jeff." Unlocked her apartment door and stepped inside.

*

Jeff smiled as he pulled his truck from the curb. He was back. The Jeff he'd been. The Jeff he admired. The 'Jeff' that was a true gentleman.

The one he had become made him cringe. The damage left in that Jeff's wake made him remorseful. So many women. So many hearts crushed. None of them deserved what he'd done. Especially Dajah.

He'd thought of her tonight. Sitting across from Mya, she'd come to mind. He wondered how she was making out. Hoped she had forgiven him; that life had gotten better for her.

Life was giving him a second chance to get it right. Tonight, solid proof of that. Jeff prayed that Dajah, Jill, Joy and Lisa had all been given the same opportunity. If he, who had been the least deserving, had been granted a new life, it was only fitting that they be granted the same too.

*

Mya didn't open her eyes until a little past noon. A quiet panic thumped her chest as she reached for the phone. Jeff answered third ring. Told her to give him about forty-five minutes and he'd swing by to pick her up.

They had breakfast at a diner on the Queens/Long Island border. He asked if she wanted to see a movie. "The second installment of *Lord of the Rings* is playing. Want to catch the matinee?"

Fantasy wasn't her thing but there was an excitement in Jeff about seeing it that was infectious. She told him yes. Two hours into the three hour movie, Mya fell asleep. Jeff let her be, waking her as the end credits rolled.

She rubbed an eye. "Sorry. Tired I guess."

"Or boring to you."

"Well, I never saw the first one, so I wasn't sure what was going on. And that little monster guy…,"

"Creeped you out?"

"Yes. Just creepy looking and weird talking."

"It's cool….hungry?" She told him yes. "How about I make you dinner?"

Jeff was always a master in the kitchen.

*

They stopped and picked up her coat from the cleaners. Outside of a faint spot near the bottom, the coat was fine. What she wasn't too thrilled about was the huge Irish setter that charged her the moment she stepped into Jeff's apartment. Mya screamed, tried to run, but Jeff stopped her, instructing the huge red hairy beast to 'sit.'

Kelly did. Eye-brows twitching, tail wagging.

"You got a dog?"

"Yeah, a while ago. Had her, what? Going on five years now?"

"She?"

"Yep, female. Her name's Kelly. She's a sweetie."

"Who nearly knocked me over."

"She's just happy to meet you…pet her head."

The idea of touching any part of the dog didn't sit well. She gave Jeff a look like he was crazy.

"Go ahead Mya. Just pet her head. She won't bite."

"She has teeth right? Big old doggy teeth?"

Jeff laughed. "So do you. But when was the last time you bit someone?"

Mya looked at Jeff, down at the Setter, whose wet eyes looked so sad and needy Mya relented. Tentatively, she patted the dog's head once, twice. Pulled her hand back.

"No Mya, don't pat her. *Pet* her, like this," Jeff's finger gliding over the red mane on top, an act Kelly seemed to love as she lifted her head to meet them.

Mya reached out a second time, changing her mind as Kelly licked her palm. "Ugh." She wiped her hand dry on the side of her coat. Looked at Jeff, needing reassurance.

"Go ahead."

Steeling her nerves, Mya stroked the fur, once, twice. A third time, each passage making her less fearful.

"See? Okay Kel, that's it, go lay down." Kelly gave one last sad look at Mya, Jeff, then Mya again. Made a quiet retreat. "I have to walk her. You want to come or stay here?"

It was brisk outside and the temperature inside Jeff's apartment was too comfortable to leave. "No, you go ahead. I'll watch TV or something."

For the first time all day, she thought about Alex. Hoped his trip south for Christmas would go well. Hoped his life was turning for the better, too.

*

After dinner, Mya fell asleep on the couch. Jeff tossed a blanket over her and took Kelly for a final walk. When he got back, she was still sleeping. He hated to wake her but the hour was getting late.

"Did I fall asleep?" she said coming to.

"Yeah."

"Man, I must be tired."

"Or something."

She sat up. "What time is it?"

"A little after eleven."

Sleep left her. "That late?"

"Yeah."

Being in Jeff's apartment was cozy. But so far things had been platonic. Mya wanted to hold onto that for as long as she could.

"I better get going."

It was on the walk to Jeff's car that Christmas came up. "What are your plans?" he wanted to know.

With you, her mind decided. "Dinner with family. What's your plans?"

Jeff shrugged. "I was hoping I could spend it with you."

She had just brought Alex to the Thanksgiving table. There was no way she could show up with Jeff. Told him so.

"We could get together before then after your family dinner."

Mya thought about it. Told him okay.

*

The winter sun of December 23rd washed the entire city in brilliancy. Car visors were flipped down, sunglasses donned and anything reflective gleamed a hundred fold.

The island of Manhattan sparkled like a diamond as the sun descended towards the day's end, bringing little warmth but a glow that was blinding. It turned asphalt streets copper and made tiny novas through the empty boughs of trees.

Mya walked along Eighth Avenue, the setting sun bathing her. She closed her eyes for just a second, lifted her face and inhaled.

The city was festive. Office workers headed home for the long holiday, thoughts of work, deadlines and screaming alarm clocks vanishing the moment they left their desks.

Salvation Army volunteers rung bells beside red kettles and poinsettias lined the fronts of fruit markets. The smell of hot charcoal, roasting chestnuts and the sound of Christmas carols filled the air while street corner vendors hawked cheaply made toys, scarves and decades old DVDs.

Tis the season, she thought, as she eyed the subway station half a block away. *It will be a good one,* she decided as she headed down the subway steps, the chilly underbelly making her shiver the moment she got to the platform.

She hoped the train wouldn't take long. Her toes were already cold and standing on the cement platform would make it worse. A nice warm train with some good heat would do her good. God did her one better. Not only did the train have heat, she got a seat.

Her joy was short lived as she left the station an hour later, dashed as she answered a call from Alex.

"He bailed on me," was how Alex began. "He left for South Carolina without me."

She knew who the 'he' was. Felt the devastation behind the news. This was supposed to be the start of a new relationship between Alex and his estranged father; the road trip, cementing the deal.

"I can't believe he did that, Mya? How could he do that?"

She wanted no parts of the pain in his voice. But she used to love him, still did, and so, she had no choice but to listen, feel, and ultimately empathize. "I'm so sorry Alex."

"Just messed me up."

"What did he say?"

"Say? He didn't say anything. We were supposed to be leaving tomorrow. Share the driving, the whole nines. So I call him to get a time and he doesn't answer. I call him again, still no answer. So I finally text him and he texted me back saying he decided to leave early. He's already on his way."

"Oh."

"Yeah, *oh.* I bought gifts for my aunts and uncles. Put together a whole album of photos to show them. Was looking forward to it…" His voice slipped over the edge, disappeared.

"Well, can you still go? Drive yourself, I mean?"

"I don't know them, Mya. Those are his people. I never even met them. He was supposed to…" Silence.

Up ahead Mya saw her bus. She wanted to run after it, but suddenly had no strength.

"I'm just so—"

"Upset? Hurt?' she offered. "Yeah, I know." But that's all Mya knew. She didn't have an answer for him.

"Can I come over?" That request was so left field Mya didn't know how to respond. So she said nothing. "Well, can you come over here, just for a little while? My head is all jacked up now."

Could she? Did she even want to?

The answer was no, but she knew what it was like to have the world fall apart and nobody there to at least look at the scattered pieces with you. She knew what it was like to have your soul crushed to ash and not have the strength to even start gathering them up.

It was nearly Christmas and once upon a time, she had loved him with all her heart. "Yeah. I'll drop by."

*

He opened the door with red eyes and she knew he had been crying. Mya thought about the strong virile man she'd met those many years ago and wondered where he'd gone.

She didn't expect the first words that came out of her mouth: "You have to get over it," but she let them ride. She said it again because in her soul she knew she was giving him gospel. "You do Alex. And as terrible and hurt and disappointed that you're feeling about what happened and what didn't, you have to push past it."

It wasn't what he expected her to say; how he expected her to greet him. It showed on his face. Sadness slipping into annoyance as he turned and walked away. "I don't need to hear that right now."

Mya closed the door. "I know you don't, but what's done is done and there's not a thing you can do about it but get past it."

His apartment looked the way it had months ago. There was a TV, a couch, and she spied a small dinette set in the kitchen. But nothing hung on the walls and boxes were still stacked in a corner.

"You've been here, what four, five months and you haven't even finished unpacking. You? Of all people? Mr. 'self-empowering-is-the-key-to-everything'." Mya sighed. "Alex, this is not who you are."

"I know."

"So if you know, you need to do something about it. You want a pity party? I'm not going to join you."

He looked at her. A tear slid down one cheek. It hurt her heart to see him like this. Empathy made her hug him. She did it because she understood the power of touch. But she didn't linger. "It's about you, you know. Not me. Your father. Just you. And I know you can't see that right now. Can't feel it or nothing, but it's true."

"I'm trying."

"No, you're not. You're waiting for something to change. But nothing is going to change until you start making it change. Those boxes, for instance. How long are you going to let them sit there?" Mya's cell phone rang. She reached into her pocket, pulled it out, put it on mute and slipped it back in. "You think they're gonna move themselves? And what about your motto? Kwaleed's House of Hope motto?"

"I don't want to do this now."

"What's the motto, Alex?" she insisted.

He looked at her. "I never stopped loving you."

Mya ignored him. "The motto?"

He moved to the window. Peered out. "Even when I slept with Dawn, I never stopped."

She sighed. "But you did Alex and talking about what went wrong with us isn't why I'm here. So cut the bull and tell me the freaking motto."

"…Believe and you can achieve," he said reluctantly.

"This," she indicated his half finished place "is what you're believing now? Six days a week you are down at that center, preaching to people how they can make their life better and then you come home to this?...you need to take a page from your own lesson book."

He faced her, humbled. "You're right."

Her smile was cautious. "We get so caught up in the wrong, we can't find our way to the right. And Alex Cornelius Connor, on the day I met you, you were on the right. You slipped, big time, but there's nothing stopping you from getting back to where you used to be." Her smiled raised a bit. "Because the Alex I met back then? Well, he was the *shizzle*."

A tiny smile found him. His eyes closed. He nodded a bit. "Thank you."

"No biggie." She looked at her watch. "I better be heading home."

"You want to grab a bite or something?"

Mya knew his hurt. Knew his trials. Knew that he had taken one step through the newest disappointment. That there would be many, many more.

"We could go to that West Indian spot on Merrick. Just a few blocks from here," he went on to say.

She thought about Jeff. The call she had already ignored. Looked at the man who had been her husband and soon wouldn't be. Considered the holiday and the disappointment it had brought him. Dinner with him would be her parting gift.

"Sure. But we go in separate cars."

*

She phoned Jeff on the ride to the restaurant. Explained as best as she could what had happened. He wasn't feeling the whole idea of her going to dinner with Alex, but told her okay. The eatery was warm and fragrant with food. They took a window table. Watched the folks of Laurelton, Queens move huddled up and down the sidewalk. Talked about non-issues. Laughed a bit.

He asked her about her Christmas plans and she told him she was going to her folks. She sensed he wanted an invitation but gave him an alternative. "You can still go."

"Go where?"

"South Carolina." Reluctance filled his face. "Those are your aunties, your uncles, your cousins. Your blood. And yeah, your pops left, but maybe the idea of spending seventeen hours in a car with you after being absent from your life all those years was too much. Maybe he needs to be with you in increments, y'know? People get scared. And being scared makes you do dumb things." Mya paused. "But I do believe that when he made that offer, he meant it, and I do believe that he chickened out because the reality was a little too much. But I also believe that if you go, it will be good for both of you."

"I don't know where we're supposed to be going."

"Well, how about this? How about you call your father and say: Dad I really would like to meet my other family. I'm willing to come on my own. Would that be okay?'

He'd looked as if she'd stuck him in the chest with her fork. "I can't do that."

"Why? Because you're scared he'll say no? You won't know until you try…fear keeps you stuck. How about starting the new year unstuck?" She eased out of the booth. "I'm going to go the ladies room. While I'm gone, call your daddy."

Out of the frying pan into the fire? Mya wasn't sure as she opened the door marked *Mademoiselles*. There was a good chance his father wouldn't answer. A greater chance that if he did answer, he would tell Alex he couldn't come.

All she could do was pray. Pray that Alex made the call and his father answered. But the look on his face when she got back to the table said those prayers weren't answered.

"What did he say?"

"He didn't even pick up."

"Text him. Send him a—,"

His hand on her wrist stopped her. "It's done Mya. I'm done." The rest of the meal was eaten in silence. Mya avoiding Alex's eyes, Alex avoiding Mya's.

*

Jeff was standing in the doorway of his apartment when Mya arrived. Standing and waiting, standing and pensive. Standing and pinched-faced.

"Don't." One hand landed midway his chest for emphasis. "Just don't." Mya moved past him, grateful when she heard him close and lock the door.

"He was hurting, the only reason why I went." She wasn't going to give Jeff a chance to say anything about nothing. She'd get it straight before the whole thing got muddled by insecurity and stung feelings. "And I don't know if you know what that's like, but I sure do."

She undid the buttons on her coat, eased it off her back. "It's the worst pain in the world. Just having somebody there to hear you talk out loud is everything. So, that's why I went. I didn't go because I want him back; I didn't go to sleep with him. I think I hugged him once the entire time." Her eyes found Jeff's. "I went because it's almost Christmas, he used to be my husband and he was hurting."

What Jeff had thought in the time since Mya had called him was all Jeff had known since. Mya's words were having a hard time chipping into that.

He'd flashbacked to how right before they were supposed to get married, Mya had slipped off and crawled into the bed with Vincent, as if Jeff, the love between them, or their then up-coming marriage hadn't mattered.

He'd imagined Alex's hand on the rise of her behind, the cream between her thighs. Imagined Alex's tongue on Mya's belly, a thick hard penis gliding into her juicy wetness. Jeff imagined Mya clinging to Alex like he was the best thing ever. That's what Jeff imagined.

"Say something."

Even though he had been looking directly at her, Jeff hadn't seen her. He had been lost in the fantasy of his brain, images twisting his gut. Jeff blinked. Blinked again. Saw Mya and didn't. Saw the Mya that she'd been and suddenly couldn't see the one she'd become.

That newly built foundation of trust was gone.

CHAPTER EIGHTEEN

*D*ajah Moore had become a tourist.

She hadn't skated in the ice rink of Rockefeller since childhood, but here she was, wooly hat on her head, bright red scarf around her neck, and rented skates on her feet, holding onto the rail with a death grip.

"You're holding up traffic," Rick said back gliding.

"Come back," Dajah insisted, scared to death to move. She'd forgotten just how smooth ice was, how to hold her body to prevent falling over and how to stop.

Rick laughed. "No, you come here."

Dajah looked behind her. She was holding up the line—six other scaredy cats were standing at the entrance waiting to grab a hold of the metal railing. Taking tentative steps until she was five feet from the entrance, she sighed a sigh of relief as the back log moved past her.

"You can do this," Rick insisted, easing backwards with grace. *Where did he learn to skate so well?* Dajah took an instant dislike toward him as he took off leaving her rail clinging.

People whizzed by her frontward, backward and even sideways. She suddenly felt cold and foolish. Couldn't believe that this had been her idea.

She'd been watching a special on TV and when they showed Rockefeller Center with the huge tree and the skating rink, suddenly she wanted to go. Rick liked the idea. They decided to do it Christmas Eve.

They caught the train into the city. Had lunch down on Thirty-fourth then caught the train to Rockefeller Plaza. Took the two-block walk over toward the NBC headquarters; the restaurant and rink below, their final destination.

They rented skates and Dajah took care in lacing them up. The first surprise came when she tried to walk on the carpet. The skates were heavier than she remembered. They also tilted her ankles and made them hurt. Stepping onto the ice almost landed her on her butt.

"Chicken."

By the time she turned to see who was calling her names, Rick was whizzing past her again. Dajah inhaled then exhaled. Tested the slickness of the ice—very—and readied her heart to let go.

She *weeble-wobbled* as she stood with no hands for three seconds before grabbing the rail. She pushed off a little, one hand still holding on and was surprised she'd glided two feet.

By the time Rick passed her a third time, she was scooting along with no hands. By the fourth, body bent and arms swing, Dajah was skating too.

He skated over to her. Took her hand. "I knew you could do it. That's why I let you be."

"No, you abandoned me. Left me scared and stuck at the rail." Suddenly the conversation didn't feel like it was about ice skating at all.

"But you're out here now. Look? You are out here on the ice, with me."

Dajah looked around. The huge Christmas tree towered to her left and the buildings with a thousand office lights glowed on either side. *The Ronnettes* were singing about a sleigh ride. Dajah felt it then. The wonder that was New York City at Christmas-time.

She understood why people came from all over the world to experience it; why they put shows on TV about it. The experience was just that special.

But even more, Dajah felt the blessing that was Rick by her side during this very special time of year.

She smiled. "My ankles are killing me."

"Hot chocolate?"

"Of course." She leaned in. Kissed him. "Thank you."

"For?"

Dajah couldn't answer. Her heart was too full.

*

Mya hadn't planned on putting up her tree. The stand-off with Jeff had dimmed her holiday and now she just wanted to get through it.

Her merry little Christmas had vanished. Everything had fallen apart in a blink of an eye.

There was talk of snow, but even the chances of that had diminished. On the verge of *Bah humbug*, Mya knew that if she didn't put the breaks on it right now, she'd dive in and never re-emerge. She wasn't feeling merry, but put on her Vanessa Williams Christmas CD and pulled her artificial tree from the closet.

It took two songs before she began to sing along. It wasn't until she hurt her throat trying to reach a high note, that she felt the shift. Life may not have been the way she planned, but it was *okay*.

She looked at her unfinished tree and wanted eggnog. Just because Jeff was mad at her didn't mean she had to be mad at herself. The Key Food across the street was out and the bodega only had the Borden's brand in the can.

She'd go to the other Key Food. A bigger store, they were certain to have the kind she liked.

*

Kelly was whining.

It wasn't because she wanted to be walked. She had just come back from one. Jeff checked the water bowl—filled, but the dog food bowl was empty. Jeff would have to go to the store.

He had no plans of leaving his apartment tonight. He had planned on staying inside, by himself, licking his wounds until they were raw.

He was still stinging over what Mya had done, and though she had said it was just a hug, having some compassion and going to dinner, it was still feeling like a whole lot more.

So much more, he hadn't talked to her since she'd left his place yesterday.

That imaginative mind that allowed him to make a good living as an architect was in overdrive. *She'd done it before,* the loop that was in continuous play in his head. She'd done it with a man she wasn't still married to. Done it with a man while she was engaged to him.

Mya had been married to Alex for years. Those feelings ran deep. They couldn't just disappear over night.

Kelly whined again. "You hungry, girl?" Jeff went to get her a dog biscuit, but he was out of those, too. With a sigh he got his coat, his keys. Jeff had no plans of leaving his place that night, but he was very much aware of what could be said of plans.

*

Dajah was wincing. She was trying not too, but her ankles felt like someone had beaten them with metal pipes. It took every thing she had just to walk up the front steps to her place.

"Hurts that bad?" Rick wanted to know.

"Worse." She confessed. Those few minutes on the ice had wreaked havoc on her. She unlocked the door. Looked at the seventeen steps she had to climb to get to her apartment, frowned. "God Rick, I don't know if I can make it."

"Want me to carry you?"

Dajah grimaced. Shook her head no. "I think I can." She did, one painful step at a time.

"You have some Epsom salts?" She didn't. "You need to soak your ankles. I'll run to the store and get you some."

*

Rick circled the parking lot six times before he could find a space. So many shoppers were coming and going, you'd thought Key Food was giving away free food. He even had to wait for a shopping cart.

Dinner came to mind and he placed an order at the Chinese restaurant. He picked up pancake mix, a pack of bacon, syrup, orange juice and a small quart of milk for breakfast.

He thought about snacks for the evening and hit the chip aisle. Considered the holiday and headed to the diary section to get some eggnog. He was reaching for a quart when he bumped into a woman. Their eyes met. Rick smiled sheepishly. "Got to have that eggnog, right?"

She smiled. "What's Christmas without it?" But there was sadness in her. She stepped back. "Go ahead."

Rick knew his manners. Not only was she a woman, she was a bit older, so that meant she should go first. "No, my momma would slap me sideways if I didn't let you go first."

"I know what you mean." Except it wouldn't so much have been her mother, but her daddy. Scotty Williams was no joke, a bit crazy, undeniably selfish, but she loved him just the same.

She would be with him tomorrow. Him, her mother, her brother, her uncle, aunts. Cousin. Everybody would be there except...she lost her smile. Felt the man studying her. Grabbed a carton of eggnog. "Well, Merry Christmas," she offered, noticing his eyes. Big brown ones. Felt envious of the woman who claimed them. She paused. "Did anyone ever tell you that you have eyes just like Allen Iverson?"

Rick laughed. Told her that he'd heard it before. "Yeah, but I don't see it."

"Well, you do." Words left her before they could be checked. "...whoever she is, she's lucky."

"Yeah, so I am." With that he got his eggnog and headed towards the health and beauty. Everything was in his cart except the Epsom salts.

*

The check out lines snaked down aisles like ribbons made of people. Mya was in the express lane, the container of eggnog in her hand feeling heavier by the minute. There were twelve people ahead of her and the 'express' was feeling anything but.

"Excuse me."

She moved to the side, Jeff moving past her, his cart filled with a huge bag of dog food. By the time she got her mouth to open, to call his name, he was gone. Even if he was pissed at her, he would have still spoken.

He didn't see me. That's what she told herself. But a bigger truth tapped dance in her head: *No, he thinks you did something with Alex and so you've become air to him.*

Mya watched the retreating Jeff. Go after him or not? It took her a few seconds of debate before she chose the not, even as her eyes watered; the feelings she'd put at bay since yesterday arriving at the check out line of the supermarket.

*

A pulse of energy hit him in the middle of his back. Jeff stopped, turned. Looked behind him. He saw a sea of faces undistinguishable from the rest. Shook his shoulders a bit to lose the sensation and continued towards the bread aisle.

Christmas dinner wasn't until three o'clock. He'd need some breakfast in the morning, *all by my lonesome.*

It wasn't supposed to be that way. Jeff felt it more and more as the whole store seemed to be enjoying a festive party that he had been escorted out of.

He had been right there, all happy and merry and jolly. Right there, Mya bringing light back into his life and then, true to her style, dashing it.

He should call her The Dasher. The Hope Killer. *He should call her*…the thought not new. He had been thinking it since yesterday. But he was afraid. Afraid she'd betrayed him, again, and to reach out meant he was okay with it. To reach out to her meant she had a green light to cheat on him any time she wanted.

Fool him once, shame on them. Fool him twice, shame on him. And she had.

His cart bumped into someone. Jeff looked up, muttered "Sorry."

The man smiled. "It's cool."

The two men looked at each other, something familiar. One frowned, tilted his head to the right a bit. "Do I know you?"

Jeff had seen that face before. "I think so."

A pause. Then. "You used to date Dajah, right?"

The name was so out of place in Jeff's tiny universe it widened his eyes. "Yeah?"

"I'm Rick." A beat. "We were all at the same Italian restaurant years ago."

Jeff was surprised the man even remembered that far back. But there was something to Rick's smile, the ease in which he spoke Dajah's name. A test question fell from Jeff's tongue. "How is she?"

Rick's eyes drifted. His voice, soft as left out butter. "She's good."

"Tell her I said hello," an automatic response Jeff wasn't feeling.

"Will do." Then the smiling buttery-voice Rick was slipping around a corner, disappearing from sight.

*

Four people from the cashier, Mya searched for Jeff. Maybe if he saw her, she'd wave and he'd come over. Say hello.

It was Christmas Eve. He wasn't talking to her. Being in the same place at the same time was a perfect ice breaker. But he'd have to be the one that broke the ice.

She put her eggnog on the conveyor belt; watched it glide toward the cashier. "That will be Two dollars and seventy-eight cents." She handed over a five. Took her change, her bag and headed out of the store.

*

He was putting the dog food in his shopping cart when Mya passed by. There was no way she didn't see him. She walked right passed him without even a glance his way.

If that's how she wanted to play it, then fine with him. She'd cheated with her husband and tried to convince him she hadn't. Just like the old Mya...*no Bro, you're wrong.*

The old Mya had cheated and said so. The old Mya had done what she'd done and came straight away and told you. She didn't try to hide it, deny it or anything. So, did that mean this time around she'd told the truth, too?

It was about trust; the thing that she'd broken and the thing he'd broken himself. He watched her go through the exit doors. By the time he got there, she was no where to be seen.

*

A strong wind flapped around her. The sky was murky with clouds. The smell of snow filled the air. A white Christmas after all?

She didn't need that right now.

Mya didn't need to be stuck in her apartment on Christmas Day. She didn't have a thing to make a meal with if she did. She sniffed the air, considered the weather forecast and knew she had to go back inside the supermarket. Pick up a chicken, some canned yams, Luck's collards, some Stove Top stuffing.

A just-in-case plan, she turned and headed back toward the supermarket.

*

Mya was walking so fast Jeff thought that she was racing towards him. But her head was down against the wind, so there was no way she could have seen him. He turned his back a bit from her approach, but last minute faced her.

Ten feet away she stopped, pulled something out of her pocket. When she flipped it open and put it to her ear, he knew she was taking a call.

She huddled next to the wall. He couldn't see her face. But her body language was on display and he watched her shoulders hunch, her head move from side to side. Whoever it was, the news wasn't good.

A minute later she was walking his way, her eyes blooming then dimming when she saw him. "Hey," reached him before she did. She looked real sad.

"I'm sorry I tripped," his first words. Mya nodded, distracted. "Can we try this again?"

"Jeff, I-,"

"I'm not perfect Mya," an admission that took a lot of will to say. "I'm not. I make mistakes. Think wrong things. Assume wrong assumptions." He paused, gazed around him. "It's Christmas Eve. So we can we try this again?"

The sorrow on Mya's face deepen. She thought about the phone call she'd gotten a few seconds ago. "I have plans for tomorrow."

Jeff didn't ask with who. "Day after, then?"

Maya smiled. "Sure."

"Can you watch my cart while I got get my car?" When he came back, she asked him about snow for tomorrow.

"If it does, it won't be much, why?"

"I was going to go back inside and get some things – just in case."

"No, I think it'll be mild. Want a ride to your car?" she told him sure. He drove, the two of them sitting for a few minutes before she got out.

"It takes a minute," Jeff admitted.

"For?"

"To truly let go of what happened in the past and embrace what the present is."

Mya nodded. The fact that she'd extended her family's holiday one more time to Alex proved it. He had been the phone call she'd gotten, asking for a final favor. *The New Year is around the corner and I know life is going to get better. But for right now, I would like to be with people who care about me. So, can I spend some time with you for Christmas?"*

She'd been impressed that he didn't say he *needed* to be with people who cared, but that he wanted to. Jeff hadn't called her and, at the time, she didn't think he would, so she'd told Alex yes, weather permitting.

Now here she was inside Jeff's car, heat going, another try before them. She wasn't going to volunteer why she was unavailable tomorrow, but if he asked, she'd tell.

He didn't.

Jeff was determined to rebuild that trust. As much as his brain was trying to go all over the map about why, he refused to take that trip. Christmas was but one day. The rest of their lives were before them.

"So, what are you doing for the rest of the night?" he wanted to know.

"Drinking eggnog, listening to Christmas music and finishing putting up my tree." She paused. "…what about you?"

"Kelly's waiting for some food. I ran out."

"How is Kelly?"

"Missing you."

Mya smiled. "Well you tell her that I hope to see her soon."

"How about now?"

"Now?"

"Yeah. Follow me home. Let me fill her bowl then I can come over to your house and help you finish the tree. Promise to be gone before midnight."

Mya said okay, her *Bah Humbug,* vanished.

*

The thirty-something pieces scattered on the floor became a completed six-foot Spruce pine in no time. "You're good," Mya declared.

Jeff stood back. Admired his handiwork. "It's all in the approach."

"Bells will be ringing, this sad, sad news." The voice from the radio was railroaded with hard life—gin drenched and prickly. *Oh, what a Christmas,"* images of juke joints and twenty-five cent back-kitchen dinners rode the words. *"...to have the blues."*

Mya frowned. "What is that?"

"You mean 'who.'"

"Well, who is that?"

"Charles Brown," Jeff answered.

"Charles Brown? Like in Charlie Brown?"

"No. Not Charlie Brown. Charles. *Charles* Brown. My momma and daddy used to play it all the time when I was a kid."

"Why does he sound so sad?"

"Cause it's the blues, Mya." Jeff reached out. Pulled her close. "And the blues is old," his feet began moving. "... and sad, and good and real and honest." The more Charles Brown sang, the tighter he held her. The song ended. Neither let go. It wasn't until Michael Jackson crooned about people making lists and buying special gifts did Mya step away.

But the deed was done. Sealed by the blues-soaked Christmas song and the bare Christmas tree by her window. Sealed by how Jeff's body felt next to hers and what her own heart felt. A part of her wanted it. But she'd promised herself. Made Jeff take the promise too. Platonic until she was no longer Mrs. Connor.

She headed toward the box of decorated bulbs and ornaments. She wanted something soothing this season. Decided on blue with gold accents.

She took out the tree topper. Handed it to Jeff. "Normally I use the step stool, but you're here."

He asked about an extension cord. "You need to make sure it works before you hang all the lights."

She went and got one, the tree finished up forty-five minutes later. Afterward Jeff had a glass of eggnog with her before announcing he was heading home. "I promised to be gone before midnight and its ten minutes to."

"That late?"

"Yeah. That late."

Coat was retrieved; a brief kiss at the door, exchanges of Merry Christmas and then Jeff was out.

Mya looked at the clock, saw the hour—five before midnight. Word, was indeed, bond.

CHAPTER NINETEEN

*F*ive inches of snow blanketed the streets of Jamaica, Queens by morning, bringing softness and a poetic hush. The sound of chains on snow plows and city buses jingled like bells and it felt, if only in that moment, peace enveloped the earth.

Mya stood, looking down on the boulevard, a cup of warm coffee in her hand. Jeff had called her around eight that morning to wish her a Merry Christmas. They chatted for over half an hour before he had to get going.

He was off to his parent's house for Christmas breakfast and then he would drive them all up to his aunt's house in White Plains.

"Tell them I said Merry Christmas," she told him.

"Really?" Jeff surprised by her request.

"Yeah."

"They might ask questions."

"Tell them the answers," Mya volleyed back.

"But I thought we were going to keep us on the hush-hush."

"It's just semantics at this point."

"So I can tell them?" The excitement in his voice, high.

"Well, yeah. I mean you don't have to go into detail, but yeah. You can let them know."

"What about your folks?"

"No, not yet."

"I love you Mya."

A pause. A swallow. "I love you, too."

That confession rested around her shoulders for the rest of the morning. Hours after she'd said it, it felt as if they were just leaving her mouth. She had no intentions of confessing any such thing, but the truth had been with her since last night.

Her phone rang. Alex on the other end. He wanted to confirm what time he should pick her up. She told him in about an hour. He asked her if she'd had breakfast and she told him yes. He seemed a bit disappointed by that but Mya left his disappointment with him.

At the end of the day, who they were now had been his doing. If there was one thing Mya knew: if you danced to the music, eventually you had to pay the band.

*

The gift card, hard, plastic and red, was in her hand. A part of her didn't want to tuck it away in her pocketbook. A part of her wanted to give it back. She hadn't gotten Alex anything for Christmas because he wasn't even supposed to be in town. But he had gone ahead and got her a gift card from Macy's.

"After all our years together, still couldn't figure out what to get you." He took his eyes off the road for a second. Looked down at the card. "Figured you could get what you want."

Get what she wanted. But if she could truly 'get what she wanted,' then she'd be sitting in Jeff's Jeep with Jeff behind the wheel on their way to Jeff's relatives in Upstate New York.

If she truly had that power, she would have never met Alex and certainly wouldn't be about to divorce him.

"You're quiet."

Mya looked at Alex, seeing all that he wasn't. "You got to want it," she said softly.

"Want what?"

Mya stared at him a long time before she replied. "Happiness."

They rode in silence the rest of the way to her aunt's house, the sun in hiding, washing the day in gloom.

*

Dajah awoke to the smell of cooked bacon and brewed coffee, the space next to her empty. Christmas morning came as it often had in the past—not feeling much different from any other winter day.

She stretched, yawned, rolled over to the side of the bed that only saw her rarely. She pressed her nose to the pillow Rick had slept on. Inhaled.

Tongues would wag, eyes would pop when she showed up at her folks with Rick. But life was what it was and her life, these days, were about Rick.

"Smell good?"

She didn't see him standing in the door, a tray of food in hand. She smiled. Sat up, the sheet slipping to her waist, revealing high perky breasts.

"Cover those up," Rick said distracted.

"What?" But Dajah knew. She looked down, nipples hard and pointy in the slight chill. "These?"

"Yes."

"Why?"

"Because I made us breakfast," He placed the tray on her lap "and we need to eat it before it gets cold." Rick left, came back, a cup of coffee in one hand, his plate in the other. She scooted to her side, took her toast off the plate and put the plate on her night stand. Moved some more dishes around. "Here, there's room."

"You say grace?"

She hadn't. "Was I supposed to?" toast in her hand.

Rick took the toast away. "Yes." Bowed his head. Dajah followed suit. "Dear Lord. We thank you for this day, this day that your son Jesus was born and we pray that you bless this food that we are about to receive for the nourishment of our bodies. In Jesus Christ name, Amen."

Dajah looked at him, surprised. "Wow. That was good."

Rick grew shy. "Just grace."

"But you did like the real one. Not like the one I used to say…the God is Good, God is Great…impressive."

Rick forked up cheesy eggs. "Yeah, well. You should always say it." He looked at her. "You should always be grateful for what you have."

All too soon Rick was downing his coffee and taking his plate to the kitchen. He had to get to Gina's house. Collin had manned up and had been over there since last night, relieving Rick of the super early morning visit. But it was after nine and he knew Kanisha was waiting for her gifts.

He came back into the bedroom, coat on. "Got to get to Kanisha. Should only be there for about an hour, then I'm gonna swing back home. Call you when I get there?"

"Yeah." Dajah swallowed, missing him already. "Tell her I said Merry Christmas."

*

The gray day seemed to grow grayer by the time Mya and Alex arrived on 198th Street. It was Christmas, but it was hard telling. The streets were empty of new bikes and their riders, and ball bearing wheels looking to lose their sheen against concrete. Not even the echo of a new basketball hitting the asphalt could be heard. Mya's aunt's block looked empty of children.

"Where are the kids?" she wondered out loud.

"Inside playing with their new video games, on their new cells and computers probably," Alex said reflectively.

"Man. Christmas Day? We couldn't wait to get outside and show off our new stuff. Even in the snow, we'd be riding bikes, roller skating. The boys would be putting up imitation hoops on light poles just to show off their new basketballs."

"Nothing stays the same forever."

She was glad he was smiling when he'd said it. He had shown up at her front door a bit gloomy. Mya was happy to see his mood lighten just a little.

She unlocked her door. "Well, let's go get our eat on." Standing on the street, Mya tried to find joy in the air, but it was absent. The world seemed stunted and locked away.

*

The sight of the poor shoveling hit Jeff like a ton of bricks.

Huge patches of packed snow still littered the sideway both in front of his parent's house and along the walkway. It looked like his father had just given up by the time he got to the stairs. Jeff had to be careful walking up them.

His father had always boasted that no one ever slipped in front of his house. That he was always the first with the shovel, the rock salt. What Jeff had seen was nothing to boast about.

His father was getting old, seeming older with each passing day.

The once strapping man was turning into one with bad knees, sciatica of the back and hands that had began to gnarl. Even his father's eyes had begun to milk over.

Jeff's parents had been up in age when he was born and had only gotten older in the time he'd become a man. Eighty-one to the day, his father had truly fallen off his game.

The patches would become ice by sunset. Jeff knew what he had to do. He fished his gloves and ear wrap out of his pocket. Slipped them on after ringing the bell.

"Merry Christmas, Daddy."

"Same to you, son. Same to you."

Jeff hugged his father, asked where his mother was and reached for the bright orange shovel by the door. "You missed a few, partner."

Mr. Gingham smiled. "Partner? I got your 'partner.'" But the relief in his father's eyes showed through. "Well, since we're partners, you shovel and I'll sprinkle the salt."

Twenty-five minutes, later both men went back inside, Jeff's mother in the kitchen, a pot of hot cocoa waiting for them. There was no missing her smile, her joy as they came in, stamping snowy boots and blowing on their hands.

"Look at my men," Mrs. Gingham declared. *Alive and breathing*, the real source of her joy. Though she didn't say it, it was all in her eyes. It grew brighter as Jeff's father leaned in and rubbed his cold nose against her cheek. "Milton. Your nose is like ice."

He took her hand and placed it to his chest. "But my heart is still on fire."

Jeff rolled his eyes. "You two ever gonna stop?"

"No," they said in unison.

"Good. Don't. Not ever," he found himself saying.

He watched his mother pour hot chocolate into ceramic mugs. Watched as she took care to hand it to his father and how that simple act made him touch her face.

Jeff realized that before him had been his real instructor in the way of love—his father. He'd always made his mother feel special and needed.

"How's the roads?" his father ask, blowing across the top of his mug.

His mother extended him his cup. "Not too bad." Jeff took it, and blew across his, too.

"Apples don't fall far from the trees, do they?" Mrs. Gingham decided.

Jeff looked at his father. His father was looking back. Words raced to both men's tongue, but Jeff's father was quicker. "Now in some ways, yes. Other ways? Well…"

Jeff nodded. "Guilty. But all the good ways I learned from you, Pops." He leaned over tapped his father's shoulder. "And you are the master."

Milton Gingham liked that. Liked that a lot. "That's my boy."

Jeff's mother placed breakfast platters in front of them. "You all hurry up and finish. We have to get a move on. We're already behind and you know how Judith likes everyone to be on time."

The men did as they were told.

It was over breakfast that Jeff shared that Mya wished them all a Merry Christmas.

Jeff's father choked on his eggs. Coughed and coughed again. "Mya?"

"Yeah Dad, Mya."

"She's back around?" Jeff's mother asked, surprised.

"Yeah Mom, she is."

Silence. The food in Jeff's mouth suddenly tasteless as he looked down at his plate.

"Well," Mrs. Gingham uttered.

"I thought that was over a long time ago," Jeff's father said carefully.

"Me too," Jeff answered just as careful.

"She's making you happy?" his mother's question.

A smile came into Jeff that lit his entire face up. "Yeah, Mom. She does."

"Real happy?" his father wanted to know.

"As happy as Mom makes you."

Mr. Gingham smiled. Patted his back. "Well, that's all that matters."

*

As always, the dreads put a bad taste in Rick's mouth.

They were neat, not too long and lint free, but too many prisoners at Rikers sported them and Rick couldn't help but make assumptions about the man sitting on Gina's floor handing Kanisha pieces of a toy.

It was disturbing to see how comfortable Kanisha was sitting next to him. By the time Rick realized it was okay, Kanisha spotted him and raced his way.

"Daddy! Daddy!" As always, Rick bent down low to receive his hug, but discovered he didn't have to go as low as he used to. His little girl was growing up. She hugged him hard, thrusting an oversize-headed doll his way. "I got Bratz! Mr. Collin brought me Bratz!"

It hadn't been on the list he'd gotten from her. But obviously it was highly prized. "Wow. Its head sure is—,"

Gina cleared her throat. "Rick, you remember Collin, right?"

Rick nodded in Collin's direction. "What's up, Man?"

Collin got up. "What's up?" He gave him a fist bump. "Merry Christmas, Brother." *Brother.* Collin making peace with whatever mini war was raging in Rick's head about him.

Rick eased up. Smiled a bit. "Yeah, Merry Christmas to you, too." He looked down at Kanisha. "Guess who I ran into on the way over here?"

Mirrored eyes looked up at him, wide, curious, anticipative. "Who?"

"Santa Claus!"

Kanisha frowned. One hand going onto her non-existent hip. "Daddy. No such thing." Innocence lost. It stung. He was ten before he stopped believing. Kanisha was just seven. "He just some made up man," she went on to say. "You and mommy and Granny and Grandma Trimmons and, oh, yeah," she turned, looked at Collin, "Mr. Collin. Y'all buy my gifts. Santa ain't even real."

Kanisha had come to the hard truth three days ago when Kevin Owens told her in class right before winter break. When Tarshanay Smith agreed with him, sharing how she'd seen some of her gifts under her parent's bed before Christmas, Kanisha knew it was true. Because Tarshanay always told the truth. She told the truth about everything all the time.

"Kevin and Tarshanay told me. Told me how parents hide gifts and make you go to sleep early to pretend Santa's coming. But there ain't no Santa."

A part of him wanted to insist that there was. A part of him wanted to chastise her for her attitude, tap that hand off that hip. But the bigger part of him could only smile. There was no knocking wisdom. "Yeah, well."

"So, what you bring me?"

Rick opened the hall door, grabbed three big boxes; Kanisha's eyes growing wide at the sight of them, just like a little seven-year-old should. She tore through the gifts, opening the big box first, screaming when she saw her play kitchen, complete with a micro wave, coffee maker, toaster and oven.

Rick begged off breakfast. "I ate already." Hung around long enough to put together the play kitchen. Kanisha sat it in the corner of the real kitchen and got busy making everyone fake lunch. "'Cause we already had breakfast," she decided.

Rick, Gina and Collin sat in the living room, pretending to cut a fake T-bone steak, munch fake French fries and sip play coffee. Just like a true hostess, Kanisha gathered their plates and took them to the kitchen when they all agreed that the lunch was delicious.

Gina watched Rick look at his watch for a third time in ten minutes and realized Dajah was waiting for him. She was happy that Rick had gotten a second chance with her. Lord knew how hard she'd tried to break them up. And the Lord knew that she'd succeeded.

But she also realized that sometimes relationships went through bumpy roads. Sometimes they crashed and burned. But if the emotions and the feelings were real, there was always hope. The fact that Collin was sitting with her Christmas morning and not up in the Bronx, said as much.

But seeing Rick with Kanisha flipped it for her and not in a good way.

She didn't expect Collin last night. Didn't know who was ringing her bell a little after eleven. He was the last person she thought it would be, shopping bag in hand. Gina hemmed and hawed for a few seconds before she opened her door to him. When she tried to ask about what changed his mind, he stopped her.

"I'm here because I want to be here, okay?"

When she found out he had two gifts—one for her and one for Kanisha—she put the asking away. But Rick's arrival had brought it back into focus.

"You still going to your folks for dinner?" Gina asked Rick suddenly.

"Yeah."

"Well, I know how your moms' likes everybody on time, so you better head on back." *You sure?* His eyes wanted to know. "Traffic is already crazy, so you need to get a head start."

Rick stood. Called out to Kanisha who was working on 'dessert.' "Daddy has to go."

She came, a fake cupcake in her hand. "This is for you."

"For me?"

"Um hum."

"Won't you need it later?"

"Nah. I got another one. So, you take this one."

Gina disappeared into the hallway before Rick could slip the fake food into his coat pocket. Kanisha hugged him again. Rick hugged her back. Within her tiny embrace, he felt her spirit and there was no doubt that for her, it was a great Christmas.

Saying good-bye to Collin, Rick headed downstairs, Gina by the front door when he got there.

"Thanks," she offered meekly.

"It's who I am Gina."

"I know that. But I still appreciate it…you know, as much as I wanted Collin here, seeing you with Kanisha. I realized it was a bad move…Collin should have been with his son."

"Feeling bad about it?"

"Yeah," the confession surprising her. "I mean, sometimes I just want what I want and I don't be considering nobody else." She frowned. "And that's not good. I got to do better."

"But you are."

"That's not what I mean Rick." She looked off. "I'm tired of tripping over stupid shit, I mean stuff." She extended her right arm.

A sterling silver charm bracelet dangled off her wrist. "This is what he got me." She picked out a charm. "See this one? It's a graduation cap." She reached for another. "And this one? It's a computer, 'cause he know how I want a job with my own office." She dropped her arm. "He gets me, Rick. I mean really gets me. That's like, everything."

"I agree."

"So now I got to do better, see what I'm saying? And pulling him away from his son on Christmas over my bullshit and insecurities?" she shook her head. "That ain't even cool or right." Gina inhaled, let it go. "Just want a better me."

"If you really do, then you can start with Collin. Tell him what you just told me because I know he's torn inside. Yeah, he's here with you, but he *knows* he's supposed to be with his son."

"You right." She gave Rick a quick hug. Opened the door. "Thanks for never giving up on me."

"As long as you don't give up on yourself, I'll be right here rooting you on."

"Tell Dajah I said Merry Christmas."

"She told me to tell you the same thing."

"I guess us great women think alike."

They were so different Rick wouldn't even know how to begin to state just how much. But the glow that came into Gina eyes when she said that was bona fide and hope-filled. There was no way Rick was going to tell her different.

*

The hair on Kay-Kay's head was short, stylish and all her own. But that sophistication was lost in the gold tooth on the right side of her mouth, a size too-small blouse that exposed her gave-birth-to-three-babies stretch marks every time she moved and slacks fitted so low, she had muffin tops above both hips.

But this was who Kay-Kay McKinner was and her ensemble didn't surprise Mya in the least.

"Mya Angelique," she called out; the name music on her tongue. She opened her arms wide and Mya accepted the embrace. Kay-Kay may have been her married uncle's baby momma, but she'd been Mya's life saver, literally.

Years back, Mya decided to test fate and her own abilities and had gone into near heat stroke trying to run on a day that was too hot to be out-doors. It had been Kay-Kay who'd come along and found her passed out. It had been Kay-Kay, pregnant at the time, who half-carried Mya back to her room at the women's shelter, letting her rest and giving her ice water and cold compresses until her body cooled down.

What-ever ill-will Mya had against her faded after that. Yes Kay-Kay was street, wild, irresponsible, too young and uncouth, but that same woman had stopped and helped her, when in truth, she could have left Mya out there to die.

"Uncle Brother here?" Mya wanted to know. Despite her uncle's immoral ways, she loved him.

"Jimmy? Yeah. They down stairs." Heavy foot steps raced up behind her. Kay-Kay whirled around, face ugly, tone sharp. "What I tell you two about running? Don't make me say it again, hear?"

The two were Kay-Kay's sons, Uncle Brother's illegitimate children, Mya's cousins and her Aunt Martha's legal keep. Everybody thought Aunt Martha was nuts when she adopted both of her husband's sons from a woman who was young enough to be her granddaughter. But there was no denying that their life was much better with Aunt Martha than with Kay-Kay.

"Auntie Mya!" they exclaimed, running towards her, ignoring Kay-Kay's warning. Yaya—Aunt Martha—was their mother. Yaya did everything a good mommy should. Kay-Kay was just a lady who used to be their mommy but wasn't any-more. She only came around sometimes and when she did, all she did was yell.

"Little Man? Daniel? How are my two favorite cousins doing?"

"Fy-in," they sung in unison.

"Where's Yaya?"

Little Man spoke up. "She in the kitchen with your momma and their sister." Mya looked into his eyes. Saw the Williams gene strong in the honey and cinnamon color. She looked at Daniel's eyes—dark as midnight—and thought what she'd always thought when she saw him: there wasn't a drop of Williams' blood in that little boy, but both her uncle and aunt claimed him as their own.

Little man tapped his baby brother. "Come on Danny. Let's go finish the game." Off to the living room they went.

"Where's Sabria?" Mya wanted to know. Sabria was the third child Kay-Kay had birthed. Uncle Brother wasn't the father because they had been split up for over a year when she was born.

"With her daddy," Kay-Kay said wistfully.

Kay-Kay knew who the daddy was? Mya found it hard to believe. She had been running the streets, sleeping with Tom, Dick and Harry, Peter, Richard, Stanley, Steve and anyone else who had cold cash.

But Mya played it cool. Played along. "Oh, yeah. How's he's doing?"

"He alright." Kay-Kay studied her a minute. "DNA, that's how I know. Everybody told me not to, but I went on Maury. Crazy cause I had like five Negroes on stage with me, but good because I found out who was her father. Got to stay in a hotel and everything."

"You were on Maury?" Alex's question. He had been content to let the two woman converse, waiting for Kay-Kay to notice him, give him the chilly hello. They had been fine with each other until Alex cheated on Mya. When Alex messed up on Mya, Kay-Kay was through with him.

Still, in all of his life, Alex had never known anyone who had to go on Maury to find out who their child's father was. His curiosity was peaked.

"Yeah," she said testy. "And ain't no shame in my game either. Now, I know, he know, and Sabria know."

Alex raised an eye brow. "I guess you right about that."

"And I got to fly to Connecticut. Didn't cost me nothing. Stayed in a fly hotel. Ordered room service. Rode in a Town Car and was on TV. Maybe not for the greatest of reason, but a real one."

"I hear you," Alex said carefully.

"No, you ain't really hearing me, but that's cool." Kay-Kay took Mya by the arm. "Let's go downstairs. Let Jimmy know you here."

Mya looked over her shoulder. "You coming?"

"I'll see them later."

Mya frowned. Kay-Kay snickered. Mumbled something unkind under her breath.

*

Alex waited until Mya and Kay-Kay disappeared into the basement before heading into the kitchen. He put a fake smile on his face, self conscious about who he had become in Mya's family's eyes—a no-good, nasty, lying, dirty, cheating dog.

He'd caught nearly all of them glaring at him in such a way on Thanksgiving that there left no doubt about how they felt about him. But he was here now, fake smile plastered on his face. Time to face the music. "Merry Christmas, everyone."

Mya's mother and two aunts looked totally surprised to see him. Weren't him and Mya getting divorced?

Mya's mother was the first to make a move. Her palms up and open to him. "Alex? I didn't even know you were coming?" She hugged her soon to be ex-son-in-law. Let him go. "I don't have a gift for you."

His smile was careful. "I wasn't expecting one. So it's fine."

Aunt Martha was next, taking a sec to dry her hands on the dish towel. Coming over to him, surprise still rode her cheek bones. "Well, Merry Christmas." She kept her arms down to her side. Alex, getting the message, did the same. Awkward, he eventually leaned over and kissed her check.

It took everything Aunt Martha had not to wipe it.

Yes, her husband was a scoundrel. Her husband's brother was a scoundrel and her husband's brother's son was one, too. It seemed that was all the Williams men could do—produce male scoundrels. Even Mya had her time of troubles. But when she married Alex, Aunt Martha felt that the awful Williams curse had gotten broken and she thanked God.

Four years into the marriage, God tossed her 'thank you' back at her because it turned out Alex was no better than the man he was son-in-law to.

"Better check those yams," Aunt Martha said, walking away.

Aunt Martha's sister didn't even rise from the table. She went on cutting up potatoes like he wasn't even standing there.

Alex backed out of the kitchen. "Let me go say hello to everyone else." But nothing in him wanted to go down into the basement, so he headed to the living room, watching Little Man and Daniel play video games until dinner was called.

*

Christmas dinner was dismal.

Mya's father started in on Alex the second after everyone muttered 'Amen' to the grace. He had been cordial before the meal and Alex dropped his guard. But Scotty Williams had been waiting for everyone to be gathered before he tore into him. "You got a lot of nerve showing up a second time."

"Mya invited me," Alex said hotly. Which was a lie. He had invited himself.

"Yeah, well this ain't Mya's house or table and nobody—,"

"Enough!"

No one saw her stand. But in a blink of an eye Mya was up, hands firm on the dining room table; the power of her voice shell-shocking the room. She'd scared herself but she was in the middle of it now and could not back down. "Alex… is a guest." She paused, demanding anything of her family – new shoes she was walking in. "And no, Aunt Martha didn't invite him, but he's here with me and you treat him like he's somebody."

Someone giggled. Out of the corner of her eye, Mya saw Kay-Kay covering her mouth. "Something funny Kay-Kay?"

"Who me? Nah. I'm good."

Mya eyed her father. "You, of all people. How are you going to even try and go there with all the mess you've done? Got stabbed in your wife's kitchen by your other woman and you still was out there." That shut her father up.

They didn't stay for dessert, the festivities feeling like a chore they had to complete. The sun was still up by the time Alex pulled up to Mya's apartment. He cut the engine and reached for her hand. She allowed it.

"It wasn't the best Christmas I had, but at least I wasn't alone. Thank you for that."

"You're welcome." But Mya was tired of the day and just wanted out of Alex's car. She'd gone far and above her call of duty and just wanted out of his car and his life.

The love they'd shared left shore a long time ago. It was so far gone she had to remind herself that she had loved him at all. It was amazing what betrayal could do. More amazing was the power of second chances with the one that got away.

She unlocked the car door, swung it open. Took one final look. "I wish you well."

Alex nodded, lost in her soon-to-be departure. His dance card was empty and the music had stopped long ago. But true to the woman that Mya was, she'd let him keep dancing—solo and all by his lone self.

"See you in April?" he asked, half joke/half serious.

Mya told him no. Got out the car. Free for the first time in months.

*

Rick stepped on the tab at the bottom of the garbage pail, happy to see the lid spring up. Too often those types worked one day and just quit the next. He dumped the paper plate, a plastic fork smeared with sweet potato, the sound of joyful voices drifting in from the living room.

It had been a good Christmas.

"You make her happy."

He didn't hear Dajah's father come in, but wasn't surprised that he had followed him into the kitchen. All day Rick sensed her father wanted to speak words with him. Now, he was getting his chance.

"Mr. Moore. I didn't even hear you come in."

Hank Moore smiled. Did a little move with his arms. 'Because I'm stealth like that."

"Yeah, I see."

"That's all I really care about, y'know. Making my little girl happy. And I've seen over these last few months how you did just that."

Rick looked down, self-conscious. Looked up. "She makes me just as happy."

Hank Moore nodded. "Just don't stop, hear? Don't ever stop making her happy." There was a warning in his voice.

Rick wanted to say that he was going to try his best to, but Hank Moore walked out. Rick waited a beat and left out too, settled in the love seat next to Dajah.

He leaned into her, whispered "Your daddy read me the riot act."

"When?"

"In the kitchen."

Dajah looked across the living room at her father, surprised that he was looking back. He winked at her. Nodded his head. Dajah found herself winking back.

"You two got some kind of Morse code going on?" Rick wanted to know.

"No, he just wants the best for me."

"It's what I want too."

"I know you do."

She hadn't expected anything fancy or too serious from Rick for Christmas, but the gold ring on her finger said her expectations had been set too low. An intricate weave of golden lines, Rick said it was based on an old Irish design that indicated a deep friendship.

There were no diamonds, nothing flashy about it, but the simplicity was just as appealing. It was a token of Rick's commitment to her and every time she looked down at the soft brilliant metal, it told her so.

Dajah chose to wear it on her right hand as opposed to her left because it wasn't an engagement ring and she wanted anyone who saw it to know that.

He looked at his watch. "It's getting late."

"Yeah and we have to get to your peeps." She looked around, her family scattered about. Didn't want to leave, but understood they had other obligations. She scooted off the love seat. Rick got up too. "We're getting ready to go."

Dajah's mother stopped talking mid sentence. Frowned. "So soon?"

"Yeah, we have to get to Rick's family."

"You want to take anything with you?"

"A piece of that sweet potato pie would be nice," Rick said quickly.

Dajah's mother cocked her head to the side. "So you liked my pie?"

Rick smiled. "Mrs. Moore, you've given my mom's pie a run for her money."

Dajah's mother smiled, liking him even more. "Why thank you, Rick." She got off the sofa. "I'm gonna give you an extra slice." Headed to the kitchen.

CHAPTER TWENTY

*H*old her. That's all he wanted.

Go to bed with her in him arms, wake up with her pressed against him, the way they used to do.

But the idea of sleeping in the same bed with Jeff and doing nothing but sleep was hard to imagine. It had been months since she'd slept with anyone and while Alex had been good in bed, Jeff had been much better.

He was asking too much. She told him so.

"Well, then no bed. We'll snuggle on the couch, clothes on."

Mya laughed because her funny bone was tickled. She laughed because it was the cutest, sweetest, most unrealistic thing she'd heard in a while. "Seriously, Jeff? Seriously?"

"Yeah. Why not?"

She was already snug as a bug in a rug against him stretched out on her couch, watching *A Christmas Story*, munching homemade cookies his aunt made and sipping eggnog spiked with rum. She was already turned on and, if he kissed her, she'd turn to jelly.

He had positioned a decorative pillow between his waist and her behind, but her imagination had done away with the pillow and Mya swore she felt him, all of him. Her panties were so wet she needed to get up that minute and change them and he was talking about sharing a bed.

"I've been good so far," he piped in his defense.

"Yes, you have. But you know what's gonna happen."

Lips kissed the back of her ear. "What?" Warm breath tasted the flesh there.

She spilled out of his embrace, stood, pillow tumbling to the floor, a turned-on Jeff making a tent of his jeans. Knew.

Knew, but loved the game. Knew, but wanted to take these last few moments as far as they would go.

She picked up the remote to the TV. Clicked it off. Stood there. Arms folded. Playing along. The mouse waiting for the cat to pounce.

Mya stood, one leg slightly in front of the other. The pajama bottom hugging her hips, the top, tight and snug, revealing nipples getting harder by the minute.

Mya stood while Jeff remained on the couch until she spoke what he knew had been in her soul for a while. "You coming to bed?"

*

Better than before.

Mya didn't think such a think was possible, but it was as if Jeff had taken more lessons on top of the lessons he had already known. She was so tight and so wet, she made Jeff moan in a way she'd never heard him do before. And he felt so good deep down inside of her, his name became a song that her mouth parted just to sing.

Better. Everything was.

*

Alex was in the bed, but not the least bit sleepy. He was trying to get his mind beyond his present situation but all he could think about was what he didn't have. He imagined families all over the world settling down into warm beds with spouses next to them and children sleeping soundly down the hall.

He imagined Christmas trees gone dark and dying embers in fire places. He thought about the one gift he'd gotten this year, from his assistant. It was a tie because "you're always having those business dinners, keeping this place open" Morris told him.

Yes he had. Struggled hard to keep Kwaleed's House of Hope going. But what about his own 'house?' Alex had been so in love with Mya. How did he do what he'd done?

He'd blamed his father, tainted family history, but at the end of the day, he was a grown man who made the wrong choice. His daddy didn't do it. Dawn didn't do it. Alex and Alex alone had done it. And here lay the consequences. All alone.

Something snagged onto his consciousness. Would not let him go until he got up, went to his book-shelf and pulled out a tome. It was leather bound, old with cracks on the cover. He stared at the faint gold letters, barely discernable after all the years of use.

His grandmother had given it to him when he was twelve. Alex had barely cracked it open. But he did now, the soft nearly translucent pages trimmed in gold, a strange comfort. Seven times seventy was what he was searching for. Seven times seventy, the number of times a man could sin and still be forgiven.

He found it only after turning on his computer and doing an internet search. But the most important thing was he'd found it. In the book of Matthew, it was Jesus' reply to Peter asking how many times could a person sin against him and he would forgive them.

Alex had sinned against Mya and she was in the process of forgiving him. It was now time to forgive him-self.

The phone rang.

Alex looked at the clock, saw it was a little after ten. Answered. "Yeah."

"Alex. It's your father."

"Dad?"

"I couldn't let this day go without calling you. You've been weighing on my mind every since I left New York. I knew it was wrong to leave without you, but I couldn't bring myself to take you."

"I don't understand why you did that?"

"Because I was feeling guilty about so much. I didn't want to deal with it."

"I called. You didn't even bother to pick up the phone."

"…I'm sorry."

Sorry. A word used too casually; tossed out without real consequence. "I don't need your sorry…I need you." The confession left Alex feeling exposed and raw.

"No, no you don't need me. You've done just fine without me."

"Have I? Really? I ruined my marriage. Lost the best woman I ever had. That's doing just fine?"

His fathered swallowed. "Nobody's perfect. We make mistakes, some bigger than others. But you don't let one mistake stop you from trying. You can't. If you do, you'll be stuck in that mistake forever." There was a heavy weight to those words. It spoke truth to

Alex and exposed his father's own realizations. "So don't be stuck, son. Stuck don't serve nobody."

Anger sizzled inside of him. "What about you? You still stuck in your mistakes? Mistakes that hurt me? Momma?" Wetness dampened the corner of his eyes. Anger and tears. His father had reduced him to a little boy again.

"I know I hurt you all. I'm trying to apologize. I can't make you take it. All I can do is offer."

The ball was back in Alex's court.

Alex wiped a corner of one eye. Blinked. Blinked again, head spinning. Heart aching. "I needed you to be there for me. I needed to be in that car with you."

"I know. I know." His father said softly.

"But once again the great Samuel Connor ditched me."

"I did."

"At least you admitted it."

"Because it's the truth. And like I said, I couldn't lay my head down until I called you to apologize. To say sorry. To ask your forgiveness."

Alex took a breath. Let it go. "It's cool."

"No, it's not cool but I really want another try. I really want to put this all behind us and start anew. The new year is coming and I've wasted too much time already. So, I'm asking for a second chance."

"To do what? Jump ship on me again?"

"No," his father said softly, "To be a father. A real one."

"Kinda too late for that, isn't it?"

"Alex, it's never too late if you're willing to try." *Was he?* "I'll be back in New York on the twenty-eighth. If you want to get together then, you call me…I just wanted to tell you that. Hope you had a good day. Love you son."

The line went dead. The silence, making Alex's ears buzz.

*

Gina was trying to get the words out, but they stuck like a sandwich with too much peanut butter and not enough bread. Most of her life she'd ducked responsibility for anything wrong she'd done. Speaking out loud about just how wrong she'd been was going to take her a minute. But she didn't have a minute. Collin was getting ready to go.

His North Pole jacket was on his back, his hat on his head and gloves were in his hand. He had given Kanisha a hug and was standing by the door—her cue to show him out. She needed to tell it, just like Rick suggested. Needed to confess, take the weight off Collin's shoulders, but Gina had spent so many years being 'fearless,' owning her own fear had her turned upside down.

"Hope the trains are running good," he said.

"Yeah. Me too."

He opened the door because she didn't seem to want to. Headed down the steps, knowing she would follow. He was beyond late getting to the Bronx and his baby's mother would rag him the whole time he was there. Collin wasn't looking forward to that, but he had been itching to see his son all day.

He was turning the locks when Gina came up behind him. "We ain't never gonna do this no more."

He turned, confused. "Do what?"

"You here and missing Christmas with your son. That's not right."

"You didn't give me a choice."

Gina looked down. Shamed. "I know and I—, it ain't happening again." She slipped her arms around his neck. Kissed him, deep and slow. Released him. "Call me when you get there. Want to make sure you got there okay."

He smiled. "I'm a big boy. I can take of myself."

Gina smiled back. "Yeah, you are. But you got to keep safe." The rest of her words were unspoken, but they lay deep in her softness of eyes.

*

Three days later, Alex sat in his office at his center, working the calculator. He had run the numbers three times already and all three times said unless he got some cash flow soon, by May, he'd have to close his doors.

He looked out into the main room, the sound of a foosball game in progress, the slap of checkers hitting the paper board and low toned conversations drifted in. Classical music eased out of the classroom full of high school students getting extra math help. Behind him, his 'Wall of Success' overflowed with over one hundred photos of kids he had helped get their life on track.

But there was no game, no music and no class that could help him do what he had been trying to do all day—call his father.

"Mr. C?"

Alex looked up. Saw Kenneth, one of his students standing in the door.

"Yes?"

"There's some dude, I mean, man here to see you. He says he's your pops?"

"My 'pops'?"

"Yeah, that's what he said." Kenneth tilted his head a little to left. "He do sorta look like you tho'. You want me to send him back here?"

Alex stumbled to his feet. "I'll come out."

The man standing near the front was indeed his father. But it was a father Alex had never seen. A little shorter, a bit stooped. What had once been dark brown hair peppered with gray was now all white and an inch from the scalp.

Alex had not seen him in fifteen years and as he moved toward him, he tried to see the father he remembered inside of the slightly stocky older man now standing before him.

"Sometimes, Mohammad has to come to the mountain," his father uttered with a cautious smile. "Sometimes we got to take the first step." His father looked around. "It looks good, this thing you've done." Pointed to a wall of framed artwork. "Some nice stuff here."

"Dad," Alex admonished, "will you just stop looking around and just look at me?"

It took a few tries; Alex's father's eyes whizzing pass him like cars passing a stranded motorist. But his eyes finally settled. Dropped down, slowly lifted up. Dropped back down again. A little grunt, a slight shake of the shoulders and then his father's eyes were upon him.

"Always said you had your mother's eyes." But there was pain in that delivery.

"I always thought I had yours."

"No. Everything else, maybe, but not the eyes." He looked around again. "Can we go somewhere, talk?"

Alex told him sure. His hand slipped around his father's shoulder. Stopped and introduced him to everyone in the center that day. By the time they reached his office in the back, Samuel Connor began to feel like what he hadn't in way too long – Alex's father.

CHAPTER TWENTY-ONE

"*I* used to come out here all the time."

Rick nodded, the sub freezing wind blowing in from the Atlantic, no friend of his. Even though the sun was out, it was a bitterly cold day. Being at the beach was the last place he hoped to be.

No one else was out there and there were chunks of snow clinging to lamp poles, along the shore and dotting the sand. But Dajah wanted to come on New Years Eve, *because*. She had no real answer, just a strong need to do so, so Rick bundled up the best he could and brought her.

"It's real cold now, but in the summer, even late spring, it's not so bad."

Rick stamped his Timberland-clad feet. Nodded. Even though he had put on thermal socks, his feet were starting to freeze up. He had his back to the ocean because the cold air was brutal. Dajah faced it, closing her eyes, lifting her face to the sun. Enjoying it.

"There were times when it seemed like I was always here. Trying to get my head straight. My heart. You, Gina, just driving me mad..." she stopped talking for a moment. Watched a seagull soar along the beach. "Just tough times. Rough times. Met my almost-husband out here."

That caught Rick's attention. He turned around, needing to see her face. Watch it as she shared what she hadn't shared before. "Did you say husband?"

"Yeah," Dajah answered, her smile careful. She had never told Rick the extent of how she'd come to move two blocks from his house. He never asked. Tomorrow was a new year and Dajah wanted to clear her slate. "Yeah. I met him here, a few months after we broke up. You were trying to come back and I wasn't trying to hear it. Came out here one day and this dog runs up to me. Beautiful huge red Irish setter. Scared the crap out of me." She looked towards the sun. "He belonged to Jeff. The dog introduced us." She chuckled. "I should have taken it as a sign, but I didn't." Lost her humor. "He wasn't perfect, but after going through what we went through, he was more than perfect, you know what I mean?"

Rick nodded. Those had been some crazy rough times. He couldn't begin to imagine what it had been like for Dajah.

"He has issues, but he fixed them. At least it looked like he did. So we're dating. I'm happy again."

"You loved him?"

"Yeah. I did. It was different from how I felt about you, but yeah, I loved him. Enough to say yes when he asked me to marry him."

"You were engaged?"

"No ring or nothing, but yeah, we'd set a date, the whole nines."

"So, what happened?"

Dajah looked away again. "He happened. He happened to cheat on me. And the woman he cheated with told me, that's how I found out. He had been sleeping with her and living with me."

"So that's how you came to move?"

"Yeah. By the time I left him, my apartment had been long rented out. I wanted something good, y'know. Some new place where I could start all over."

"So you moved two blocks from me." He was smiling.

Dajah nudged his arm. "I moved two blocks from you not because you lived there. I moved two blocks away from you because it was a good place to live."

"No wonder he looked like he'd sucked lemons when I saw him in Key Food last week."

"You saw him?"

"Yeah. We were in Key Food Christmas Eve."

"And you didn't tell me?"

Rick shrugged. "I didn't think it was important."

"He remembered you?"

"No, not right away, but I remembered him. I'll never forget that day we all ran into each at the restaurant."

Dajah remembered. "Yeah, that was kind of wild."

"It was hard for me. I didn't show it, but it was like a knife in my heart…seeing you had moved on with somebody who was, well."

"So put together?" Dajah nodded. "Yep, that was Jeff." She paused. "Did he say anything?"

Rick realized that even though Jeff was her past, it mattered that she still mattered to him. "Yeah. He said and I quote: "How's Dajah?"

"He said that to you?" Rick nodded. "How did he even know we…?"

Rick moved behind her, slipped his arms around her waist. Bulky winter wear made the hold hard, but he managed to latch his fingers together, holding her tight. He angled his head until his mouth was near her ear. "How did he know? My whole world *is* you, that's how."

She wanted to ask more questions, but realized the trip to the beach was about that clean slate. In her head, she wished Jeff well. In her heart, she was grateful for Rick.

*

Snuggled up tight on the boardwalk was how Jeff and Mya found them.

Mya knew that Jeff was a nature freak. Still coming out to the beach on a day when the temps were just seventeen degrees was insanity. Mya didn't care if Kelly 'had to run,' as Jeff put it. It was just too cold to be outdoors, especially on the beach.

She had bundled up, but the cold air still felt like acid on her cheeks the moment they left the car. She was sure they were going to be the only fools out there, but there was another car parked in the lot.

Jeff recognized the car. Knew what it meant.

But the past was the past and he would not turn around and duck the second woman he had wanted to marry. He'd be open and honest and real with his life.

He let Kelly off the leash the moment they hit the boardwalk. Jeff was almost certain Kelly would find Dajah before he would. It felt better that way. Let Kelly announce that he was at the beach too, so that by the time he showed up, she wouldn't be caught totally off guard.

"I can't believe somebody else is out here? They must be nature freaks, too."

Jeff leaned into her, slipping his arm around her waist. "You love this nature freak."

Mya relented. "Yeah, I do."

But his heart began to pound in his chest as he saw Kelly take off. It was all he could do to stay calm as he saw her charging along the boardwalk, Dajah the destination.

"Jeff, she's going after those people?"

"It's fine."

*

Face to the sea, Dajah didn't see Kelly, just began hearing the faint clang of a metal leash scrapping along the boardwalk. It was dim over the roar of the ocean, but the sound grew louder. She frowned. "What is that?" She looked and saw a big red dog charging her way. She squinted. Whispered. "Kelly?"

Rick was looking too. "Oh shit. There's a dog coming after us." Instinct made him want to hop up on the rail. He grabbed Dajah's arm, wanting to flee. "We better get out of here."

But she pulled her arm back. "No, it's fine. It's Kelly."

"*Who*-see?"

By the time Dajah went to answer, Kelly's hug paws were on her coat. The slobbery tongue, licking her face, Dajah laughing under the attack. She spied Jeff and someone else heading her way. Ruffled Kelly's thick red fur.

She had come out to the beach to cleanse and clear her soul. It appeared that her wish was coming true.

*

Dajah was introducing Kelly to Rick by the time Jeff made it to her. She smiled his way, the woman's way, genuinely.

"Funny meeting you out here," she piped, meaning it. She turned to Rick. "You remember Jeff?"

Rick extended his gloved hand. Jeff accepted it, the furrow in Jeff's brow, slight. "Hey again."

"Yeah. Hey. Happy New Year's Eve." Jeff turned to Mya. "This is my lady Mya. Mya this is Dajah and her—?"

"Boyfriend, Rick." Dajah said. But her eyes were on Mya. On the woman Jeff had found after her. She was closer to Jeff's age and pretty. Not beautiful, not stunning, but pretty. Dajah resisted the urge to touch her own face.

"I thought Jeff was the only one who does this," Mya said, a smile careful on her face.

Dajah laughed. "Oh no. There's a few of us in the world."

Mya was trying hard not to stare at Dajah, but it was difficult not to study the only other woman Jeff had deemed good enough to marry.

Jeff had told her about his engagement to Dajah and how he'd wrecked that by stepping out on her. Mya had been surprised, saddened but also glad. If he hadn't done what he'd done, the two of them wouldn't have the life they were having together. Still, Mya never expected to actually run into Dajah.

She didn't expect her to be so young. Jeff must have had her by ten years. She had a style to her that couldn't be missed. Classy and elegant in the same breath. And gorgeous. She had smooth skin to die for. And even though she wore a hat and a hoodie, her braid extensions looked good enough to be real.

"Well," Rick joining in the conversation, "seems like me and you, Mya is it?" She nodded. "Seems like me and—," it was Rick's turn to pause. "You look familiar?" Rick wasn't great with names, but he remembered faces.

"I do?"

"Yeah." He thought a moment, "That's right. We both were reaching for eggnog what, a week ago?"

Mya frowned. Scanned her memory. Blinked in surprise. "You're right! We were." She laughed. "Oh my God Dajah, he remembers everything?"

It was weird hearing her name come off of Mya's tongue. Weird for all them to end up at the beach in the middle of winter on New Year's Eve. But Dajah took it as it was—a crazy coincidence.

While Mya knew it was fate.

"Yeah." Dajah ran a mitt hand over Rick's head. "Mind like an elephant."

Rick's eyes slipped towards hers. His smile, wide. "That's a good thing, right?"

Dajah agreed. "Yep, it is."

Kelly whined pulling everyone out of where the meeting had landed them. Jeff patted her head. "We're going, girl. We're going." He looked at Rick. Extended his hand. "Good to see you again, Sir."

Rick wasn't sure what the 'Sir' was about, but he took it as a compliment. "Same here."

Jeff looked at Dajah, glad to see both joy and forgiveness in her eyes. "Dajah. Good to see you."

She nodded. "You too." Picked up the farewell. "And Mya, nice to meet you. And a little FYI…you might want to invest in some real good thermals. Coming to the beach," her head tilted toward the ocean, "it's his year-round thing."

"I will keep that in mind." Suddenly Mya felt overwhelmed. Understood the source. Dajah had loved Jeff enough to marry him, but had swiftly cut those ties and had found someone new. Mya envied that. She had never stopped loving Jeff, even when she loved someone else.

She wanted to know how Dajah did it, but it was a question that would never leave her lips. In that moment, she just wanted to get away from her. Disconnect the fated meeting. Close Dajah out of things, forever.

"Happy New Year," Mya piped as she turned and walked away.

"Yeah. Happy New Year," Jeff added, urging Kelly towards the steps. Then they were down on the beach, the Frisbee tossed into the air and Kelly on the mad chase to retrieve it.

Dajah was silent as she watched. Rick just as silent beside her. And when she had her fill, she told Rick she was ready to go.

*

The pot was stirred.

The life she had with Jeff, upon her. *Because no matter how great things are with Rick, there are things about Jeff I miss. Incidental stuff, like how he always opened doors, pulled out chairs, hand-fed me strawberries. Knew when I was in the mood and wasn't.*

I miss how tall he is. All the things he knows. That he draws. His intelligence. How he played my body like I was a delicate cello and I would just vibrate to his touch. I miss playing Frisbee in the middle of winter on a beach with a dog...

"You don't want one."

Dajah was so deep in her thoughts she forgot she was even in the car with Rick. "Huh?"

"I said, you don't want one." Rick was taking a huge chance, putting in front of them what was inside of Dajah right now. He knew by her face, the way she was quiet; chose to look out the window than rattle on about something, that she was missing some of the life she'd had with Jeff.

Her brow furrowed. "Don't want one what?"

Rick paused a beat. His smile hitching a ride on his silly smile. "A dog."

Dajah's brow creased more. Her nose turned up a bit, but the end result was laughter, big, hearty and needed. There was no such thing as perfect and no one was. Rick wasn't and Jeff certainly wasn't.

She had a great guy in Rick. She wasn't going anywhere. As he reached out and gave her hand an 'it's okay' squeeze, she knew he wasn't going anywhere either.

"But if you did, I'd be cool with it," he said carefully.

"Having a dog is like having children. They have to get shots, go for doctor's appointments. They have to be played with and walked and potty-trained. You got to keep them clean. Keep them fed...no thanks."

"You sure?" Rick wanted to know.

"Absolutely. If I'm gonna take care of another thing then it's going to be a child for real."

"You want kids?"

"Doesn't everybody?"

Rick nodded, tucking that information away. "Good to know."

"I mean, I'd have to be married first. Not trying to be anybody's baby momma."

"Of course not."

"But yeah, I do." Dajah paused. "What about you? You want more kids?"

Rick smiled. "A whole tribe."

Dajah laughed. "A tribe, Rick?"

"Yep. At least a starting five."

"Five kids?"

"Absolutely."

Dajah looked away, chuckled. "Well, good luck with that."

"You mean to say you wouldn't help a brother out?"

"Do you know how old I am?"

"I do."

"Then do the math. No way on God's green earth this here body is going to pump out five kids."

His face grew serious. "But if you could, would you?"

Dajah looked back at those incredible soft brown Allen Iverson eyes looking her way, words leaving her before she had the chance to check them. "Yeah, I would."

CHAPTER TWENTY-TWO

A blizzard arrived New Year's Day and it snowed so much it felt like God had left the snowmaker in the 'on' position for the rest of the winter.

The City of New York began to run low on salt and had to borrow from other states. Auto accidents went way up as New Yorkers, determined that nothing could stop them, ventured out on streets of packed snow and slippery ice.

Homeless deaths rose and antiquated furnaces gave up the ghost. It was a great season for Sanitation workers, repair shops and plumbers, but for everyone else, it was miserable.

The snow continued to blow and fall right up until the first day of spring. The Parks Department had to clear ground just to make sure the ground hog could see his shadow. But there was no need for that early predictor. As far as New York City was concerned, winter was going to hang around until June.

The snowy season ended in late March, but true to the month, an ice storm hit soon after. By April, the greenery was still brown and bare trees still shivered in a deep cold snap. Attempts at outdoor planting failed. They all got frost bite and died.

But something of a miracle occurred the seventh day of April. Temperatures shot up to the high fifties and the earth sprang forth with new growth within a day. The very air smelled of turned earth and hints of bloom. The sun shone bright, warm and long overdue.

It was a beautiful day, all Mya could think as she stood at the top of the court house steps on Supthin Boulevard, her divorce decree signed, sealed and delivered.

She thought about summer. Thought about the very special day that was on its way – July twenty-fourth. Mya thought about what it meant and how she wasn't going to blow that second chance. Jeff had proposed to her on the first day of the New Year. He wanted to marry her and he didn't want to wait.

"My parents aren't getting any younger and I just want my pops to be able to hold at least one of his grand-children," he explained.

Mya understood. Felt the same kind of pressure. Both of them would be forty-one this year. It was time to get on that horse and ride it all the way.

Mya dug into her coat pocket and pulled out the velvet gray jewelry box. Carefully she opened it, temporarily blinded as the sun hit the diamond fixed center the gold band. She exhaled as she slipped it on the ring finger of her left hand. Felt the power of the moment as her heart swelled.

Jeff had given it to her New Years Day and she had toted it around like a super secret every since. It felt good to wear it in public. It would feel even better to tell her friends and family that she was getting married.

She had kept it from Gail and Chloe because she didn't want to risk judgment. Mya didn't want anything to dampen the hope that she'd rediscovered.

Life took dips and turns. Spins and loops. Sometimes you held on. Other times you tumbled. Mya had been through all that and more, but here, in this moment, she was standing tall. Standing tall in the love she'd lost and against all odds, had regained; the love of Jeff but more importantly, the love of herself.

THANK YOU's

It takes a village…
If you are reading this, then you are a part of mine.

To my family: I love and appreciate you. To my friends, my life is so much richer because of you. To my fans, readers and anyone who has ever picked up one of my novels ~ I truly appreciate you.

To my friend and phenomenal business mentor Mary Kelley ~ there aren't enough words to express just how much I appreciate you. You took me by the hand and showed me a whole new approach to life. For that, I am truly grateful.

To fellow authors Bernice L. McFadden, Phillip Thomas Duck and Timmothy B. McCann ~ thank you for inspiring me; your works challenge me to be better…

To my advance readers for *Tumbled*: Marsha Cecil, Fongie Lanier, Marshel Crittenden, Jackie Bolds, Stacy Campbell, Kendra Carter, Denise Pitcher Samuel, Lori M. Legette, Tamara Ella Palmer, Cherrie Woods and Nandi Crawford ~ thank you for your invaluable feedback ~ smooches!

And to God: there aren't enough words in the English language to begin to say how grateful I am for your Mercy, your Love and your Grace. Thank you for always being in my corner and for always having my back; for making a way out of no way. You are my rock…

Jeremiah 29:11

ABOUT THE AUTHOR

Margaret Johnson-Hodge is the author of 10 novels, many receiving national acclaim. She has garnered rave reviews from Publisher's Weekly, Booklist, Midwest Book Review, The Dallas Morning Star, The Quarterly Black Review, Essence Magazine and Ebony Magazine. She is the recipient of the Reviewer's Choice Award for her first novel *"The Real Deal"* and her seventh *"A Journey to Here,"* earned her an "Author of The Year" nomination.

Her works were considered by Showtime and Hallmark for book-to-movie options and have made bestseller lists numerous times. Her novels have been used as part of the curriculum at University of Wisconsin – Eau Claire and she was invited by Harvard University to submit a short story for their literary magazine. Originally from New York, Margaret continues to pay that great city homage with every story that she writes.

"Tumbled" is her 11th published novel.

Made in the USA
Lexington, KY
17 May 2014